My Fairy Grandmother

My Fairy Grandmother

Aubrey Mace

Bonneville Books
Springville, Utah

Other books by Aubrey Mace:

Spare Change
Santa Maybe (coming fall 2009)

ISBN 13: 978-1-59955-217-0

Published by Bonneville Books, an imprint of Cedar Fort, Inc., 2373 W. 700 S., Springville, UT 84663
Distributed by Cedar Fort, Inc., www.cedarfort.com

LIBRARY OF CONGRESS CATALOGING-IN-PUBLICATION DATA

Mace, Aubrey.
My fairy grandmother / Aubrey Mace.
p. cm.
Summary: A fairy tale about a 10-year-old girl whose Grandmother claims to be a fairy.
ISBN 978-1-59955-217-0
1. Grandparent and child--Fiction. 2. Grandmothers--Fiction. 3. Fairies--Fiction. 4. American fiction--21st century. 5. Fairy tales--United States. I. Title.

PS3613.A2717S628 2009
813'.6--dc22

2008048221

Cover design by Nicole Williams
Cover design © 2009 by Lyle Mortimer
Edited and typeset by Heidi Doxey

Printed in the United States of America

10 9 8 7 6 5 4 3 2 1

Printed on acid-free paper

This book is for the three most important girls in my life.

To Avery:
When I started this book you weren't even born yet, but I still loved even the idea of you. I wanted you to have a fairy tale of your very own from your Lady. But what began as a warm, fuzzy story of a fairy princess with a beautiful voice took a few unexpected dark twists and turns, as fairy tales—and sometimes life, for that matter—often do. So put it on your shelf and when you get a bit older, it will be there waiting for you.

To Avery's mum, my best friend in the world. I want to be just like you when I grow up.

And to my mum, the one who always reads it first and wants to know the end at the beginning. I'd tell you, but you'd only be disappointed later.

⋆ Acknowledgments ⋆

Thank you to all my friends at Cedar Fort: to Kammi for your invaluable help with the early edits, to Jennifer for keeping me in the loop, to Nicole for another awesome cover, and to Heidi for smoothing out all the rough edges and making me look like a better writer than I really am. You girls consistently exceed my expectations.

I would also like to mention my family and friends who have taken on the role of faithful editors/pre-readers: Merrillyn Butterfield, Glenn and Elaine Eyre, Ron Mace, Lindsey VanAntwerp, and the entire team at IMC Infusion Services. You pass around my early rubber-banded efforts with so much enthusiasm that I feel more like a rock star than the little fish that I really am. If I ever get rich and famous, I will see that you are all compensated with something more substantial than my gratitude.

Fairy Tale

1. Story about fairies: a story for children about fairies or other imaginary beings and events, often containing a moral message
2. Unlikely explanation: an improbable invented account of something, often a false excuse

—Encarta World English Dictionary,
1998–2004, Microsoft Corporation

"Fairy tales are more than true—not because they tell us dragons exist, but because they tell us dragons can be beaten."

—G. K. Chesterton

"Dicon ch'oltre mare se cade in man dell'uom,
ogni farfarla,
da uno spillo e'trafitta ed in tavola infitta!"

"They say that in your country if a butterfly is caught by man, he'll pierce its heart with a needle and then leave it to perish!"

"Un po' di vero c'e.
E tu lo sai perche?
Perche non fugga piu.
Io t'ho ghermita . . .
Ti serro palpitante. Sei mia."

"Some truth there is in that, and can you tell me why? That you may not escape. See, I have caught you. I hold you as you flutter. Be mine."

—Giacomo Puccini, *Madame Butterfly*

* ONE *

It was hot in the back seat, and the old leather seats stuck to her skin. Kaitlin shifted around, trying to find a place that wasn't uncomfortable. The seat made her sweaty, and no matter how she situated herself, it clung to her like a magnet on her soft white skin, drawing her inexorably to it. The air in the car felt like someone had opened the oven at home while something was cooking. She was discovering a new kinship with chickens, imagining them roasting and sweating their juices away behind the glass oven door. But chickens were treated more humanely. Even chickens weren't cooked while they were still alive.

"Grandma, could you turn on the air?"

"I'm sorry, Katie, but there isn't any air conditioning. The heat doesn't bother me," Grandma Viola rasped cheerily. Her voice was quiet but crinkly, like torn-up tissue paper.

Kaitlin rolled down the window, but that didn't help much. Apparently, they didn't make cool air in Arizona. She scooted back in the seat, peeling her legs from the burning leather and hugging her knees close to her body. That seemed to be the only way to keep the seats from sticking to her. For a few seconds, even the hot air felt cool on her sweaty legs.

"Katie, please don't put your feet on the seats," Grandma Viola's voice drifted back from the front seat.

Reluctantly, Kaitlin put her feet back on the floor, surrendering her skin again to the unforgiving seat. Why should she do what this woman asked anyway, when she couldn't even manage to get her name right? She was definitely a Kaitlin. She had never been a Katie, and no one else called her that. Her mother, Megan, popped her head over the passenger seat and gave her a sympathetic smile. Kaitlin had been excited to go on vacation and visit her grandma, but everything here was different. From the moment they got off the plane, she wanted to turn around and go back home to where things were normal.

Her grandmother was a stranger who she barely remembered from the only other time they met. Kaitlin's dad was excited for her to finally be able to spend some time with her grandma—He had told her that it would be hot enough in Arizona in July for them to fry an egg on the sidewalk, and she was looking forward to testing the theory. They were supposed to be taking this trip together, as a family. But at the last minute, her dad had to tell her that he wouldn't be able to go with them. He was an officer in the National Guard, and his unit was being deployed to Baghdad the day before they were supposed to leave for Arizona. Kaitlin didn't understand why he couldn't just go to Baghdad when they got back, but he laughed and said it didn't work that way.

They talked about postponing the trip, but her dad insisted that she and her mother go anyway. He said it would be easier for them: they would be distracted by the vacation when he left, and by the time they got home, they would already be used to his absence and wouldn't miss him at all. Somehow, she doubted that would be the case.

So, the adventure Kaitlin had been looking forward to quickly became nearly two weeks of unbearable heat and loneliness in a strange place. Plus, they were going to be in Arizona for her tenth birthday, something she was not at all pleased about. She wanted to have a birthday party at home with her friends, not some lame dinner at her grandma's. At least her mother was there to suffer with her. Megan was trying to make conversation in the front seat, but her tone sounded forced and unnaturally bright.

Kaitlin reached over and unzipped the bag on the seat next to her, sifting unsuccessfully through underwear and socks.

"Mom, do you know what happened to my DS?" she called into the front seat.

"It's in one of the other bags, sweetie—in the trunk."

"What about my books?"

"If they're not in the bag you're looking through, they're probably in the trunk too."

"Do you like books, Katie? I've got hundreds of books. I bet there are some you would really enjoy," Viola said enthusiastically.

I doubt it, Kaitlin's mind echoed sarcastically. She sat, sullen and silent, looking out the window at the arid desert landscape crawling by.

"Don't worry—it's only about an hour to my house, and then we'll get you all settled."

Kaitlin leaned back against the seat and sighed loudly, wishing she could melt into it and disappear. This might just be the longest thirteen days of her life.

"Mom, can't we just go home?"

Kaitlin's words got caught in the web of stifling air that lay between her and her mother. They'd stripped the double bed of the robin's egg blue chenille spread and were lying on top of the sheets, trying to stay cool. Apparently, Grandma Viola actually did have air conditioning in her house, but it broke down last summer, and she hadn't bothered to fix it yet. The man who came out to look at it said it might be up to eight hundred dollars in repairs, and she sent him away, promising to think about it. The truth was she wasn't inconvenienced enough by the heat to justify the cost.

Megan sighed, rolling over to face her daughter. "How do you think that would make your grandma feel, if we just got up in the morning and left?"

"I know, I know. We have to stay." Kaitlin lay as still as possible so she wouldn't generate any excess heat by her movements. She played a little game with herself, trying not to even breathe until it was absolutely necessary. "What's the deal with Grandma's voice? It's like she's whispering all the time."

"You know, I'd forgotten about that. I'm not really sure. I was going to ask your father the first time I met her, but I never got around to it."

"I wish Dad were here. He'd fix the stupid air conditioning. We'd be laughing about this if Dad were here."

"Well, we'll just have to make it fun, you and me."

"But how are we going to survive here for two weeks?" Kaitlin persisted.

"We'll work on our tans."

"You can't tan out there—you'll melt!"

"We'll drink a lot of lemonade."

Kaitlin kicked her legs petulantly, immediately regretting her hasty display. The kicking seemed to awaken the hot air, alerting it to her presence. It pressed her down into the mattress with suffocating precision, ready and waiting to choke the remaining air from her lungs.

"You need to look on the bright side. At least we have each other. Dad is by himself, and believe it or not, it's even hotter than this in Baghdad. Do you hear him complaining? We've got to stop moping and feeling sorry for ourselves, and be strong like Dad. Okay?"

Kaitlin had no response. She wasn't strong like Dad—she was just a kid. Maybe it was a good idea to go to sleep. Things would look better in the morning; she was sure of it. She half dozed, imagining herself outside in the middle of winter. The clouds were stuffed with snow, and were ready to pop. The flakes drifted down, and she could feel the chill when they landed on her face, like frozen kisses.

"Maybe we could get a big fan," Kaitlin mumbled sleepily.

Her mother giggled, momentarily forgetting her problems at this abrupt change of topic. "We'll go to Wal-Mart tomorrow, as long as it isn't too far away. I think another long drive in that car just might kill me."

When Kaitlin woke up in the morning, her mother was still asleep. There was a delicious smell of chocolate wafting down the hall into their room. For a minute, she couldn't figure out where she was, but the overwhelming heat quickly reminded her. Her face felt hot from the sun shining through the window, pooling mercilessly onto the pillows. It was like adding insult to injury, and she pictured a giant bully in the sky, using the sun like a magnifying glass, trying to fry their brains as they slept.

The chocolaty aroma provided any additional motivation Kaitlin may have needed to escape. She carefully eased off the bed, not wanting to wake her mother, who didn't look as if she were in any immediate danger of suffocation. She wandered down the hall in her pajamas toward the kitchen, where she discovered her grandmother removing a pan of brownies from the oven. She was actually wearing a sweater. How she could bear to even turn on the oven in this heat was a mystery to Kaitlin.

"Good morning, Katie. How did you sleep?"

"Okay, I guess." She picked up the newspaper from the table and used it as a makeshift fan. The idea was to move the rising heat away from her, but there always seemed to be a fresh wave waiting to take its place.

"Good. Would you like a brownie? They're still warm."

"Brownies? For breakfast?" Kaitlin wrinkled her nose.

"I think brownies are good any time. Sometimes I eat brownies all day long. It's one of the perks of being an adult."

Kaitlin shrugged. "Okay." She was hungry, and she was afraid if she declined the brownies that her grandmother might present her with a steaming bowl of oatmeal. Viola nodded her approval, and Kaitlin watched as she expertly cut the brownies into squares. She sprinkled them with powdered sugar, which almost immediately morphed into a sticky mess upon contact with the hot surface.

"Oh, dear, I guess I should have let them cool a little longer. They still taste good, even if they aren't very pretty." She put the two largest brownies on little rosebud plates from the cupboard and placed one in front of Kaitlin, and took the other for herself. "Would you like a cup of cocoa?"

The idea of drinking anything hot made her shudder. "I like milk with brownies," she said tactfully.

"An excellent choice." Viola stirred the cocoa in her own cup and placed a large glass of milk in front of her granddaughter. She took the seat across from Kaitlin, taking a bite of her brownie and smiling contentedly. "Now, tell me about yourself, Katie."

Kaitlin nearly choked on the huge chunk of brownie she'd just stuffed into her mouth. "What do you want to know?" she mumbled.

"I want to know everything. It's been far too long since I've seen you, and I want us to catch up. How about school? What kind of books do you like to read? Do you have lots of friends?"

"What about school?" she said, trying to figure out which question to answer first.

"Are you a good student? What is your favorite subject? Do you like your teachers?"

"School is okay."

"But what do you like best about it? What's your favorite part?" Viola pressed.

"I don't know. What was your favorite part about school?"

Viola looked away wistfully. "I didn't get to go to school; not for very long, anyway."

Kaitlin's curiosity was piqued. "Why didn't you go to school?"

"A big part of my childhood was spent in a place where there was no school."

"Lucky," she said jealously. "Where did you live?"

"A castle in Spain."

This short statement jarred Kaitlin. She would have been less surprised if her grandma had claimed to have grown up on the moon. Viola took a sip of her still-steaming cocoa and happily munched another bite of her brownie, completely oblivious to the fact that there was anything strange about what she said. Of course, Kaitlin knew almost nothing about her grandmother; it could be true. "A castle. In Spain." she finally said, dubiously.

"Yes. Spain is really far away, it's a completely different country—"

"I know where Spain is," Kaitlin interrupted.

"See, you are a good student!" Viola beamed. "Even though I

didn't get to go to school very long, I know things now. I went to college, after I was married," she said importantly.

Kaitlin wanted to steer the conversation back to the Spanish castle, but her mother appeared suddenly in the doorway, yawning and looking decidedly pink and sweaty. She leaned down to kiss Kaitlin.

"Some daughter you are. You left me in there to roast!"

"Sorry, Mom, I wanted to let you sleep."

"I guess I must have been more tired than I thought." Megan sat down at the table, looking at the plates with a puzzled expression. "Are you eating . . . brownies?"

"Grandma eats brownies for breakfast all the time. Sometimes she eats brownies all day long."

"Does she?" Megan looked at Viola, who was suddenly wearing a guilty expression.

"I guess I'm just used to living on my own," Viola said sheepishly.

"Maybe we'll get some cold cereal at the store. Kaitlin, why don't you go get dressed? We can go this morning, before it gets any hotter."

"But, Mom, Grandma was right in the middle of a story!"

"Don't worry, Katie. You're going to be here almost two whole weeks. We'll have plenty of time to chat." She winked.

Kaitlin went back to their room, which seemed even hotter than when she left it, if that was possible. She wondered if it was true what her grandmother said, about the castle in Spain. Surely her dad would have mentioned something like that. Maybe she was really a princess! Didn't you have to be a princess or a queen or something to live in a castle? That would make Kaitlin some kind of royal person as well. Wouldn't that be something to tell her friends when she got home! Maybe there was even a crown somewhere, hidden in Grandma Viola's house.

Kaitlin sifted through her suitcase and picked out the most lightweight outfit she brought. She had plenty of questions for her grandma, who suddenly seemed a lot more interesting; mysterious, even. Maybe this trip wouldn't be so terrible after all.

✶

Kaitlin sprawled across the couch in the living room with a book, sucking on the melting ice cubes that lingered in the bottom of her glass. When she looked at the clock on the wall, she was amazed to see that it was 9:00 already. What kind of place was still this hot, even after the sun went down?

After they got back from the store, the rest of the day passed in a sort of heated haze. As hard as she tried to get her grandmother back onto the topic of her childhood castle home, Kaitlin was never alone with her, and she wasn't sure she wanted to share the story with her mother. She liked the idea that she might be the only one who knew the story of her grandmother's secret life. Kaitlin was sure of one thing, though—if the rest of the days were like this one, she would definitely run out of books.

"What are you reading, Katie?" Viola was standing in the doorway, watching Kaitlin with a curious smile on her face.

"*Peter Pan*. My dad used to read it to me when I was a kid."

"I never really liked that book. I think it was the idea of being young forever. When I was a little girl, I was always in such a hurry to grow up."

"I like the parts with Tinkerbell."

"Yes, but fairies aren't really like that."

"What do you mean?" Kaitlin cocked her head quizzically.

"Well, fairies aren't like they are in books. At least, they weren't when I knew them."

"You *knew* them?" Kaitlin could hardly believe what she was hearing, but it was hard to doubt her grandmother when she seemed so sure of herself.

"Absolutely. Everyone knew a fairy when I was a girl, whether you were aware of it or not. But fairies weren't tiny, fluttery things—they were just like people now, albeit somewhat shorter. They looked just like you and me."

"So they didn't have wings?" she asked, her voice heavy with disappointment.

"Of course they had wings; you just couldn't see them under their clothes!"

This made the castle in Spain story look positively normal. Kaitlin reached down and nonchalantly pinched her leg, just to make sure she wasn't dreaming. The pinch stung and left a red mark, so she could only assume that this was really happening. "But why doesn't everyone know about the fairies, if you were surrounded by them?"

"Most people who were old enough to remember have passed on now, and the rest of us are dismissed as crazy if we mention them. Besides, a lot of people would rather forget."

"Why?"

"Fairies didn't exactly have easy lives."

"Why?"

Viola sighed. "For one thing, people were afraid of them. I don't know why. It wasn't as if they had any strong magic, and certainly nothing that could harm anyone."

"Couldn't they fly?"

"Goodness, no. Perhaps in the days before my time fairies could fly. But ever since my grandmother lived, wings were nothing more than a visible reminder of your distant heritage."

"I don't get it. People didn't like them because of their wings?"

"That was only part of it. People have always been afraid of things they don't understand, and they don't like variety. Being a fairy meant you were different. If you were known to have a fairy in your family, you were shunned, or worse, persecuted."

"What?" Kaitlin wasn't sure she knew what persecution was, and she really just wanted to get back to what fairies looked like.

Viola blinked. She was taken aback at just how much she'd revealed so easily to her impressionable granddaughter. "I think we've talked about this enough today. Maybe when you're a bit older, I'll tell you the story."

"But, Grandma, I want to hear! How many fairies did you know?" Suddenly, her face lit up. "Wait a minute—are you a fairy?!" Kaitlin squealed.

"Shhh. If you're a very good girl and go to bed, I'll tell you a little more about it tomorrow. Good night, Katie."

Kaitlin pouted just long enough to realize it wasn't going to do her any good. She jumped off the couch and scampered down the hall to the bedroom she was sharing with her mother.

✶

"Why aren't you asleep? It's past your bedtime." Megan pulled up the blanket and tucked it tightly around her daughter.

Kaitlin gasped for air and kicked off the covers. "Are you kidding with the blanket? It's got to be a hundred degrees in here!"

"Oh, but we have this lovely fan now. It's like an Arctic breeze." Megan paused, pulling her sticky shirt away from her body. "It doesn't really help much, does it?"

"Not really. All it does is move the hot around."

"I was just going to kiss you good night and crawl into bed. Why are you still awake?"

"I couldn't fall asleep. I was thinking about something."

"Was it about Dad?"

"Yes," she said quickly. Kaitlin didn't want to tell her mother about the fairies just yet. She was fairly certain her mother would have issues with the story, and she didn't want her to interfere before she had a chance to hear more. Furthermore, her mother had given her the perfect excuse, and it wasn't completely untrue. She had been thinking about Dad earlier, so it wasn't really a lie.

Megan rolled over onto her side, propping herself up on one elbow to face her daughter. "Sweetie, I don't want you to worry about Dad. He's going to do his job, and he'll be home before you know it."

"I know."

"Well, if you ever need somebody to talk to, I'm here." She rubbed Kaitlin's arm comfortingly.

"Thanks, Mom." She felt slightly guilty for using Dad as an excuse, but it wasn't as if she'd done anything wrong.

"Well, I don't know about you, but I'm really tired," Megan said, yawning.

"Yup, me too. Really tired," Kaitlin echoed.

"So, I guess I'll see you in the morning. Don't stay up reading all night," Megan trailed off, her voice drifting into sleep.

Kaitlin grinned. Her mother always fell asleep super fast, which worked out perfect with her plans for the evening. She waited about five minutes to make sure she was sound asleep before easing out of bed slowly, being careful not to jostle the bed and risk waking her mother. Perhaps if Grandma was still awake, she might be willing to provide Kaitlin with a bedtime story.

"Grandma?" Kaitlin lingered hesitantly in the doorway.

Viola sat at the kitchen table, drinking her bedtime hot cocoa. "Katie, you startled me. What are you still doing up?"

She shrugged. "I couldn't sleep."

"Would you like a glass of cocoa?"

"That would be nice," Kaitlin lied obligingly. She didn't want to seem ungrateful. There was a cup of cocoa waiting on the table in front of the chair opposite Viola. Kaitlin thought this was odd but sat in the chair and tentatively took a sip.

Viola frowned, as if trying to recall something or reconcile an item that was out of place. She shook her head, brushing the errant thought away and smiled at her granddaughter. "I'm so glad that you and your mother decided to come, once you discovered that Kevin would be unable to make the trip with you. You don't know what it means to me to be able to spend this time with you. You're my only grandchild, and I barely know you."

"I was just thinking the same thing! In fact, I was hoping that you might want to tell me more about yourself. You could start with the fairies."

"I would like to, but I'm afraid that you're not old enough yet."

Kaitlin decided to try another tactic. "It's okay. My dad

already told me the story. I just thought you might want to fill in the blanks."

"Really? What did he tell you?"

"That his great-grandmother had wings," she said, trying to be as nonchalant as possible.

"Now I know you're fibbing, Katie," Viola said, pursing her lips.

She panicked. "Why?"

"Because your father couldn't have possibly told you about the fairies."

"You think that just because I'm so little, he wouldn't have trusted me?"

"Your age has nothing to do with it. The fact is Kevin doesn't know anything about it."

"Why didn't you tell him? I'm pretty sure he's old enough."

"My dear, fairies pass their history from mother to daughter . . . or granddaughter," she started patiently. "The sons don't come into it. As much as we love them, they really can't relate. That's why I wanted to tell you now. It's important that you understand your history so that one day, you can share it with your daughter."

"So tell me."

Viola shook her head. "I'm afraid it's not that simple. It's a very grown-up story. Maybe the next time you visit . . ."

"I'm a very grown-up person for my age. I'm almost ten," she pleaded.

Viola smiled. "I know, but this story is quite scary. It's full of danger and suspense. I don't want you to have nightmares."

"I promise I won't have nightmares."

Viola looked furtively around the kitchen, as if she expected company at any moment. "I don't know . . ." she hesitated.

"It might be ten more years before we come back!"

A shadow crossed Viola's face. "Maybe you're right. I suppose it couldn't hurt to tell you just a little bit of the story tonight."

"Yessss!" Kaitlin said loudly.

"Not so loud!" Viola hissed.

Kaitlin clapped a hand over her mouth. "Sorry," she whispered through her fingers.

"Now . . . where to start?"

"Maybe you should start at the beginning," Kaitlin said encouragingly. "Tell me about when you were my age."

"But that wasn't the beginning. The story certainly didn't start with me. The trouble is, which beginning to begin with?" Viola brightened a little. "Did you know I was kidnapped as a child?"

Kaitlin was so surprised she nearly fell off her chair. "Really?" she breathed in awe.

"I was. The man who took me made it look like I was dead, so my parents weren't even looking for me. I was missing for years."

"That might be a good place to start," she urged.

"No, too many important things happened before that; not important to me necessarily, but important to the story."

"You start wherever you want. Any story with fairies in it is cool with me."

"I'm glad you approve." Viola closed her eyes momentarily, gathering her thoughts. Just when Kaitlin thought she might have fallen asleep, Viola cleared her throat dramatically, the sound seeming loud enough to wake the sleepy neighborhood.

"Once upon a time, there was a girl in a cage and a servant boy who could not speak." She looked momentarily disoriented, trying to figure out how to proceed from there. "No, that's leaving out the beginning. Let me try again." Viola cleared her throat once more, as if she had been planning it this way for years. "Once upon a time, there was a boy who loved to collect things."

Kaitlin waited expectantly, having to restrain herself from shaking the story out of her grandmother. Viola scratched her head and waited for the next part to come to her.

"I apologize, that's still not far back enough." She cleared her throat a third time, and Kaitlin began to worry that Viola might lose what little voice she had left before she could even say the word *fairy*.

"Once upon a time, there was a boy who fell in love with a girl. The girl had a secret." Again she hesitated.

"*And?*" Kaitlin said desperately, no longer able to control her outburst.

"Oh, forget it. I had a picture in my head of the way this was supposed to happen, but it obviously isn't working." She sighed and settled back in her chair, the drama and flair of her previous delivery absent. "I suppose I'd better tell you about Cordelia first," she said simply.

"Who is Cordelia?"

"Cordelia was my grandmother."

CORDELIA

Cordelia didn't dare spend any more time on the road. She ducked into the forest, trying to escape the mess of vines that tangled about her feet in a green web. A thousand years of undisturbed growth slowed her down considerably, and several times she found her ankles so entwined with the plants that she very nearly came crashing down to the dirt. As she glanced behind to assure herself she wasn't being followed, she lost her balance and slid unexpectedly into the bowl-shaped valley below, filled with even more twisted foliage. The vines were up to her knees now, and Cordelia tried not to imagine the green ropes as snakes, seething and writhing. The undergrowth rasped and scratched against her bare legs as she struggled, the hissing sounds making the reptile analogy even more believable. She stopped momentarily, squeezing her eyes shut and repeating in her mind that vines cannot hurt you. Besides, compared to facing what was pursuing her, she would gladly wade through the green snake bowl.

Her pulse throbbed, the pounding in her chest so loud that she could barely hear over it. When the pain in her side became too great to go on, she crouched behind a thick tree, allowing herself a few moments of rest. She gulped the air greedily and ignored her better judgment, which told her to keep moving at all costs while making as little noise as possible.

Cordelia leaned her head back against the rough bark, feeling the tiny river of sweat as it trailed neatly down her spine. She was so tired of running. Her mind told her to get up and start moving again while she still could, but her exhausted body encouraged her to lose herself in the bed of vines for a well-deserved nap. As her breathing began to slow, she slid a bit lower until she was in a sitting position. The same vines that looked threatening only a minute ago now appeared cushiony and inviting. If she could just close her eyes for a few minutes. . . .

Cordelia never even heard the footsteps. She woke to find an impossibly large net spread over her, and no matter how much she thrashed around or tried to bite through the rope, there was no escape. The men scooped her up, net and all, and started back the way they came. When they got tired of trying to carry her as she struggled, they dropped her unceremoniously on the ground, dragging her instead. Her arms and legs were welts of bumps and scratches. As they pulled her carelessly across the rugged terrain, she hit her head on a sharp rock, and everything around her became painful and fuzzy. She tasted blood on her tongue and finally surrendered to the blackness at the edge of her vision.

. . . * . . .

There was a noise in the background before Cordelia opened her eyes, a sort of tapping noise that hovered at the edge of her conscious mind. At first it was soft, like the gentle pattering of rain, but it quickly progressed to someone smashing rocks with a hammer. She tried to block out the sound and return to the peaceful place she was before, but the thumping noise refused to let her slip away. Soon, it was the deafening fall of a giant crashing to the earth again and again.

Frustrated, she finally opened her eyes to identify where the sound was coming from. Cordelia discovered that she was in a bed in a hospital ward, but to her surprise, she could find nothing capable of making the noise that was tormenting her. The only other person in the ward was a guard sitting in the chair next to her bed, but he was concentrating on something else and hadn't yet noticed she was awake.

Cordelia watched, mesmerized, as he effortlessly rolled a coin back and forth across his knuckles. Now that she was awake, she felt the pain begin to increase, the rhythm pounding mercilessly in her head. She realized this was the illusive tapping sound from earlier. On top of all that, her nose itched as well, and as much as she wanted to reach up and scratch it, her brain was unresponsive and couldn't convince her hand to move. Her arms felt too clumsy and heavy to lift under the blanket.

The guard accidentally fumbled his coin, cursing softly when it clanged on the floor. When he leaned forward to retrieve it, Cordelia took the opportunity to ask him a question.

"Could you please tell me what is wrong with my arms?" she said timidly, her voice smaller than she remembered.

Startled, the guard jumped and went into the hall to call for a nurse. He returned to her bed, staring at her warily. "Your arms are fine, but you should be asleep. Just lay back and close your eyes," he said gruffly.

"But I cannot move my arms! I need to go home. Please help me."

The guard said nothing, and Cordelia was frightened. She started to thrash around, trying to shake off the blanket so she could see her arms, but the pain searing through her shoulder blades forced her to be still. Her breath came in quick gasps, and drops of sweat ran into her eyes, stinging and burning. In her brief struggle, she had succeeded in inching the blanket up on one side, and was horrified to discover the reason for her suddenly useless arms; her hands were tied to the bed rails with torn pieces of cloth.

She remembered then—the men chasing her, sleep overtaking her in front of the tree, struggling in the net. . . . The moment rushed back on her with impressive violence, and she began to scream. She screamed and tugged at her restraints, and when the pain roared again, she roared back even louder. The guard was at the door again now, and he was yelling too, hollering for the nurse to do something. Cordelia didn't stop screaming until the nurse put a bitter smelling cloth over her mouth and nose, and the world went dark again.

. . . ✶ . . .

When Cordelia awoke, she didn't know how much time had passed, but there was a different guard this time: a tall, solid man with a shaved head, standing at the foot of her bed. Her throat was so dry; she felt she must have been asleep for months. She was barely able to conceal her relief upon discovering that her hands were untied now.

"Could I please have some water, sir?" she rasped.

The guard said nothing but retreated into the hall, returning with a glass of lukewarm water that she gulped greedily. She handed him the empty cup, gingerly stretching and testing her back. It was not the searing torture of before, but the dull ache that heralds healing. Cordelia was certain now what must have happened in the time between being captured in the net and waking up in the hospital, and strangely, she felt a flood of relief. No more running and hiding, pretending to be something else. She knew that somewhere down the road, once the shock wore off, she would have to deal with what had been lost. But right now, she felt like she could finally breathe again without having to look over her shoulder to see who was watching.

The guard refilled her glass with water, watching her curiously. She took a few sips, a bit more delicately this time.

"Thank you. Would it be all right if I asked you a question?"

The guard nodded his head, still not speaking.

"Why are you keeping me here? Obviously, I am no longer a threat."

"The law says we hold you for thirty days, to be monitored for signs of regeneration," he said softly. His quiet voice did not match his appearance, and Cordelia had to strain to hear his words. In spite of her disgust, she found herself strangely intrigued.

"Does that ever happen? Regeneration, I mean?"

"Occasionally."

"What then?"

"They repeat the procedure."

"And you get thirty more days?"

"Naturally."

"What if the . . . growth began again?"

The guard smiled. It was not an inherently cruel smile, but Cordelia understood its meaning all too well. "I could tell you, but I am not the kind of person who enjoys scaring young women."

"So, I am trapped here."

"It is for your own good. I will be back every day to check on you. When your quarantine is over, if there are no signs of regeneration, you will be free to go home."

"Home?" she said with a hollow laugh. "Yes, I am certain they will welcome me back with open arms at home."

The guard ignored her sarcasm. "You look tired—best get some rest. Sleep will make the time pass more quickly. And do not bother trying to escape. Our security makes it impossible, and if you tried to leave before your quarantine was over, we would be forced to keep you here much less comfortably. I know you would not want me to have to tie your hands again."

"Why would I try to escape?" Cordelia said bitterly. "You have what you want from me already."

"Such boldness and fire!" he jeered. "You hardly seem like the same girl we bagged a week ago."

"Has it really been a whole week?" she marveled.

"When we found you, you were fast asleep, right out in the open, limp as a dishrag," he taunted in the same quiet voice, a self-satisfied smirk on his face. "You were no more trouble to net than a new butterfly. Is that why you quit running—because you wanted to be found?"

"I had been running for three days without resting. I did not stop because I wanted to; I stopped because it was physically impossible to keep going."

The guard nodded matter-of-factly, as if he were simply gathering research. Cordelia was exhausted by her conversation with her captor. She lay back against her pillow and closed her eyes, willing him to be gone when she opened them again. And he was—the room was empty and silent, and she wondered for a minute whether she had imagined the whole encounter.

Cordelia got to her feet carefully, her legs wobbly from her week in bed. Her feet felt numb, and her legs were prickly and painful as the blood began to circulate. She staggered to the small mirror on the other side of the room, taking a deep breath and trying to prepare herself. She slowly eased her hospital gown below her shoulders, revealing the crudely bandaged sutures where her wings used to be.

"I think that's enough for tonight." Viola washed out her cup and placed it in the sink.

"But what about your grandma? Did her wings grow back? Did she escape? I want to hear the rest of her story!"

"That is the rest of her story."

"I don't understand. Did she die?"

"No. After her thirty day quarantine, she went home. Her father blamed her for exposing and shaming the family, and he married her almost immediately to a man who was much older than she was, who was only interested in someone to bear his children and do the housework. They had only one child—my mother, Claire."

"But I want to know what happened to Cordelia!" Kaitlin said impatiently.

"I just told you! Her part of the story is over."

"That doesn't make any sense," she said stubbornly.

"Katie, everyone comes to this earth and lives their life. It might be a long life or it might be short, but most of the basic details are uninteresting. We go about our daily chores, we might marry, we might have children, and we die. No one wants to hear about all of it."

Kaitlin opened her mouth to say something but couldn't find the words.

"This might be hard for you to understand at your age, but each of us has one story worth telling, one moment of glory and triumph or pain and despair; something that defines us. It might be one second, or it could extend over several years, but for better or worse, it is the most interesting part of who we are. That was Cordelia's story."

"I guess that makes sense. Grandma?"

"Yes, dear?"

"What was your story?"

She smiled. "You mustn't be impatient. To fully appreciate my story, there are others you have to hear first. Now, you need to get to bed before your mother discovers you missing."

"It's cool. I'll just tell her that I couldn't sleep, and you wanted to tell me about your family."

Viola paused briefly in the doorway, turning to look back at Kaitlin as she gulped the rest of her drink. "I would have made you your own cocoa, you know. You didn't have to drink that one."

Kaitlin's brow furrowed. "I thought it was for me."

Now it was Viola's turn to look confused. "How would I have known you were still awake?"

Kaitlin ignored the question. "But if the drink wasn't for me, who was it for?"

"For Will, my brother."

"I didn't know you have a brother. Where is he?"

"He used to visit me on our birthday, but I haven't seen him in years. Somehow, I knew he'd come tonight." Viola was looking in Kaitlin's direction, but her eyes were fixed on something else. It was almost as if she were looking inside Kaitlin . . . or through her. Despite the heat in the room, Kaitlin shivered.

* Two *

Kaitlin perched on the edge of the bed, painting her toenails a scarlet red.

"Heaven help you if that ends up on the carpet," Megan warned, leaning close to the mirror and concentrating on her mascara.

"I'm being really careful."

Her mother frowned. "I'm not sure that's such a great color for you anyway. Maybe when you're a little bit older."

"I'm so sick of everyone telling me I have to wait until I get older to do things. I'm going to be ten in a few days, you know. That ought to count for something."

Megan looked at her curiously. "What else have you been waiting to do?"

Realizing what she said, she started to backpedal. "Well . . . piercing my ears, for one thing. And getting a cell phone."

"Kaitlin, we've discussed this. Your father and I think that you should wait until you're twelve to get your ears pierced. And as for the cell phone, that's a long way down the road."

"But, Mom . . ."

"Honey, you don't need a cell phone. I barely need a cell phone."

"All my friends have cell phones," she pouted, secretly pleased that she'd managed to cover her mistake. She'd almost slipped and told her mother that Grandma wasn't going to tell her the fairy story because she wasn't old enough. She'd have to be more careful in the future.

"Just because all your friends are doing something doesn't mean you have to."

Kaitlin groaned. "Yes, peer pressure. I get it. We don't need to have the talk again."

"I'm sorry, but I'm your mother, and I love you. So I'm afraid you'll be forced to suffer through these little chats for years to come."

"Maybe when Dad gets home, we can talk about the cell phone?" she asked hopefully.

Megan smiled and kissed her daughter on the top of her head. "We'll see. I thought maybe I would try to do some chores for your grandmother today. I noticed that her windows need cleaning. Do you think you could keep yourself busy for a while?"

"Sure. I brought plenty of books with me," she said, patting her bag. "And if I get bored, I can always talk to Grandma. She mentioned that she wanted to tell me about her family," she added, rolling her eyes as if it was a terrible imposition.

"You're a good girl, Kaitlin. I really appreciate this."

After breakfast, Megan decided to broach the topic of the windows. "Viola," she said delicately. "I thought that while we were here, I might be able to do some things for you."

"What kind of things, dear?"

"Well, maybe some chores that might be difficult for you . . . like your windows?"

"You know, I used to pay a neighbor boy to wash them for me, but he moved away. It's embarrassing how dirty they are."

"Not at all. I just don't think you should have to pay someone when I could do them for nothing," she said kindly.

"Nonsense. I can't have you out there like a slave, scrubbing the windows. You're a guest," Viola protested.

"I don't mind at all. Besides, Kaitlin wants to catch up on her reading, don't you?"

Kaitlin nodded, winking at Viola when her mother wasn't looking.

"Maybe when you're ready for a break from your book, I can tell you some stories about my family, Katie. I've always thought family history was fascinating."

"Uh, yeah," she said, giving her mother a "poor me" look as

she bolted for the bedroom, pulling the door almost closed so that she could still see through the crack. Kaitlin waited as her mother gathered Windex and paper towels, watching as she went down the steps and out the front door. She counted to three hundred just to be on the safe side, in case she came back for something. She felt important, like a spy on a secret mission. When there were no signs of her, Kaitlin crept down the hall and back into the kitchen where Viola was still sitting at the table. Viola gave her an innocent grin.

"Are you through reading already?"

"I just thought you might be bored in here by yourself."

"How very considerate of you."

"And I thought you might be ready to tell me more of your story," she admitted. "I could hardly sleep last night, wondering what happens next."

Viola poured Kaitlin a glass of fruit punch. "Well, I suppose that since your mother is busy, this would be a good time. But there's something you have to understand. I wouldn't go behind her back if I didn't have a good reason. I don't want your mother to know about the story because she wouldn't believe me. She might even think I was crazy, but I'm not."

"I don't think you're crazy."

She hesitated only momentarily. "I guess I should tell you about my mother next. You're sure I'm not boring you? We could go out and do something instead, if you want."

"How could I be bored when you're telling a story about fairies? Plus, you're a really good storyteller," she added for good measure.

Viola beamed, starting in with her dramatic throat clearing. Kaitlin took a big swig from her drink to keep from laughing. And Megan, who had come back to ask Viola for a ladder, stopped abruptly just outside the kitchen door. She had no intention of eavesdropping, but the word *fairy* made her curious, and she hovered quietly, waiting to see what would happen next.

Claire

Claire hummed a happy tune to herself, barely able to contain the raucous joy that threatened to spill out of her at any moment. She peered at her face in the mirror, checking to make certain that everything was as it should be. Her cheeks were pink and healthy, her eyes were bright, and her smile was contagious. She stepped back from the mirror and curtsied before launching into an impromptu dance that consisted of skips and twirls. She admired the way her dress flared around her legs as she spun. It was definitely a dress made for twirling, and Claire should know; she had made it herself. She was becoming a more accomplished seamstress every day.

After exhausting her burst of energy, Claire dropped into a giggling heap on her bed. She indulged in a lengthy stretch, wondering what she had done to deserve such good fortune. Then she jumped back out of bed, smoothed out the creases in her dress, and wandered back to her dressing table. She sat down at the chair, took a pink ribbon from the top drawer, and tied a careful bow in her hair. She dabbed the tiniest bit of honeysuckle water on her neck and wrists before skipping down the stairs, pausing for the briefest of seconds.

"Mother, I am off to Stephan's for supper, to meet his parents. I will be back before dark."

And then she was gone, without even a chance to say goodbye. Cordelia stood over the kitchen counter, both arms white to the elbows with flour as she kneaded the bread dough. She watched Claire through the window, gliding down the street like an escaped kite, drifting away on the slightest breeze. She shook her head wryly as she brushed the sticky bits of dough from her fingers. She tried not to be envious of her daughter while at the same time wondering idly if that was what being in love was like.

Claire told herself not to be nervous at dinner, but despite Stephan's assurances that his parents would adore her, she felt uneasy. Claire wasn't normally a clumsy girl, but she hadn't been at the table more than three minutes before she knocked over her water glass, sending a tidal wave across the table. Her cheeks flushed bright red, but Stephan gave her hand an encouraging squeeze under the table, and for a minute, she felt a little better. But overall, things didn't seem to be going very well. She tried to make conversation but found Stephan's family to be as good as a brick wall as far as chatting was concerned. His mother and sisters ate their dinner in near silence, their eyes carefully trained on their meal. Claire could see that Stephan's father was the source of absolute authority in this house, and if she wanted to marry Stephan, it was his father she needed to impress.

Claire praised the meal and the china and the house and everything else she could think of. But Stephan's mother hardly glanced at her twice, and her progress with his father wasn't much better. He directed the piercing stares usually reserved for his wife to Claire, and she shifted uncomfortably in her chair under his watchful eye. He studied her as one might a unicorn that showed up at the dinner table. Stephan kept her well supplied with hopeful smiles, but it wasn't enough to counteract the potent effect of his father's blatant sizing up.

Almost before the last bite of peach cobbler disappeared from their plates, the children begged to be excused and were waved away impatiently by their father. The remaining occupants of the table spent a few minutes of quiet, miserable contemplation, at which point, Stephan's father rose unexpectedly from his chair.

"Well, this has been most . . . pleasant. It was a pleasure to meet you, Claire. However, I have more important things to attend to this evening, if you will excuse me."

"Father, wait," Stephan interjected quickly. "If you will remember, there was something I wished to discuss with you . . ."

"Yes, I know. Some other time, perhaps."

"But, Father, the talk was the reason that I asked Claire for supper this evening."

"This is not the right time, Stephan. Come and see me later tonight, after your friend has gone home," his father said coldly.

Claire directed her eyes at the floor, embarrassed that she was being discussed as though she were absent. Her face was still red and hot, and she began counting the flowers in the rug, wishing that she were small enough to slip underneath it and hide.

There was a distinct edge to Stephan's voice now, and Claire got the feeling that she was about to become the cause of a family brawl. She stood quickly, putting on a bright smile.

"It is all right, Stephan. I really should be going anyway. I told my mother I would be home before dark, and I would not want her to worry."

Stephan stood as well. "Claire, wait. There is nothing that my father might say that you could not hear, especially since I hope you will soon be my wife."

Stephan's father snorted derisively, but said nothing.

"So, Father, if you will give your consent, Claire and I would very much like to be married," Stephan finished, pushing out a short breath and waiting anxiously.

Stephan's father took one last quick glance at Claire before shaking his head firmly. "I am afraid that is impossible," he said bluntly.

"Why? Father, I cannot understand why you are so opposed to this. I love Claire very much."

"Yes, but does she love you?"

"Of course I do," Claire interjected.

"Then why are you dishonest with him?" Stephan's father said, his arms spread in open challenge.

"I have never lied to Stephan about anything," Claire said stubbornly.

"Fine, if that is the game you wish to play. You are an unacceptable choice, and we shall leave it at that."

"With respect, that is simply not good enough, Father. You obviously have some reason for your decision, and I demand to know what it is," Stephan said firmly. He grabbed Claire's hand in plain sight as a show of solidarity, and she knew that she had never loved him as much as she did at that moment.

"I had hoped to spare you this, but now I see it is unavoidable. It is her heritage."

Stephan looked confused. "What about her heritage?"

"She is from a fairy line—their blood runs through her veins. Stephan, she is impure!"

Stephan sighed in relief. "Is that all? Father, I already know she has fairies in her distant family. Nearly everyone does, if you go back far enough."

"Not as distant as you might think," he spat out. "Ask her about her mother."

"What about her mother?"

"Tell him," his father said, looking ominously in Claire's direction.

Stephan still gripped Claire's hand tightly in his own, but she could feel the suspicion seeping out of him and spied the first signs of distrust forming when she forced herself to look into his eyes. She took a deep breath.

"I did not want you to find out like this. My mother had more . . . fairy characteristics than I do."

"Fairy characteristics?" his father said, leering. "That is putting it mildly. Stop trying to sugarcoat it—your mother has wings!"

"*Had* wings," Claire shot back. "She was rounded up by hateful people like you—she and all the others like her, and when she returned home—her 'unnatural differences' had been remedied." Claire looked to Stephan for support, only to discover him suddenly studying her back carefully. "Are you trying to see if I am tainted as well?" she asked sharply.

Stephan's face reddened, and he quickly pulled his hand away from hers. Claire looked away in bitter disappointment. Her Stephan, who she loved and was hoping to spend the rest of her life with, couldn't even look her in the eye. He was slipping away, and there was nothing she could do about it. He finally gave her the briefest of glances before resuming his place at the table and fixing his eyes on the floor.

Claire knelt on the ground beside his chair and put her hand on his arm, wincing when he recoiled from her touch. Still, she was determined to try. "Stephan, look at me. I am just Claire, the same girl you wanted to marry only minutes ago. Nothing has changed. What are you so afraid of?"

"Everything has changed. We can never be together now," he said, his voice so quiet that she had to strain to hear the awful words.

"Because my mother had wings?" she said in disbelief.

"Because you were not honest with me," he said, his voice icy and distant. He squared his shoulders but looked beyond her at the wall, avoiding her eyes. "We are different, you and I. You could never understand."

"You are right. I will *never* understand."

Claire left in a hurry, torn between wanting to stay so she could try to persuade Stephan, and wanting to leave with her head held high. She knew if she said anything else, her broken heart would betray itself through the quiver in her voice. So she left, stumbling through the streets in a painful haze.

When Claire reached home, Cordelia was seated at the table, waiting anxiously to hear about her evening, but Claire was tired. She was too tired to tell her mother the story, and too tired to make something up. So she went straight past the table, past her mother and her concerned gaze to her bed, where she stayed.

For thirty days, Claire refused to go out and wouldn't eat. She lay quietly under the covers while the tears made fresh tracks from her cheeks to the pillow. After a while, they began to pool on the floor around her bed. No one understood where the endless well of salty sadness was springing from, as Claire refused any food or drink that was brought to her. Nevertheless, whenever she wasn't sleeping, she was crying. The sea of tears grew deeper and deeper, and when Cordelia opened Claire's door to check on her, they started to seep down the hall. Before long, they were up to her mother's knees, and she was afraid that Claire might drown. She had to make multiple trips up and down the stairs with a bucket, emptying the tears in the garden.

Unfortunately, the salt killed all of the vegetables and the flowers; theirs was the only house in the neighborhood where nothing would grow. And still, Claire continued to weep. Her beloved sewing lay untouched on the chair by her bed. Her mother was nearly hysterical as she watched her once lively daughter disappear into the bed sheets, her cheeks hollow and her eyes empty.

"Claire, darling, I know you are unhappy, but this has gone on long enough. If you don't eat something soon, you're going to fade away completely. Is that what you want?" Cordelia pleaded.

"Yes."

. . . ✶ . . .

When Claire's father came home that night, he was puzzled to find his wife sitting at the kitchen table with a faraway look in her eye. He sat down in the chair next to her, and she blinked a few times, turning to stare at her husband as if he were a stranger.

"What are you doing home so early?" she said finally, looking around as she attempted to orient herself.

"This is the same time I come home every day. Where is supper?"

Cordelia glanced briefly around the kitchen, as if hoping the food would appear by her simply wishing it into existence. "The last thing I remember was coming in here to start the meal, but I was so tired. I sat down at the table to rest for a minute, and then you walked in."

"Maybe I should call the doctor," he said brusquely, pushing his chair back.

"We should call the doctor, but not for me. It's Claire—I thought she would get over her grief and improve on her own, but she is getting worse."

His hard face softened a little. Claire was his beautiful daughter, his only child. How anyone could humiliate and degrade her the way that Stephan boy did was beyond his comprehension. After all, Claire couldn't help what her mother was. He told himself for the hundredth time that if he were twenty years younger, he would have taught that scoundrel a lesson he would not soon forget. Instead, he went to fetch the doctor, who examined a listless

Claire thoroughly before rendering his diagnosis.

"Your daughter is very low in spirits, and I am afraid her health is failing," the doctor said, his face a serious mask. "She must be treated immediately if she is to recover."

"Of course; anything that can be done, we will do. What do you recommend to restore her health, Doctor?" Cordelia asked anxiously.

"In cases of her particular illness, I have found fish oil to work remarkably well."

"Fish oil? Is there not some sort of treatment or medicine that would be better?" Her father was already beginning to wish he'd waited for their regular doctor, who was out of town. But he was surprised to see how far Claire had deteriorated in the past few days, and he was afraid that if they didn't get her some help soon, by the time their doctor returned, it might be too late.

"I know that it does not sound very impressive, but trust me when I say that fish oil is the very best thing for someone with her condition." The doctor opened his bag and removed a vial of greasy yellow oil and a folded slip of paper. "This should be enough for the first day, and here is the name of a fisherman who can supply you with additional oil. Dose your daughter with the fish oil every night at bedtime, and she will soon be feeling more like herself again. I will check on her in a week, but you may contact me if there is anything you need before that."

"We will never be able to thank you, Doctor," Cordelia said, trying to keep the tears from her voice. She showed him to the door, all the time gripping the vial tightly, as if it were liquid gold instead of something she could find in the market.

"Would you like to take the oil up to Claire?" she asked her husband.

"What good will it do? The man is obviously a charlatan."

"Nonsense," she bristled. "We must have faith in the doctor. Besides, we have to give the right impression to Claire. She has to believe that it will work, or she might not even try it." She thrust the vial into his open hand, closing his fingers around it.

"I still think it is ridiculous, but we have to do something." He climbed the wooden stairs to Claire's room, muttering under his breath about how silly it all was, stopping briefly in front of her door to compose himself. He put on his best smile.

"And how is my girl?"

"The same as I was when you left me ten minutes ago, Father." Claire's eyes were fixed on the ceiling, and even when he sat down on the edge of her bed, she didn't look at him.

"The doctor said this is going to help you start feeling better again. He said that fish oil is the best thing for someone with your condition."

"What did he say my condition is, exactly?"

Her father thought the doctor was a fraud, with his vague promises of a miraculous cure, but he wasn't about to tell her that. "He has it narrowed down to a few possibilities, and he is still trying to decide what exactly is wrong with you. He said if you take this every day, you will be back to the way you were before in no time."

"Nothing can do that. There is no medicine on this earth that will fix me. I will never be back to the way I was before," she said calmly. Her voice was monotone, but tears began to leak from the corners of her eyes as she spoke. It was almost more than her father could bear to look at her.

"Please, Claire. Could you try it? For me?"

Obediently, she opened her mouth, and her father poured the contents onto her tongue. If it tasted anything like it smelled, it must have been dreadful, but Claire didn't complain.

"Good girl."

"I am very tired, Father. I would like to go to sleep now, if that is all right." Claire turned toward the window and closed her eyes. Her father slipped out of the room, joining Cordelia back in the kitchen.

"Well?"

He shook his head sadly. "I lied and told her it would make her feel better, and she swallowed it without a word. But I could tell she did not believe me." He took his jacket from the hook on the wall. "I am going out for a while."

"I will have dinner ready when you get back."

"Do not trouble yourself; it seems that I have lost my appetite."

. . . * . . .

Cordelia peeked through the crack in her daughter's door, trying to decide if she was sleeping. Everything was always so silent and still in Claire's room now, it was difficult to tell whether she was even breathing. Even if Cordelia left the window open so Claire could get some fresh air, the room still felt stale and unused. The air seemed to bypass the room, afraid of catching whatever illness had settled there. It was as if Claire had disappeared one day: all her things were still in their places, waiting for her to return.

"Claire?" Cordelia whispered. "Are you awake?" Even her own words wanted nothing to do with the room. They bounced back toward her in an effort to escape the haunting presence of her altered child. When there was no response, she tried again, a little more urgently. "Claire?"

"Yes, Mother, I'm awake." The phrase floated uncertainly from the direction of Claire's bed.

"I've run out of flour, and I have to go to the market. Is there anything you need?"

"What would I need?"

"I was being polite. It does not have to be something you *need*, you know. Is there anything you would like? It could be something wild and impractical; I would not care. I could spend a fortune, and as long as it made you happy, your father would be overjoyed. If you ever dreamed of having something that seemed impossible, now would be the time to ask."

"You cannot find the impossible thing I want at the market."

"What is it? Honestly, I think your father would sell this house and live in the street if he thought he could buy something that would put a smile on your face again."

"I want Stephan. That is the only thing I want."

"Claire," she said uncertainly.

"No, that is the one thing that would make me happy. So you can tell Father that if he wants to see a smile on my face again, he can make Stephan come to me. He can make him love me again."

"I know you cannot mean that. You would not want to be with someone who would run at the first sign of trouble. Stephan did not really love you, or he would not have deserted you as soon as he discovered something outside his ideal. And not even something about you—it was about your family. It was something you had absolutely no control over."

"Stephan did love me," Claire said violently, her thin face distorted by rage. "He simply dared not disobey his father."

"Would you really want to be a part of that family, where they have no respect for you?" Cordelia said gently.

"I just want things to be the way they were before. I cannot go on feeling like this anymore."

Cordelia brushed the hair from Claire's face. A faint blush was struggling to rise to the surface of her pale cheeks, and Cordelia caught a fleeting glimpse of Claire as she once was. Tears swelled in her eyes as she tried to find the words to explain.

"Oh, Claire. If only it was possible for me to give you what you really need; a glimpse into the future. If you could only see a little farther down the road, you would understand how very little this will all matter to you. I know it is hard to imagine now, but this will not be the great tragedy of your life. You will be happy again, in time, with someone else."

"You had better get the flour, or dinner will be late. You know how Father hates that." Claire attempted a half-hearted smile, for her mother's sake.

"I will be back soon. Are you certain you will be all right here by yourself?"

"You have no need to worry about me. I am not going anywhere." Her voice was tired again, and her eyes drifted away toward the ceiling.

. . . ✶ . . .

Claire was having a hard time falling asleep after her mother left. Lately, she slipped in and out of consciousness so easily that she sometimes had difficulty distinguishing the difference between sleep and reality. All she had to do was close her eyes, and she could escape to her place of nothingness. No dreams ever dared disturb her there, and she had no worries. It was almost like she had never existed at all.

But not today. Suddenly, for the first time in over a month, Claire was forced to sit awake with her thoughts. There was a bird in the tree outside her window, perched on a branch with its little blue head cocked sideways. The bird opened his beak and sang the same little tune, over and over, looking encouragingly in Claire's direction.

This would never do. Claire closed her eyes again, waiting for the familiar burn of tears to come. But nothing happened. She squeezed her eyes closed tightly, willing a few drops of saltwater to appear. When there were still no signs of weeping, she allowed her mind to rest on the one thing that she knew would cause her the greatest pain. She conjured the picture of her beloved in her mind, settled into her pillow, and waited for the thundering squall that accompanied it. Stephan who abandoned her, Stephan who destroyed all her hopes, Stephan who was the source of her endless grief.

Claire's nose started to run a little, so that was something. Of course, the window was open, and the trees were heavy with pollen-filled blossoms, so it might not be grief at all. It could just be an allergy. Was it possible she had finally run out of tears?

A sudden, loud knock at the door downstairs brought Claire out of her reverie. Startled, she jumped a little and made a slight squeaking sound. Her mother hadn't mentioned that she was expecting anyone, but she should be back from the market any time now. She closed her eyes again, concentrating on Stephan and the shameless way he discarded her. She was rewarded with another knock, a little extra pounding thrown in for good measure, and of course the same persistent, happy bird with his hopeful song.

Claire sighed in frustration. She would never be able to focus on producing any tears with that racket going on outside. Surely whoever it was would give up and go away soon.

"Hello?" someone shouted. "Is anyone home?"

A man's voice. For one happy moment, Claire thought it might be Stephan, coming to beg her forgiveness. But she knew his voice almost as well as her own, and it was definitely not Stephan. A strange man at the front door—maybe he was looking for her father. Well, he would just have to come back later, when there was someone who could answer the door. Claire snuggled farther into her blankets and waited to see what the voice would say next. As if on cue, he yelled, "I have an important delivery for this house, and I was told someone would be here to collect it. Is there anyone at home?"

This was getting ridiculous. Soon, all the neighbors would be at their windows, wondering at all the shouting. Something had to be done. Claire took a deep breath.

"There is no one here, but someone should be home soon. Go away and come back in about an hour!" she shouted.

"I knew someone must be home! Let me in—I have something that has to be delivered."

"Just leave it on the porch and go!" she yelled frantically.

"I cannot. Someone must sign for it, and I was told specifically to give this to the young lady of the house. Is that you?"

"I am afraid there has been a mistake. We do not need it anymore."

"Oh. Well, I suppose I will just go away then. I am sorry to have bothered you, miss."

Claire let out a huge sigh of relief. Her parents might be cross when they got home, but since they had both been tiptoeing around her lately, she was certain no one would be too upset. The delivery man would go and leave her in peace, and he would come back later when someone else was home. No real harm was done. To top it all off, the noisy bird was nowhere to be found. He must have been frightened away by all the yelling. Maybe now she could get back to the task at hand. Claire closed her eyes, not really expecting any tears, but willing to settle for sleep at this point.

From the window, she heard the sound of branches rustling. Claire groaned. It must be the bird back again, ready for another impromptu concert. She rolled over and opened her eyes but saw something much more sinister than the bird. In the branches directly outside her window, she saw a hand. Paralyzed by fear, she could do nothing but watch as another hand appeared, followed by a head. It grinned.

"Well, would you look at that; someone really is home."

Claire shrieked.

The man momentarily lost his grip and nearly fell out of the tree. "Calm down, woman! Do you want to have the policeman at your door?"

"What do you think you are *doing*?!" Claire screamed.

"I told you, I have a package to deliver. And I am not a man who gives up so easily." One hand dipped below Claire's sight, only to reappear with a small vial.

"And I told you, we do not want it!"

"Who is this 'we?' Is there a mouse under your bed?" he said, amused.

"My mother will be home any minute," Claire threatened.

"Good. Maybe she will sign for this package so I can get on with the rest of my work."

"You are going to be in a heap of trouble."

"Why? Because I climbed your tree and startled you? I would not have had to do any of that if you just came to the door like a normal person."

"What makes you think I am not normal? What have you heard?"

"Just sign for the package, and I will take my leave."

"I am afraid I cannot sign for the package."

"Can you not write your name?"

Claire bristled. "Of course I can write my name. I am educated," she said haughtily.

"Go on, then; impress me. Get out of bed and sign for the package."

"I cannot get out of bed."

"Why?"

"Because I am ill."

"Forgive me for saying so, but you do not look very sick."

"Well, I am," she sniffed.

"Oh," he said, his face brightening with sudden understanding. "This must be for you," he said, shaking the vial, laughing a little to himself. "It does explain a lot, does it not?"

"What are you talking about?" Claire was quickly losing patience.

"Well, sometimes when a young woman of a certain age who does not look very sick cannot get out of bed, they dose her with fish oil," he said, as if it were the most natural thing in the world.

"And just what is this magical fish oil supposed to do for me?"

He grinned again; a charming, slightly lopsided smile. "Nothing."

Claire was exasperated. "That makes absolutely no sense at all."

The man readjusted his grip on the tree, checking to make certain his footing would hold before settling in against a large branch.

She tried again. "I was told that fish oil is supposed to be very good for my condition."

"Oh, yes. Any doctor would tell you that fish oil is the best thing to treat your particular ailment."

Claire looked satisfied.

"It comforts the parents; helps them believe that they are doing something for their sick daughter and it makes the patient feel . . . validated."

Claire's face fell, and she found she suddenly couldn't look at the man in the tree anymore.

"What I meant was, when a doctor cannot find anything physically wrong with a young woman, they treat her with fish oil. It plays a little trick on your mind, convinces it that you are cured. Fish oil is the most readily prescribed cure for what you are suffering from."

"And does this mystery ailment have a name?"

He tossed the vial in the air, catching it neatly. "A broken heart."

"A broken heart?" she said angrily. "Is that what you think is wrong with me? Because I assure you, I have a legitimate illness. And since you are a delivery boy and not a doctor, I have to assume that there are more uses for fish oil than you are aware of. So maybe you should just stick to delivering things instead of handing out diagnoses."

"Which is what I was trying to do, if you recall? And just so you know, I am a fisherman, not a delivery boy. By the way, does your 'legitimate illness' have a name, if you do not mind me asking?"

"They have not decided exactly what it is yet—"

He snorted a laugh.

"—but you can rest assured that it is very serious. My parents are very concerned. I will probably die."

"Well, I would hate for that to happen."

"Why?" she said quietly, as if the small fire that had been sustaining her had burned out.

"Because then I would have no reason to come here again, and this has definitely been the most interesting part of my day."

Claire was speechless. Her heart, which had quit beating a month ago, suddenly started pumping again.

"By the way, you were right about your condition being serious. Plenty of people before you have died of broken hearts—it is up to you whether the condition is terminal."

Before she could come up with a reply, the stranger set the vial carefully on the window sill and began to climb back down the tree. Claire couldn't remember when she'd been so elated and disappointed at the same time. She leaned back against the pillow and closed her eyes, lamenting that she didn't even know the deliveryman's name.

. . . ✶ . . .

Cordelia rushed into her daughter's room like a whirlwind.

"Oh, Claire, the most terrible thing has happened! I thought the deliveryman would just leave your fish oil on the doorstep, but it is nowhere to be found. He never comes this late—he must have been here while I was gone. What will we do without the fish oil until tomorrow?" In the agony of the moment, she failed to notice her daughter's miraculous transformation. She stood dumbly, her mouth gaping. "Claire, darling, you are sitting up! You are working on your stitching!"

Claire smiled at her mother. She sat against the headboard on the bed, her sewing in her lap. Her mother's face clouded over again. "The fish oil has begun to do its work, and now we do not have any. Where am I going to get it at this hour? You might relapse!"

"Do not worry, Mother. The deliveryman did come while you were gone, and I signed for the fish oil. See, here it is." She pointed to her nightstand.

"Thank heaven for that. But how did you get downstairs to sign for the package?"

Claire smiled again. "I walked. I really am starting to feel better, Mother. But I think I should keep taking the fish oil for a while longer, just in case," she said quickly.

"By all means, if you think it is helping."

"Of course it is helping. What else could it be?"

Cordelia went downstairs to make dinner, happy in the knowledge that it was her little talk and not the fish oil that had started her daughter on her way to recovery. Claire stitched in her room and thought of the healing powers of another conversation entirely.

"So your mother got better?" Kaitlin asked.

"She did."

"And did she fall in love with the delivery boy?"

"You're getting ahead of the story. Megan must be exhausted

from the heat, not to mention hungry. We should take a break for a while and have lunch," Viola whispered, her voice almost completely gone.

Kaitlin sighed. "I'll go out and tell her to come in." She bounded out of the kitchen just in time to find Megan emerging from the bathroom. "How's it going?"

"I've been looking for a ladder. I finally gave up and came in to ask your grandma where she's hiding it. How's your book?"

"Better than I expected. But then, I had to take a break and listen to Grandma go on and on about her relatives."

Megan was careful to keep her emotions hidden. "That was nice of you. What did she say?"

"She told me about her mother. Her name was Claire, and I think she married a delivery boy, or maybe he was a fisherman."

"What do you mean, you think she married a delivery boy or a fisherman?"

"We haven't gotten to that part yet, but I'm pretty sure that's what will happen."

"You know, your dad always said that his mother never talked about her family. I wonder what made her decide to tell you now."

She shrugged. "Beats me."

"The funny thing is you probably know more now about your dad's family than he does."

"Yeah, that's funny. I'll have to tell him about it when he comes home." Kaitlin pushed away the sudden surge of guilt, thinking about what Grandma said about how her mother wouldn't believe in the fairies. In fact, if she found out, she probably wouldn't let Viola tell her any more of the story, and she was determined to find out if her grandma was a fairy too.

As they strolled into the kitchen, Viola gave Megan a sympathetic look. "It's too hot for you to be out there working. I never should have agreed to it."

"Actually, I haven't done a thing yet. I was too busy looking for a ladder."

Viola paused, her face wearing a puzzled expression. "I'm

pretty sure I left it right outside the garage door."

Megan smiled. "Silly me, I must have missed it. I'll have to look again after lunch."

* THREE *

Viola cleared away the plates and stacked them neatly in the dishwasher. Kaitlin chugged some of the lemonade in her glass, puckering a little as she swallowed.

"Grandma, why is your lemonade so sour? Did you forget to add the sugar to the packet? I did that once."

"What packet?"

"You know; the packet the lemonade mix comes in."

"My lemonade doesn't come from a packet—it comes from a lemon!" Viola said indignantly. She pointed out the kitchen window. "I have a lemon tree, right in my backyard."

"Maybe your lemons just aren't sugary enough." Kaitlin contemplated finishing her drink, and then decided against it. "Well, I guess I'll get back to my book . . ." she trailed off.

"Never mind your book. I thought that maybe you and I could play cards for a little while this afternoon."

"I know Go Fish and UNO."

Viola frowned. "What about Gin?"

Kaitlin shook her head.

"Poker?"

"You know how to play poker? Wicked!"

"Card games are not wicked, Katie. Unless you have some sort of gambling addiction, in which case—"

"No, Grandma, wicked is good. Wicked means cool."

She rolled her eyes. "Honestly, I don't understand the way children speak anymore."

"So, are you gonna teach me?" she said eagerly.

Viola looked at Megan, who nodded her hesitant approval. "I suppose there are worse people to introduce you to poker than your grandmother. I want to check my email anyway, see if there's anything from your dad before I get back to the windows."

"If you email him, tell him I'm going to beat him at cards when he gets back."

Viola took the cards and the poker chips out of one of the kitchen drawers. She shuffled the cards expertly, and Kaitlin watched her in awe. She looked like one of those casino dealers in the movies, except her hands were old and wrinkled. "I haven't played cards in ages. I used to play with my neighbor Fern all the time, until she died. She had a stroke, right in her front yard. They found her lying face down in the dirt, smashing all her geraniums."

Kaitlin was a little alarmed but tried not to show it. She wanted her grandma to see how grown-up she was, so she would keep telling her the fairy story. "Was she a good friend?" she asked in a polite tone.

"She could play pinochle for hours, but you had to watch her because she was a terrible cheater. She would never admit she was cheating, though, so we had some awful fights about it. Sometimes she wouldn't speak to me for a week. Then one day, she'd just appear with a plate of peanut brittle, like nothing ever happened." Viola sighed.

"I bet you really miss her."

"She did make the best peanut brittle. Now, are you ready?"

Kaitlin nodded enthusiastically.

"Right. Oh, I almost forgot the most important thing." Viola scurried into her bedroom, returning with her prize—a purple visor covered in little yellow flowers. She placed it triumphantly on her head, her curly reddish hair spilling across the brim.

Kaitlin gave her a questioning look.

"My lucky hat. I had to keep it in my bedroom because I was always afraid that Fern would steal it. She had a lucky hat too, but it wasn't as lucky as mine. No flowers," she said matter-of-factly, as if it was the most obvious thing in the world.

"What about my lucky hat?"

"You don't need a lucky hat. At least, not this time, because you'll have beginner's luck. But if you start playing a lot of poker in the future, I highly recommend it. If you can find one with flowers on it, that's even better. Now, where were we?"

"You were going to deal the cards."

"Yes, of course. Did I tell you about the time I was playing with Fern and got a royal flush? She lost eight dollars in that game because she was positive I was bluffing. I think it was two weeks before she came around again after that, she was so furious. And there was no peanut brittle either, let me tell you!" she crowed. "She brought half-price day-old snicker doodles and said I was lucky to get them."

Kaitlin smiled politely but could see that this was getting nowhere. "So, how many cards do you deal?"

"Well, it depends on what kind of poker you're playing. Now, I am rather partial to five-card stud, so we'll start with that and see how we do." She dealt two cards to her granddaughter, one face up and one face down, and dealt herself the same. Kaitlin immediately lifted the corner of the hidden card, trying to see what it was.

"No peeking!" Viola said sternly.

Kaitlin dropped the card, raising her hands and feigning innocence. "Now, what?"

Viola's face clouded over, and she scrunched up her forehead in deep concentration. Finally, she closed her eyes and shook it off, like a bad dream. "The trickiest part is the beginning. I got interrupted. Let me deal again—I'm sure it will come to me." She gathered up the cards and shuffled them, a little less confidently this time. She dealt again, first to Kaitlin, then to herself. She set the remaining deck on the table in front of her and waited for inspiration. Finally, she lowered her eyes and said quietly, "Are you sure you wouldn't rather play something else?"

"It's okay if you can't remember, Grandma."

"It's just been a really long time since I played, that's all. I'm sure if I could just get started, it would all come back to me." Her raspy voice had an edge of desperation, and Kaitlin thought it was strange how even a whisper could convey such a range of emotions.

"Please don't tell your mother that I couldn't remember how to play, Katie. I don't want her to think I'm getting confused. After all, it's just a card game, but she might think it was something more."

"You mean, if you can't remember how to play poker, she might think there were other things you can't remember?"

"Exactly! You're such a smart girl, Katie. I knew you would understand."

"How about if I don't tell Mom about the cards, and you tell me more about the fairies?"

"I think you've heard enough of the fairy story today. I could tell you a different story."

"But I don't want to hear a different story. I want to hear about the fairies!"

"But this is a story about me. So far, you've only been getting stories about other people."

Kaitlin still looked unconvinced.

"What I'm going to tell you, I've never told to another living soul. You and I will be the only two people on earth who know this story."

Her eyes glazed over. Perhaps this was the story about the Spanish castle, which would make sense if no one else knew about it. And wasn't the possibility of royal heritage more intriguing than fairies? "You're positive no one else knows this story?"

"Absolutely. It's a story about me and my father." Viola cleared her throat, startling Kaitlin out of her castle daydream. "My earliest memory from when I was a very little girl was walking on the seashore with my father. I remember the sounds of the gulls crying and the water lapping against the rocks. I lived on a strip of sandy beach, and when I opened my eyes in the morning, I could look out the window and see that particular blue where the water meets the sky. My father was the ruler of this domain, and the inhabitants of the seashore were his loyal subjects."

"I knew it! That's why you lived in a castle. Your father was the king, wasn't he?" Kaitlin burst out, no longer able to contain her excitement.

Her grandmother laughed, a hoarse sort of cackle. "What a strange thing to say! Weren't you listening earlier? My father was a fisherman."

Kaitlin tried to smile as the possibility of being revealed as the last of a lost royal line melted away in the oppressive heat.

✶

Meg,

Arrived safely—hope you are having a great time. You can't believe how hot it is here! Give my mother a hug from me and tell her how sorry I am about the way things worked out. I really was looking forward to seeing her.

Not much time to talk right now. I'll send you another email soon and let you know when I can give you a call. I wish I was there with you.

Love,

Kevin

P.S Tell Kaitlin I hope she's getting a nice tan laying out by the pool.

Megan wasn't sure what that last line about the pool meant. Perhaps Kaitlin would understand it. She typed out a quick reply, anxious to get back to see what Viola and Kaitlin were up to. She wasn't sure she should leave her daughter alone too long. She might not take to poker and find a way to move her grandmother onto other topics, like the strange story she was telling Kaitlin about her mother and fairies. When Megan first stumbled onto Viola telling the story, she assumed that what she heard was simply a fairy tale. She was still reeling from the shock of discovering that her mother-in-law was serious, and she found herself wondering if Viola might be losing her mind.

Kevin,

I might have more empathy for the heat situation than you think. Apparently, your mother didn't think fixing her air conditioning was a necessary expense. Kaitlin and I did think about stealing her car and escaping, but when we discovered that it didn't have any air either, the appeal was lost.

Although I am missing you terribly, I am glad that we decided to come anyway, and there's something I have to tell you. Either your mother has a very vivid imagination, or she's completely senile. She's been telling Kaitlin some stories about her life that don't quite add up. And the strangest thing is she's done her best to keep me out of it. I think she views it as Kaitlin's inheritance or something, plus the fact that she probably knows any rational adult would have serious questions regarding her sanity. I don't really know her well enough to tell if she's just prone to exaggeration or if her mind is really going. Maybe when I've heard a little more, I'll be able to decide better what to do.

Call me as soon as you get a chance—I need to see if you can corroborate any of this. I wish you were here, and not just because of your mother. I don't like being without you. It's only been a few days, and already I don't know how I'm going to get by. Please be safe.

Love,

Megan

"Your father was a . . . fisherman?"

"Of course. When I was little, he would work on the big ships, sometimes going out for days. But he had his own boat too—he loved the ocean. He used to wake up when it was still dark outside, and sometimes I would hear him moving around the house. While he was loading his nets into the boat, I liked to surprise him by sneaking into the kitchen and making sandwiches for his lunch. I'd cut slices of the bread my mother made and layer it with ham or thick slabs of cheese, and I wrapped them in newspaper. My father had a heavy coat that he always wore when he was on the water, and it had these massive, deep pockets. I would hide the sandwiches in the pockets, and I'd wave goodbye to him and watch his boat fade away until it was just a tiny dot in the distance, or until I couldn't stand the cold anymore. I remember how frozen my bare feet and hands were when I got back into bed, and how long it would take to get warm again. While I shivered in bed I pictured him waiting for his net to twitch with struggling fish, putting his hands into his coat pockets to warm them and discovering my gift. He would eat my sandwiches, the salty mist of the sea settling like a film on the bread."

Viola started to cough suddenly, so Kaitlin hurried to the sink and got a glass of water. Her grandmother took a gulp, which only made her cough more. When she finally settled down again, her voice was little more than a whisper. "I'm sorry, Katie. It must be all this talking I'm doing. I think I've talked more in the last two days than the two years before that."

"Do you need to take a break?"

She took another sip of the water and cleared her throat experimentally. "No. I am much better now, thank you. Where were we?"

"You were telling me about your father, how you got cold watching his boat sail away."

"Yes, but my favorite days were when he didn't go out on the boat at all. On Sundays, we would walk along the seashore and collect shells. My father always found the best shells, but I didn't mind. Maybe it was because the sea knew him better, so it trusted him more. But maybe it was just how patient he was. He would scoop up what looked like the least promising pile of sludge, but he would sift through it until he emerged with some sort of treasure. A tiny crab, scuttling across his hairy arm; or a scallop shell, dingy on the outside and crusted with sand, but pearly inside and still hinged at the base, like a butterfly with wings spread, frozen.

"Some of the shells he found were much smaller than your fingernail, but with the most intricate patterns you could imagine. I tried to follow his example, but when I buried my hands deep into the sand, all I ever succeeded in was making myself dirty. I preferred to stick to the more ordinary shells, the easy ones that were deposited conveniently at the water's edge. I guess I wasn't very adventurous."

"But your father was?" Kaitlin prodded.

"Oh my, yes. I was always afraid of getting pinched by the little crabs he found, and I never liked to swim. I had this terrible fear of drowning—I didn't go into the water past my knees."

"My father used to make me beautiful necklaces from the prettiest shells he found. I remember two necklaces in particular: a choker made from jagged pieces of opalescent abalone and a single spiral shell on a golden string. I couldn't figure out how he managed to thread the string through the shell. He told me the story of Daedalus, who was faced with the same challenge. Daedalus tied the string around an ant and lured him through the shell with a daub of honey. My father loved Greek myths, especially the ones having anything to do with the ocean."

"Grandma, can I ask you something?"

"Certainly, dear."

"If your father was a fisherman, weren't you poor?"

"Well, we certainly weren't wealthy, but we had enough to get by. Why do you ask?"

"I just don't get how you could have grown up in a castle in Spain and lived on the beach at the same time."

"Ah. The castle comes from a slightly later part of my life. Everything changed then."

"Could you tell me that story now?"

"Maybe tomorrow."

"But I *really* want to hear about the castle."

"We haven't reached that part of the story yet. You have to be patient."

"So the castle has something to do with the fairies?" Kaitlin asked eagerly.

"Your mother is coming—pick up some cards!" Viola hissed.

They frantically grabbed a handful of cards and pretended to study them carefully.

"How's my little card shark?" Megan asked, rubbing her daughter's shoulders affectionately.

"Grandma says I'm a natural," she said smoothly. "Even without a lucky hat."

"I got a message from Dad. He said he's arrived, and he misses us all. He sent a special message for you, Kaitlin. He told me to tell you that he hopes you're having a great time by the pool."

"The pool! I completely forgot," Viola said. "It's a good thing your father mentioned it, Katie."

"You have a pool? I didn't see a pool anywhere," Kaitlin commented.

"In the backyard; I'll show you tomorrow. Someone is coming to clean it in the morning, and I don't want you to see it until it's ready. I hope you brought your swimming suit, Katie; you're in for a real treat!"

* FOUR *

Kaitlin rolled over in bed, accidentally smacking her mother with her open palm. Her mom made a sort of muffled grunting sound and repositioned herself, too deep in sleep to notice. Kaitlin stared out the window, watching a bright orange butterfly flit back and forth and wondered what time it was. When the butterfly disappeared, she finally got out of bed and slipped into the swimsuit she had brought. Even if she wasn't going home a princess, she could still flaunt her new tan. Kaitlin had dark hair and a nice olive complexion that absorbed the sun, whereas her parents were both lighter. Her mother was blonde with fair skin, and her father was pale, red-headed, and freckled. By the end of the summer Kaitlin was always brown; her mother could ease her way into a tan, but her father stayed the same color year-round—unless he got sunburned. She hoped he had plenty of sunscreen over in Baghdad.

"Where are you going?" her mother asked groggily.

Kaitlin jumped. "You scared me. I thought you were asleep."

"Well, I was, until you decided to pummel me."

"Oops. I didn't think you noticed. This bed is just too small. I keep wondering where Dad would have slept if he had come."

"In this tiny bed with me," her mother replied. "You'd have been on the floor."

"One wrong move and I'm practically on the floor now!"

"What are you doing with your swimsuit on at this hour?"

"I'm going swimming. Grandma said someone was coming to clean the pool this morning, and the minute they leave, I want to be ready to dive in. What about you? Don't you want to cool off?"

"As much as I'd like to join you poolside, I want to help your grandma with some chores. I'm sorry, honey. I know this isn't the vacation you wanted."

Kaitlin shrugged. "I'm going to swim, get tan, read a book, and drink Grandma's sour lemonade. I can think of worse vacations. Are you at least coming to see the pool?"

"Sure, I'm as intrigued as you are. Your father never mentioned that his mother had a pool, and I would have thought that would be his biggest selling point, trying to convince you to spend two weeks in Arizona during the hottest part of the summer."

The door squeaked, and Viola poked her head around the corner, her arms full of towels. "Oh, good, you're awake! I was so excited about the pool that I couldn't wait any longer. I was afraid I was going to have to drag you out of bed myself."

"Is it ready?" Kaitlin asked eagerly.

Viola nodded, her eyes shining as brightly as if it were Christmas morning. "Here, you have to wear this." She took out a handkerchief and folded it lengthwise into a blindfold, which she tied around Kaitlin's eyes. The cloth smelled old, but not in a bad way; it was an ancient lavender sort of scent. Viola put her arm around her granddaughter's shoulder and started steering her toward the backyard. "I hope you like it, Katie."

"It's a pool—what's not to like?"

Flying in on the airplane, Kaitlin had seen numerous spots of blue, which magically became swimming pools the closer they got to the ground. She couldn't believe how many there were, but it never occurred to her that one of those backyards might be her grandmother's. She would swim in it everyday. Maybe when her mother saw how much she loved it, they might get a pool too! She'd be the most popular girl in school—the Girl with the Pool. Cool people would flock to her house, and everyone would want to be her friend. Yes, for her birthday next year, she would have a pool party in her very own pool.

Viola stopped briefly to open the door, and Kaitlin felt a wall of heat pressing against her, as solid as if it were a physical being. She allowed herself to be led through the grass, and she could sense the bright, warm yellow of the lemon tree.

"Okay, you can stop. We wouldn't want you to fall in, would we?"

"Can I take the blindfold off now?"

Viola gave her consent, and Kaitlin untied the cloth impatiently. She was greeted, not by the serene blue she'd marveled at from the plane, but the garish blue of a plastic wading pool. She opened her mouth to say something, but no words came out. This had to be a joke.

"I can see why you were worried she might fall in," Megan commented. Her face was completely blank, but Kaitlin knew her mother well enough to know that inside, she was howling with laughter.

"I don't know what to say, Grandma. It's so . . . clean."

Viola beamed. "You should have seen it before. It gets so dusty around here, and there was dried mud caked in the bottom. The man who came to clean it did a really nice job."

"Where did you hear about him?" Megan asked casually.

"I just looked up pool cleaners in the Yellow Pages. And he didn't even charge me as much as he quoted me over the phone—he said I was getting the senior discount," she said proudly.

Kaitlin thought it was more like the senile discount. The pool man must have been a saint to go through with it. Or maybe he could empathize because he had a grandmother too.

Viola deposited the towels on a rusty chaise lounge, which Kaitlin couldn't help noticing was bigger than the pool. "Well, I'm sure you'll want to start swimming right away. I'll bring you out some brownies when they're ready. I hope you're hungry—I made a huge pan so that I could give some to the pool man, but he said he couldn't wait until they were finished because he had lots of other jobs today. We're out of milk, but I'll bring you a nice big glass of lemonade."

"I'll just go get started on the windows," Megan said, glancing back at her daughter with barely time to mouth a "sorry" before Viola dragged her into the house to douse her in sunscreen. Kaitlin sighed, dipping her toe in the water and watching the ripples distort the colorful pictures of the clowns on the bottom of the pool. She flopped down into the water, enjoying the coolness while at the same time wishing it were deep enough to hide in. As she leaned back, the hard plastic dug into her back, and when she stretched her legs out, they protruded well past the edge. She was glad her grandma didn't have any neighbors under sixty-five. They probably had grandchildren who suffered the same fate when they came to visit, so they thought it was perfectly normal. It looked like the high point of her vacation would be waiting for her dad to call; as far as she was concerned, he had a lot of explaining to do.

Viola reappeared later with brownies and lemonade, but Kaitlin didn't feel much like eating.

"You haven't touched your brownie," Viola said disapprovingly.

"It looks really good, Grandma. I'm just not very hungry."

"But you didn't have any breakfast."

"Don't worry; I won't disappear from missing one meal."

"You're too skinny. Girls today walk around so gaunt, they look like they're all starving to death. I just want to take them home and feed them."

Kaitlin smiled and took a bite of her brownie as a show of good faith. "So, who are you going to tell me about today?"

Viola glanced around, but Megan was nowhere in sight. "Today, I'm going to tell you about the most evil man I ever met," she said dramatically.

"But what about Claire and the fisherman?"

"You mean Ian? Well, as I told you yesterday, they got married. A few years later, I was born."

"I think you missed a part. When we stopped, Claire was just starting to feel better, and she didn't even know the deliveryman's name."

"But I just told you—they got married."

Kaitlin smiled patiently. "I know, but what about the wedding?"

"How would I know what the wedding was like? It isn't as if I was there."

"You know what I mean. How did your dad propose? What did your mom's dress look like? You know, stuff like that."

Viola brushed it off. "That part of the story isn't really significant, except for one thing. My mother told my father that I was never to know the truth about my fairy heritage."

"Why?"

"The knowledge was always a source of great pain for her. There were plenty of fairies that were proud of who they were, but my grandmother viewed her wings as a curse. She warned my mother never to reveal the truth to anyone else. I am certain she thought that by keeping it from me, she was saving me from the heartache they suffered. When I was born, she made my father promise that he would never tell me. He thought it was quite amusing—he told her I might figure it out on my own when my wings started to grow in. My mother didn't think that was funny at all, and since it was extremely rare for the characteristics to skip a generation, she figured she would be safe."

"So, how did you find out?"

"When I escaped from being kidnapped, something happened. I knew for sure there must be fairies in my family."

"What happened?" Kaitlin asked.

"I can't tell you yet."

"Why?"

"It won't make any sense. Anyway, we still have a long way to go before we get to that part."

"Can I ask you a question?"

"You can ask me anything, but I can't promise you an answer."

"Do you have any proof?" she asked bluntly

"Proof of what, dear?"

"Well, something to prove that fairies really existed" Kaitlin said hesitantly.

"What were you hoping for? My grandmother's shriveled wings in a jar?"

Kaitlin blushed. "Of course not. I meant pictures or something that I can actually see."

Viola brightened. "There were some photographs of my mother and grandmother, and one of me and my father, next to his boat. There was also a newspaper clipping announcing my mother and father's wedding."

"Can I see them?"

"I'm afraid not."

"I'll be really careful with them—I promise."

"It's not that. I don't have them anymore."

Kaitlin bit her tongue to hold back her frustration. "Where did they go?"

"They were lost when our house was swallowed up by a sinkhole."

"A sinkhole?"

"Yes."

Kaitlin had seen pictures of a sinkhole on TV once and had watched in horrified fascination as the ground cracked and broke away, swallowing everything in its path. "My dad never mentioned anything about a sinkhole."

"Well, he was pretty traumatized. He was only in about second grade at the time, and we never could get him into a sandbox again. The poor child was absolutely convinced he would disappear! I imagine he didn't want to relive it by explaining it to you. But that's beside the point. Now, I was going to tell you about Count Diavolo."

Kaitlin didn't think Viola would appreciate the irony of her dad now being in the middle of Iraq; probably the biggest sandbox in the world. So instead, she hid her smile behind her lemonade. "Even his name sounds scary."

Viola looked stern, and there was another emotion on her face as well that Kaitlin couldn't quite place. "He was, without a doubt, the most despicable man you could ever imagine. But he wasn't always like that. Before he was the ruthless Count Diavolo, he was just Julian."

Julian

Julian liked to collect things. Many different items captured his interest, and he kept them all in assorted boxes, which were labeled with their various contents. He kept the boxes in stacks around the small room he shared with his brother, except for the most precious ones, his favorites, which he hid under his bed. It was rather like the basement of a museum, where all the odds and ends are stuffed into corners and covered with a thick layer of dust. Everyone knows that some of the most fascinating things to see in a museum are hidden in the basement, forgotten by everyone but the numerous scurrying mice.

Julian's father didn't like his collections. He wanted him to run and play and fight like the other boys—like his brother, Henri. At ten, Julian was older than Henri by a good two years, but Henri was taller and more solid. Henri was built like his father, whereas Julian had the look of his mother. At least, that's what people told him. Julian didn't remember his mother at all—she died shortly after giving birth to Henri, leaving them to be raised by a reluctant father. Henri managed to please his father with sheer brute strength, but it didn't seem to matter what Julian did. Although he was intelligent and loved to learn, nothing he did was ever good enough, and his father took no pains to hide his disappointment.

So Julian began creeping out of the house earlier and earlier, learning to find his own amusement. He didn't have any friends, and he preferred solitude to the company of his brother, who took great pleasure in tormenting him. Julian spent most of his days outdoors, where he found the first specimen of his earliest collection: a rock. He was amazed at the endless variety of nature—and that was just the stones. Julian brought a canvas bag with him and filled it with as many rocks as he could comfortably carry. Depending on how far he walked, some of the rocks were regrettably left along the way. The chosen few were placed in the box at home labeled *Stones*.

Over time, he added more and more boxes. One was marked *Leaves,* which was harmless enough and fairly self-explanatory. It was filled with many sizes and shapes, and no two were alike. Julian liked the way they looked when they were first picked—the longer they sat in the box, the duller and more brittle they became. So vibrant on the tree, once collected, they quickly faded and became ugly. He was disappointed at their decline and replaced them regularly with better ones.

Another box said *Spiders,* and Julian had two. He caught them in a jar and watched in fascination as the larger one devoured the smaller. He wanted the victor to have a more spacious home, so he placed it in the box with some grass. He was shocked to discover that when he went back to admire his sole specimen, the box was empty. From that point on, he was careful to only collect insects that were already dead. He didn't like the idea of his things wandering off the moment he turned his head, especially the crawly ones.

Another box said *Butterflies.* This was one of his favorites. He had three butterflies in the box: one blue delicately speckled with brown, one yellow with black stripes, and a tiny one that was pure white. The small white one might actually have been a moth, but he wasn't sure. And besides, he didn't have enough boxes to make a separate one for moths. The blue butterfly had one wing that was a little torn, and this vexed Julian. He had accidentally ripped the fragile, paper-thin wing when he was trying to remove the butterfly from the net. It bothered him a little to look at it, because the tear made the butterfly less perfect. Still, it was the most beautiful one in his collection, so he kept it. If you looked at it from a certain angle and in the right light, you could hardly tell there was anything wrong with it.

Julian asked Henri not to disturb his collections. Since Henri was much bigger than his brother, it was rather an idle threat and probably unnecessary anyway, since Henri had no interest in boxes of rocks and dead leaves, no matter how carefully chosen. So Julian was quite surprised when he came home early one day and stumbled onto Henri, who was lingering in their bedroom.

Julian's boxes were scattered all over the floor, as if a hurricane had blown through only their room, leaving the rest of the house untouched. Most of the boxes were overturned, their contents spilling out into a giant, jumbled pile. For a moment, Julian just stood and stared; the idea of his fastidiously sorted collections being heaped together threatened to overload his brain. To make matters worse, Henri had his fist deep into the box marked *Butterflies*. It was almost more than Julian could bear.

"What is all this rubbish?" Henri asked finally. He carelessly fished out the blue butterfly in his grubby hand, squinting.

Julian took a quick step forward, grabbing hopelessly at the box. "Careful, that one is damaged!"

"Listen to you—you're practically a girl! I can just see you, sitting here alone, petting your dead bugs. I bet you wish you could stay inside all day and sew cushions," he jeered.

"Give it back!" Julian burst.

Henri ran to the door with the box. "If you want it, come and get it!" he shouted over his shoulder.

Julian ran after his brother, chasing him to the stream that meandered past their house. Henri stood at the edge, still gripping the blue butterfly tightly. He crushed it in his fist, opening his hand to scatter it across the rushing water. He emptied the other butterflies after it, and the dead insect chased each other downstream, like colorful confetti corpses.

Suddenly, it was as if the whole world was moving incredibly slowly. The water in the stream slowed to a trickle, the remains of the butterflies froze, and Henri began to laugh. He threw back his head and emitted a great, lumbering guffaw. Julian picked up a big stick that was conveniently resting near his feet and moved little by little toward his brother, which made him laugh even harder.

Henri's face barely had time to register the shock when Julian hefted the stick and swung it at his head as hard as he could, catching him squarely at the base of his skull. The stick made a hollow, cracking sound when it connected and Henri went down, immediately unconscious. But Julian didn't stop. He hit him again and again. Every time he struck his brother, instead of feeling the rage building inside him, he felt calmer and more in control. Each blow released some incident of repressed fury, like peeling an onion apart a layer at a time, until you reach the tender green center.

With a sickening snap, the stick finally splintered and broke, and Julian set it down in the dirt. Henri lay motionless, a red trickle of blood peeking out from his hairline. A bruise was beginning to form under his right eye, a bluish black stain spreading underneath his skin, and one leg was twisted behind him at an unnatural angle. Julian couldn't believe it was so simple. After suffering through years of bullying, why had he never thought of this before? Julian wiped the dust from his hands onto his pants and went to find his father, who was cutting wood in the forest. He dreaded the confrontation, but his father would have to be told. Julian wasn't sure he was strong enough to drag Henri back to the house on his own.

When Henri woke up three weeks later, Julian wasn't there to see it. After placing Henri on his bed, Julian's enraged father chased him from the house with his axe, cursing him and warning him never to return. Wearing only the clothes on his back, Julian set off into the world. He didn't miss his father or brother, although he was a little disappointed at having to leave his collections behind. But when he saw a beautiful monarch butterfly feasting on a roadside flower, he realized he hadn't lost anything that was irreplaceable. He had bigger plans for his future collections; something to make everyone stand up and take notice.

For the next ten years or so, Julian wandered the countryside, doing odd jobs and making just enough money to keep from starving. He didn't mind working, as long as it suited his purposes. Once, he painted a barn—that provided him with several days' work. There was a large spot left unfinished when the farmer found Julian stealing a kiss from his lovely daughter. He could still remember the farmer's face, that particularly dangerous shade of red that reminded him of the paint he'd been slapping onto the barn. It made him a little nostalgic for some reason, but he was quickly jolted from his daydream when the farmer came at him with a pitchfork. The farmer was much older than Julian, and it would have been easy to get rid of him, but the idea left a bad taste in his mouth. After all, there was no reason to resort to violence, since he had already gotten what he wanted. Julian set off down the dirt road, laughing at the unpainted spot that the farmer would have to finish.

He took what seemed like hundreds of temporary jobs on farms, working in the fields. The women in the houses were all very sympathetic. They would feed him the most incredible meals—ham and potatoes, chicken and dumplings, homemade rolls with apricot jam, tender ears of corn on the cob, watermelon, and chocolate cake.

And pies. Over his wandering years, he developed an insatiable craving for pie; it didn't matter what kind. He had apple, blueberry, cherry, gooseberry, peach, raspberry, sweet potato, pumpkin, chocolate cream, pecan, strawberry, and some other berries he'd never even heard of. One resourceful woman even made an incredibly disgusting pie from green tomatoes. He managed to choke it down with a grin while her dour husband merely pushed it around the plate with his fork.

He put on his best manners when he sat at their tables, and he told them his tale of woe—a brother who despised him and usurped what little love their unfeeling father had to offer. He was a pathetic figure, and he could see them melt every time he told it. Every one of them looked at him as if they wanted to protect him from the world. He could see it in their eyes—he was broken, and they wanted to fix him. He ate their pie, soaked up their sympathy, and then he disappeared.

He never took jewelry or money, only the ladies' handkerchiefs. All the handkerchiefs were as different and varied as the women who owned them. Some were lacy or frilly, some were flowered, and some were very plain. They were either stiff and starched, or soft and worn with years. He kept them in his knapsack, and he cherished every one. They were his first new collection since leaving home.

Julian had discovered a trade that he was quite skilled at. He was mastering the art of deception.

. . . ✶ . . .

When he was about twenty-five, Julian found himself at the lowest point in his life. Word had spread of his habits as a mediocre field hand who ate more than he was worth with the strange habit of stealing handkerchiefs. He was run out of more than one village simply by reputation. The jobs had disappeared, which meant that the delicious home cooked dinners dried up also. No more warm pie with fresh cream and no more pity from the farmers' wives and daughters. No more handkerchiefs to add to his collection.

Without the regular meals, Julian became painfully thin. He managed to survive by stealing fruit from trees and sometimes preyed upon carrots or potatoes in an obliging garden in the middle of the night. But once the weather turned cold and the ground was hard, his one remaining source of food vanished. His clothing was ragged, and there were gaping holes in the soles of his shoes. His pants were too large now; he was down to the tightest notch in his belt. His hair was long and stringy, and he'd given up shaving, since there was no longer any need to make himself presentable for the tables of the farm women. His face was covered with a stubbly beard, which grew shaggier as the months went by. Although he was only twenty-five, this period of hard living made him look twenty years older.

Sometimes if he was lucky, he found a barn to sneak into at night. He covered himself with the hay in a vain attempt to stay warm, and the only bright spot was that the loud chattering of his teeth usually kept all but the boldest mice away. But mostly he ended up sleeping in the open. Sometimes he would awaken suddenly in the night to find himself covered with snow. He would gaze up into the sky at the bright, cruel stars, like pinpricks in the darkness.

His stomach growled, so he stuffed it with dead leaves or twigs. He contemplated swallowing a rock once. He even chose one—a nice smooth stone with no sharp edges, just so he could remember what it felt like to be full. He imagined it would be like that delicious feeling of having too much crusty bread or mashed potato, heavy in your belly.

As tired and hungry as he was, Julian kept walking. He followed a country road high into the mountains, where the air was even more brisk. On the chilliest nights, his beard and eyebrows were crusted with ice, making him look like a frozen walking corpse. Every morning he told himself that this would be the last day, and at night, when he could walk no further, this would be the night that he would give up. He would lie down and let the freezing snow suck what little life remained from his tired bones.

On that night when he was finally the hungriest and tiredest and coldest and dirtiest he'd ever been, when he laid down in the deepest snow bank he could find and gave himself permission to die, something extraordinary happened. He woke up the next morning, and not only did he wake up, but he awoke to spring: and not just any spring, but the most enchanting, intoxicating spring he'd ever known.

Perhaps he'd been delirious with sleep deprivation and hunger, and this had been coming on steadily for days. But it seemed to Julian that he'd fallen asleep on a frosty winter night and found himself smack in the middle of spring the next morning. It was unbelievable. He stood up and walked, feeling the morning sun melt the pain from his aching joints. He found a patch of wild strawberries and gorged himself, until the sticky sweetness filled him with the most wonderful nausea imaginable. He drank from an icy stream of rushing water near the bed of strawberries, plunging his whole head under until he had to resurface to breathe. The air was sweet with swarms of bees, and Julian couldn't imagine now why the night before he had been so ready to give up when the world was so lovely.

Invigorated by the berries and the clean water, Julian strode purposefully through the tall green grass, taking in huge draughts of the warm air. He didn't have to go very far before he was provided with the next breathtaking vision of the day. Not even a mile from where he collapsed the previous evening, he came to a spot where the trees led to a peak, overlooking the valley below. Hidden in the gorge like a glittering jewel was an enormous castle, just waiting to be discovered. Julian stood stunned, his mouth agape. He began descending the hill, never once looking away from his goal. He proceeded like a man in a trance, stumbling over rocks and walking into tree branches. His eyes were locked with the castle—he felt inexplicably drawn to it, and although he could not explain the impression, he somehow knew that his destiny and the castle were irrevocably entwined.

The loud ringing of the phone coming from the house broke the spell of Viola's story.

"How peculiar—no one ever calls here. Excuse me, dear." Viola shuffled to the door and went inside. Megan nearly beat her to the phone on the wall. She couldn't believe that according to the clock, it was almost two. She felt disoriented, like there was a fence around time, bending it and causing it to behave differently in this one corner of the universe that was her mother-in-law's kitchen. Maybe it was the heat.

"Megan?"

"Yes?"

"What are you daydreaming about?" Viola asked. "I've been trying to tell you, the phone is for you."

She shook off the feelings of lethargy and walked to the phone, still half-convinced this was some sort of strange dream.

"Hello?" she said tentatively.

"Surprise!" Kevin said, his voice tinny and small. He sounded like he was not only a million miles away, but at the end of a long tunnel as well.

Megan smiled, closed her eyes, and cradled the phone against her ear, feeling her feet once again firmly planted in the present. "You have no idea."

"I'll go and check on Katie, give you two lovebirds a moment alone," Viola said, a knowing smile on her face, as if Kevin were there instead of on another continent.

Megan mouthed a thank you. When Viola was safely out of the room, she wasted no time with pleasantries. "I think your mother may be crazy."

"So glad you called, darling; I've been worried sick. How are you adjusting to life in the desert?"

"I'm sorry, I wasn't being unfeeling. I just didn't know how much time you had to talk, and there are some things I absolutely have to tell you."

"You've always thought my mother was strange. What makes this any different?"

"Well, she's always struck me as a little eccentric, but not like this. I think her mind may be going. You can't believe the stories she's been telling Kaitlin. She has an incredible imagination—she should have been a writer or something. And she's so serious; she's completely convinced it all happened."

"Wait a minute. If she's telling Kaitlin the story, then how did you find out about it?"

A guilty silence followed Kevin's question.

"Were you eavesdropping?" he said, amused.

"I didn't do it intentionally! I stumbled onto their conversation completely by accident. I couldn't believe what I was hearing, and I had to keep listening because I was worried about her. Kevin, your mother is not well."

"What makes you think what she's saying isn't true?"

"She has no solid proof to back up her wild tales. You know what she told Kaitlin when she asked to see some pictures?"

"What?"

"She said she doesn't have any pictures or letters left, because everything was lost when your house was sucked into a giant sinkhole. Can you imagine?"

Kevin paused. "Actually, that's true."

Silence.

"Honey, are you still there?"

"How could you have forgotten to mention that your home was destroyed in such a bizarre way?"

"I don't know. It never really came up."

"I don't know what to say," she said finally. "I realize this may sound overly dramatic, but I feel like I'm married to a complete stranger right now. Maybe your mother isn't really crazy. Maybe there are just a lot of things you neglected to tell me!"

"What else did she say?"

"She said her mother was very nearly engaged to someone, but he changed his mind and she was so crushed that she almost gave up on life altogether. She did nothing but lie in bed, crying enough tears to fill the whole room."

"She was obviously exaggerating."

"She said that they had to carry out buckets of her tears and dump them in the garden!" she shot back.

"Honey, it's called poetic license. She's embellishing the story to make it sound better. Haven't you ever heard the expression about crying buckets? She's always been good at storytelling, and she's obviously gotten to you. Bedtime stories at my house were brutal—she always stopped right when she got to the best part and told us that if we didn't go to sleep, we'd never know what happened. If we were good, she'd pick up where she left off the next night."

"Did she ever tell you any stories about . . . fairies?" Megan said tentatively.

"None that I recall. Why do you ask?"

"I just wondered if that's why you always read *Peter Pan* to Kaitlin," she lied. For some reason, Megan suddenly felt it very important that she keep the fairies secret, so she changed the subject. "What about the rest of the story? Did your grandmother fall madly in love with someone who broke her heart?"

"How should I know?"

Megan blew out a frustrated breath. "Well, they're your family; she's your mother. Don't you know anything about her life?"

"It's complicated. My dad died when I was pretty young, and my grandparents went soon after. She never talked much about her childhood—you probably know more about it than I do. I can't imagine what possessed her to unload it all on Kaitlin now."

"I think she sees it as some sort of inheritance. I'm a little worried, though. Parts of it are pretty scary."

"I think Kaitlin can cope with the whole 'house disappearing into the sinkhole' scenario."

"Really? I heard you couldn't. Come to think of it, I guess that explains why you always search the area for quicksand every time we go on a picnic."

"Oh, ha ha. So, you've heard about my grandmother. What has my mother said about her own life?"

"She must be saving that part for last. I think she's taking the scenic route. Right now, she's telling Kaitlin about some sadistic man called Julian. Ring any bells?"

"I don't know anyone named Julian. Maybe when she gets around to telling the story of *her* life, I might be of more assistance. I hate to tell you, but I really have to hang up now."

"I'm sorry. I spent the whole time talking about your mother."

Kevin laughed. "It's okay. I think it's sweet that you're so concerned about her, but if you're going to convince me, try to have something a little more concrete than a sappy romantic story about Grandma Francis, okay?"

"What? Honey, are you still there?"

"I can barely hear you—the connection is terrible. I'll email you again soon. Love you."

"Kevin? Kevin?" Megan strained to hear his voice, at the same time knowing the call was already lost. She wasn't sure why she hadn't told her husband the more implausible parts of Viola's story. If she'd really wanted him to question her sanity, it seemed that the fairies would have been the sure thing. It was on the tip of her tongue several times, but she kept hesitating. She felt incredibly guilty, like she was betraying a confidence. Besides, there was no harm in hearing the rest of the story before she passed judgment.

She went to the kitchen table and sat down alone. She took a sip of lemonade from her glass, wincing at the sourness. She quickly dumped the rest down the sink before Viola returned. Her stomach was choppy enough with worry, no need to add all that extra acid. So, her husband was safe; she'd heard it from his own lips. But now she had a whole new set of problems. Who in the world was Grandma Francis, and more important, who was Claire?

Kaitlin lay on her stomach, stretched out on one of the oversized towels near the tiny pool. She reached one hand behind her and tentatively rubbed one of her shoulder blades. She could swear that it was slightly more knobby than it was a few days ago. Maybe her wings were growing in. Then again, it could just be the way she was laying—she would have to keep a close watch in case something happened. She turned over onto her back and waited for that side to fry. She stayed on one side until she felt like she was about to burst into flames, only to flip over and repeat the whole process. The concrete was hard under her back, and she idly watched a group of ants moseying toward the grass. She could feel the heat radiating through the ground and into the towel beneath her. She wondered how they could stand the searing pain on their little feet. They didn't appear to be bothered, though—they sauntered as if they were out for a leisurely stroll, stopping occasionally to change direction.

It really was getting unbearably hot outside, even in the shade. Perhaps it was time for another quick dip in the pool. Although it might help cool her off, she still had to factor in the energy required to move. It was a tough decision. Before she could make up her mind one way or the other, her grandmother appeared, looming above her. The way that she was standing with the sun directly behind her made her appear as if she were wearing a blinding halo. All she needed was a harp and wings, and she could be some sort of elderly angel.

"Katie, you really ought to get out of the sun. You're going to have a nasty burn," she scolded, in her whispery voice.

"I don't burn." She tried to shade her eyes to get a better look and was rewarded with a disapproving stare.

"Well, even if you tan the sun can still be dangerous. You should be wearing sunscreen."

"I'm not worried; the sun likes me. Who was on the phone?"

"Your father. Megan is talking to him."

Kaitlin sat up abruptly. "Dad's on the phone? Why didn't you say so? I want to talk to him too."

"He didn't have very long, and I wanted him and your mother to have a little time alone. Your mother misses him very much."

"Well, I miss him too, you know," Kaitlin mumbled, not bothering to mute the petulant tone in her voice.

"Of course you do. I didn't get to talk to him either. He promised that he would call back as soon as he could, and you can talk to him then, all right?"

Kaitlin nodded reluctantly but didn't look at her grandmother. She was afraid that if she looked into her pitying eyes, she wouldn't be able to stop herself from bursting into tears. Viola sensed that she was upset and tactfully changed the subject.

"I think we missed lunch. Let's go inside, and we'll see if we can't throw together an early dinner. That way, you'll still have plenty of time to swim later if you want. You have to wait an hour after eating before you can swim, you know."

"Yeah, I wouldn't want to cramp up suddenly and sink." Kaitlin stopped abruptly in the doorway, causing Viola to bump into her.

"Look at that!" she said, pointing excitedly toward a pinkish flowered bush under the lemon tree. "It's a bright blue butterfly, just like the one in Julian's box!"

Viola froze. "You have to be more careful, Katie. One comment like that, and your mother might get suspicious."

"She didn't hear because she's on the phone. Besides, even if she did, I'd just make up an excuse."

Viola shook her head. "I don't want you lying to your mother.

It's a bad habit to get into. Once you start telling lies, they just pile up around you until you can't remember who you told what."

"Grandma?" she hissed.

"Yes, dear?"

"You're going to tell the part about the castle next, aren't you?" The excitement flashed in her voice, like the heady shower of sparks from a firework in July.

"I'm going to pretend I didn't hear that."

* Five *

Viola added a squirt of liquid soap to the water in the kitchen sink. She always made the water as hot as she could stand, so the pans would be nice and clean. The sun was not yet up, but it seemed that she required less and less sleep these days. Besides, she enjoyed those quiet moments before the yellow light started streaming though her window. She had made a roast chicken the night before, and she wanted to give the pan a good soak before she started scrubbing it. She leaned across the counter, propped up her head with her hands and stared out the window. It was still more dark than light, but she could make out shapes in the backyard: the swimming pool, the lemon tree, the fence that bordered the yard.

"What are you looking at?" Kaitlin whispered.

"Good gracious, what are you doing up, dear?"

"I couldn't sleep. I was hoping that you might be awake so you could tell me more about the castle," she admitted. "Why are you up? Did you hear a noise or something?"

"I'm usually awake pretty early. It's like a bell goes off in my head, and after that, there's no going back to sleep. I was just letting the dishes soak for a minute before I washed them."

"Why don't you just put them in the dishwasher?"

"I had a couple of really dirty pans, and I thought they might need some extra attention."

"I'm good at dishes—can I help you?"

"Would you like to wash or dry?"

Kaitlin could see the steam rising from the water. Even though the sun wasn't up yet, it was already quite warm in the kitchen. "I think I'll dry."

Viola rolled up the sleeves on the nightgown she was wearing. "I was hoping you'd say that. I like to get my hands in the warm water."

They washed the dishes in a companionable silence, until Kaitlin couldn't stand it any longer. "You can start any time you want, you know. I can dry and listen at the same time."

Viola smiled. "Yes, I know. I was trying to drag out the suspense. Anticipation is the best part, I always say."

"It's practically the middle of the night and I'm wide awake, in the kitchen, begging. I even offered to do dishes!"

"Oh, all right." Viola hoped that Megan was still fast asleep. Viola regretted having to tell Kaitlin about the count, but it was an integral part of the story. Even if Viola shielded her from the truth, sooner or later she would learn that not everyone could be trusted to have honorable intentions.

The Castle

The closer Julian came to the castle, the more magnificent it became. To begin with, it was absolutely enormous. He had never seen anything to compare with its sheer size. He could not see the back of the castle from this angle, but he counted sixteen doors in the front alone, and he couldn't begin to number the windows, peering out like a thousand searching eyes. The walls of the castle were green with moss and growing vines, making it look as though the building itself was growing, and indeed, Julian had the distinct impression that it was expanding all the time. There was a conservatory with immense windows attached to the front of the castle under one bank of turrets, and he could spy flowers in pinks and blues displayed abundantly against the glass. The grounds around the castle were filled with trees, and the trees were filled with birds who chirped happily because they were filled with worms.

The castle was surrounded on all sides by a crystalline moat, brimming with silvery fish. The fish seemed quite content, weaving their way through the pond plants. Despite his morning breakfast of berries, Julian salivated as he watched one plump fish in particular, hovering drowsily just under the water. It would be so easy to just reach into the water and pull the fish out, and he was hungry enough to eat it raw. The only thing that stopped him was a pair of swans gliding across the surface, with three baby swans trailing proudly behind. They looked serene, but he knew that if he got close enough to disturb the fish, he could look forward to a beating from the swans' powerful wings. Just when he was ready to risk it and dive in, he caught himself. It wouldn't do to show up at the door, dripping wet and covered in blood, fish scales, and bruises. He would have a hard enough time convincing them he was respectable. Instead, he used some of the water to wash his face and smooth back his unruly hair. When he caught his reflection in the water, it was as though he were looking at someone else; someone much older.

"What are you doing in our moat?" a small voice demanded.

Julian jerked up to survey his surroundings, ready to pounce if necessary. But the threatening voice belonged to nothing more than a young boy. "Well, hello, young master." The low tone of his own voice startled Julian a little, and he couldn't remember the last time he'd actually spoken to anyone.

"You're a stranger," the boy commented.

"I am here to see your father, and I just stopped to cool off after my journey. You have some lovely fish in your pond."

"I hate fish, and it's not a pond; it's a moat."

Julian feigned astonishment. "So it is. You're quite a clever fellow. How old are you?"

"I am seven, but I will be eight soon."

"And you already know so much! Who told you about things like moats?"

"My father."

"Where is your father? Do you think that you could take me to him?"

The boy looked at Julian like he was daft. "Of course I can take you to him." He took off in the direction of the castle, holding his head high and taking great pleasure in the importance of his task.

Julian couldn't believe his luck. This could definitely work to his advantage. He had a much better chance of getting in to see the master of the house with his young son leading the way than if he'd simply knocked on the door. Let the servants try to keep him out now; he had a feeling that this boy was used to getting things his way.

The boy led Julian down a hall that seemed to go on for ages. The walls were covered with huge paintings of regal people who all looked the same. The only thing that separated one from the other was gender. The floors were some sort of dark stone, perfectly cut so that each ran into the next without interruption; no need to worry about stubbing your toe on a midnight stroll through these corridors. The ceiling was punctuated by large chandeliers dripping with strands of pinkish glass, which gave the hall a faintly rosy glow. Finally, they reached a heavy wooden door that was slightly ajar. The boy knocked without hesitation, waiting for permission to enter.

"Come in."

He pushed the door open, and the man sitting at the massive table smiled at him.

"Father, this man said he is here to see you, so I brought him in."

"That was very considerate of you, Frankie." His father had kind eyes that twinkled, barely hiding his amusement at the role his young son had taken as mediator.

"So, your name is Frankie, is it? We did not have time to be properly introduced. My name is Julian."

The boy got on his tiptoes and whispered conspiratorially. "My real name is Francisco," he said, a look of distaste wrinkling his features.

Julian nodded sympathetically.

"Francisco is my name also. It is a very good name," his father said defensively.

The boy giggled. "Yes, but no one calls you Francisco. You're the count!"

"Yes, I am; Count Diavolo. And so shall you be someday. The

cries will arise in the streets! All hail—Count Frankie the Great approaches!"

He laughed even harder, clearly tickled by his father's joke.

"I think I can take it from here, Frankie. Perhaps you should go outside and play."

Frankie nodded, stealing a cellophane wrapped sweet from his father's table on the way out.

"That is a fine boy you have. You must be very proud of him."

"Yes, Frankie is a good boy, for the most part. He seems to have taken quite a liking to you." He tapped one finger on the table in a distracted way, drawing Julian's attention to the large ring he was wearing. "You will have to forgive me, but do I know you?"

"I am afraid not. I have been traveling and looking for work without any success. I was nearly starved this morning when I came upon your castle, and I was hoping that you might be in need of my services."

"As luck would have it, one of our servants has just left us. He did a little bit of everything, and we were quite sorry to see him go. Would you be interested? We are rather isolated here, and I was beginning to despair at the thought of going into town to find a replacement."

"Sir, I could not begin to express my gratitude."

"Splendid! Sophia will be so pleased. She has been making the tea for us the past few days, and I must say it is quite dreadful."

"Sophia?"

"My wife, the lovely countess. Cooking never was her strong point. But here I am rambling about food when you must be famished. Let me take you to the kitchen and see if we can find something to fill you up."

As the count rose from the chair he was sitting in, Julian could see a monarch butterfly, trapped in an ornate frame behind him. The count noticed him staring at it, but mistook Julian's awe for disapproval. "Ghastly, isn't it? I put it on the wall where I would not have to look at it, but it still makes me feel uneasy, knowing it is there, watching me. I thought about getting rid of it, but it was a present from my wife, and I did not want to hurt her feelings."

"Of course," Julian answered meekly. The butterfly was a sign, the final proof he needed. It was no accident that he'd stumbled onto this castle. It was a golden opportunity, and he intended to make the most of it.

Although Julian felt immediately comfortable living in the castle, it took about a week before he was at ease around the family. In addition to Frankie, the count and countess had two daughters; Jessamin and Rosamund. Every time someone spoke to Julian, he flinched, as if the voices hurt his ears. It was unusual for him to be around the same people for any length of time, and he fought the urge to pick up in the middle of the night and leave because he knew that he belonged in the castle. It was the strongest presence of home he'd ever felt, certainly more than from his own uncaring family. It wasn't that he had any kind feelings for the souls who lived there, but more for the building itself. With every step he took on the grounds, he became more certain that the castle had chosen him for some grand purpose. Now all he had to do was wait for it to be revealed.

Julian never had to work very hard. He did a little landscaping, some repair work that needed to be done around the castle, and of course, made the afternoon tea. He arranged the biscuits and cookies into interesting patterns to amuse the children, and he was very punctual. The countess stressed that tea was a very important ritual and must never be late, and he was nothing if not obliging. He cleaned the delicate porcelain cups and polished the silverware until it was spotless. He didn't mingle with the other servants, but kept to himself. None of them seemed to notice that he was there anyway. He was never overly friendly or went out of his way to make conversation, but he was efficient, which was really the most valuable quality in a servant anyway.

Julian didn't mind his duties, especially the ones that had to do with the kitchen. He liked being around the food, and after going so long without, he gorged himself whenever he got the chance. He inherited several items of clothing left behind by his predecessor, who was evidently a much larger man than himself. It was impossible to see, but beneath his baggy clothing, the hollows from being deprived of regular meals were filling in quite nicely. His protruding ribs began to disappear under a thin layer of fat and muscle. Despite the fact that he was being well paid, he didn't use any of the money, not even to buy clothing that fit. He hoarded it like a rat guarding its nest of treasures, never spending a penny.

One day, the count passed him in the hall. He surveyed Julian, looking dubiously at his oversized clothing. "Are you happy here? Are we working you too hard?"

"You have been very generous to me, and I will always be indebted to you for your kindness."

"I am not sure—you still look too gangly to me. Why do you not take a break and go down to the kitchen? Have a nice thick slice of cake, and wash it down with a big glass of milk."

"I might do that, after I have finished trimming the hedges, sir."

"Oh, the hedges are not going anywhere. You need to build up your strength, and there is nothing better than chocolate cake to boost one's spirits."

"Indeed, sir. Cake is one of life's little pleasures."

"I would join you, but I have to go help Frankie with his sums." The count was halfway down the hall when he spun around on his heels. "I almost forgot. The countess said that she saw a rat run under her dresser yesterday. I am certain it was just a mouse—I cannot imagine a rat squeezing through that tiny space, but I have to humor her. There is a spot outside near the kitchen where they burrow in sometimes. Do you think you could put down some poison?"

"I will attend to it right away, sir."

"Excellent. There is a box of the stuff in the shed where the gardening tools are kept. I will tell Sophia that she has no need to worry any further, as you will be taking charge of the rodent situation."

Julian went into the kitchen. He cut a thick wedge of cake, and then licked the chocolate frosting from his fingers. He ate it without blinking; only pausing to pour himself a glass of milk. The second slice of the cake went down as easily as the first, and as he finished off the milk, he started to feel a little drowsy. He would welcome a nap, but that was out of the question. He had a job to do.

The gardening "shed" was actually a rather large outbuilding. The windows were dusty, and it was packed to the rafters with shovels, rakes, wheelbarrows, fertilizer, trimmers, and every other sort of tool or implement you would ever need. He had never really taken the time to explore the room before. Usually he would simply grab what he needed and go on about his business. It was an interesting place to wander in, so long as the cobwebs and the spiders that lurked in dark corners didn't bother you. He doubted if the count had ever been inside, and certainly never the countess. She wouldn't consciously stand for having a building this jumbled and musty on her property for one minute.

It took Julian awhile, but he eventually found what he was looking for. Perched above his head on one of the upper shelves, he located the box of rat poison. He used a fingernail to pry up the corner of the cardboard lid until he could see the grainy crystals inside. He walked behind the castle, and he could see the place the count had described—a little patch of ground worn away by mice slipping in and out. He poured a fair amount into a little dish and placed it near the spot. The mouse problem would soon be only a memory.

On his way back to the shed, Julian heard a voice. It was so loud and clear that he glanced over his shoulder to see who was behind him, and was surprised to find no one. He shook it off and kept walking, but it quickly returned. "Julian, you must never leave this castle."

"Who are you?" he asked the voice.

"It is of no importance. I am someone who is looking out for you; someone who wants to help you. So, I tell you again, you must never leave."

"But what if the count and countess order me to leave? After all, it is not my place to say whether I stay or go."

"Oh, but it is. After all, this should be yours. And it will be, if you do as I tell you."

"I do not understand."

"The grass under your feet, the trees, the birds, the castle itself—they are rightfully yours. You knew from the moment you laid eyes upon it that you belonged here. Have you ever been more content in your life?"

"No," he said honestly.

"Good. Now, listen carefully. The box you are holding can rid you of all the vermin in the castle. The mice are just the beginning."

Once the idea was planted in Julian's mind, he never heard the voice again. In fact, when he thought about it years later, he could never be entirely sure whether there was ever a voice at all.

. . . ✶ . . .

At teatime, Julian put the tiniest pinch of poison into the teapot and stirred the liquid until the granules were completely dissolved. He didn't want the whole family to perish at once—that would be too obvious. When the countess took a sip of her tea, she made a strange face.

"The tea tastes a little different today, Julian."

"Pardon me, Countess, but I accidentally put in twice the amount of leaves that I normally do, so it is a bit strong. I was going to remake the pot, but I was afraid that would make me late. Forgive me for my clumsiness."

The count smacked his lips. "Why, I think I like it better this way! There is nothing worse than weak tea." He grasped a lump of sugar in the tongs, dropping it into Sophia's cup. "A little extra sugar will make everything better, my love."

After the tea, the children went out to play. The next day, teatime came and went, and a little later, Rosamund complained of a slight stomachache. The countess sent her to bed, and Julian made her some tea and dry toast. The next morning, she was a little worse. Sophia was alarmed and sent for the doctor, but by the time he arrived, Jessamin had joined her sister in the sickroom.

The doctor advised the countess to keep them in bed, away from the other members of the family. He was not certain what sort of disease they had contracted, but as it seemed to come on quite suddenly, he wanted to take every precaution. They soon lost interest in food, taking only a little of the tea that Julian brought to their bedside.

Frankie was the next to be taken ill, and was soon followed by his mother. The count was beside himself with worry. He had dark circles under his eyes, and his skin was very pale. When the doctor came by to check on his patients, he was disturbed to note that they had doubled in number. The little girls complained that the sun from the windows made their eyes burn, so Julian quietly closed the curtains.

When the dawn broke the next morning, Rosamund didn't wake up. By noon, her sister was gone as well. The count walked from room to room in a daze, like a sleepwalker on his nightly rounds. He sat with Frankie until the color drained from his cheeks. Finally, he went to his wife. She was delirious with a high fever and blissfully unaware that her children had all passed to the next world. He watched as she too finally succumbed to the mystery illness. His mind was fuzzy, but not enough to blot out the fact that he'd lost his entire family in one day. It was more than he could bear.

Julian found him sitting next to his departed wife. "Sir, you don't look at all well. You should be in bed."

The count made no reply, but allowed himself to be led to his own room. Julian put a glass of bourbon into his hand. "Drink this, sir—it will help you to get some sleep." The count took it all in one large swig, hoping to dull the pain inside. But the bourbon tasted bitter—something wasn't right. In his haste to finish off the count, Julian had dissolved too much poison in his drink. A horrible flash of recognition appeared in his eyes as he realized the awful truth.

Julian watched him with interest, studying his response as if he were a scientist, hovering over his microscope in the laboratory. Instead of the murderous rage he was expecting, he noted only an immense sadness and fatigue. Francisco's eyes looked wet, but no tears escaped them. When he finally spoke, his voice was soft and distant, as if it had already left his body.

"You? You did this?" He started to cough, a sputtering that was surprisingly feeble. When he managed to catch his breath, he turned his helpless gaze back to his executioner. "Why?"

Julian shook his head, deliberately averting his eyes from his dying master. "Take off your ring," he said, ignoring the question.

He slipped the ring off without hesitation, dropping it into his servant's waiting palm. Julian examined the ring carefully. He'd never seen it up close before, but it was exactly what he'd suspected. The Diavolo family crest; the same ring he'd seen in numerous male portraits hanging on the castle walls. It was more than he'd hoped for.

The count watched him, unable to comprehend this most ultimate of betrayals. "I still do not understand," he said, a sob escaping from his throat. "Weren't you happy here? We treated you well, did we not?"

Julian made no response, but the count continued jabbering. "What did we do that was horrible enough to convince you that this was your only alternative?"

"Nothing. You did nothing. This is not about you or your family."

"Then, why? We would have given you anything you wanted!" The count was fading fast, his voice barely audible now.

Julian took the ring and slid it on. It fit perfectly. He admired the way it sat on his finger, as if it had always been there. He slipped it off again and tucked it away safely in his pocket. "I wanted to be the count."

While the other servants were helping to prepare the bodies

for the undertaker, Julian disappeared. He gathered his stash of money and slipped quietly away from the castle, unnoticed. He slept in the forest that night and walked into town the next morning. He went to a barber shop, where he had his beard and moustache shaved off. He also had his long locks of hair cut, instructing the barber to trim the hair until it was close to his scalp. The effect was startling—it quite literally shaved fifteen years from Julian's haggard appearance.

After the barber shop, he went to a tailor and was measured for two complete suits of clothing, in the style a noble man would wear. Then he went to the shoemaker's for a shiny new pair of boots. He got a room for the night in the local tavern, where he had a few drinks and a warm dinner. When the barmaid offered him a slice of the local roasted sweet fig pie for dessert, he gave her his most charming smile and said he'd take two.

Early the next morning, he donned his new clothing and hired the most fashionable carriage he could afford to drive him to the church for the funeral. The whole town was buzzing with the news of the unexpected demise of the entire Diavolo family. Julian waited until the last possible minute before entering the church. The overpowering aroma of flowers combined with the heat was nearly enough to send him back outside, but he stood tall and with severe dignity. He walked slowly to the front of the church and took his place on the first row. The despair on his face was not grief but claustrophobia from the five coffins crowded in front of him. Although each coffin was nearly buried under banks of flowers, it was not enough to overcome the cloying scent of death.

After the services, the priest came forward to comfort Julian.

"Are you a close friend of the family?"

"I am the count's younger brother."

The priest looked visibly surprised. "I was not aware that the count had any living relatives."

"Sadly, we quarreled a long time ago, and we had not talked in ages. But I received a letter from him a few days ago, telling me that his wife and children were all very ill. From the tone of his letter, I could tell that he was not himself, and I feared that he might take his own life, should anything happen to his beloved family. Unfortunately, by the time I arrived, he too had succumbed to whatever plague affected the others." Julian took a handkerchief from his pocket and dabbed stoically at the corners of his eyes.

"I see. You know, it strikes me as odd that none of the servants became ill."

"Yes, I wondered about that myself. My brother said in his letter that several of them went home as soon as they learned of the first death, and one of his servants simply disappeared. Perhaps he was sick and wandered off on his own. I suppose we shall never know what really happened."

"And what about you, sir? Do you have a family of your own you will be returning to?" the priest inquired.

"I will be staying on. The castle has been in our family for centuries, and I intend to see that it remains that way."

"Well, it is an honor to meet you, even if it was under such tragic circumstances." The priest took Julian's gloved hand and shook it tentatively. "I hope to see you in church, Count."

"I very much doubt it," he said icily. "Good day."

Julian went into the count's study and sank into the chair behind the desk. *His* desk—he really was lord of the manor now. For the first time in his life, he was ahead of the game. He got up and walked to the liquor cabinet in the corner. He poured himself a measure of brandy and swirled the amber liquid in the glass, sipping it thoughtfully. Everything really had gone more smoothly than he could have imagined. While he was taking a brief inventory of the books on his shelves, there was a knock at his door.

"Enter," he said calmly.

"I hate to disturb you, sir, especially when you have had such a trying day. I just wanted to introduce myself to you. My name is Lucas, and I was your brother's most devoted servant," he said, bowing at the waist.

Julian knew Lucas to be an oily little man who had always

irritated him, and he was delighted to now be in a position of power over his future. "I do not remember my brother mentioning you, but we have not spoken for years."

"A sad tale if you will forgive my saying so, considering the events of the last few days. If only you had returned in time to patch things up with your brother before he passed away. Tell me, is there anything I can do to make you more comfortable at this most difficult time?"

"Yes. Tomorrow you can go into town and pick up the rest of my clothing from the tailor, and buy some food at the market. Do you know anything about horses?"

"Of course, sir." With every reply, he made an obsequious gesture that Julian found repulsive.

"Excellent. While you are in town, you can inquire at the livery stable as to whether they know of any fine horses and carriages for sale. My brother's horses look to be very steady, but upon closer examination, I observe that they are quite old. I will require some younger ones for speed."

"And what, may I ask, will I receive in return for these favors to you, sir?"

"What will you receive in return? You are a servant!" Julian huffed. "You will do as you are told, and you will be duly thankful for anything that I see fit to bestow upon you."

"Pardon me for saying so, sir, but I should think that you might find it in your heart to be a little more charitable, since you were so recently a servant yourself."

Julian's face turned pale, and he cautiously gave the man a very slight smile. "I am afraid I do not understand your meaning."

"Perhaps I was mistaken, sir. Forgive me if I spoke out of place."

"Of course. I am nothing if not a forgiving master. What exactly did you wish in return for these things I asked of you?"

"Since I was your brother's most devoted servant, I could have been better compensated. I believe that for the . . . responsibilities I will be assuming for you, I would like a position of greater authority."

"Is that all?" Julian asked, dreading the answer he would recieve.

"I am not greedy, sir. I only want what is fair."

"Very well. You shall be my viceroy, my representative among my subjects and the other servants. I will also double your salary. Does this suit you?"

"You are most generous, sir."

"Did you know that besides being my agent, viceroy also has another meaning?"

"I did not, your Excellency."

"The viceroy is an orange and black butterfly. Collecting butterflies is a sort of hobby of mine."

"Is it that one, sir?" he asked, pointing to the unfortunate butterfly under glass behind the count's desk.

"No," he said abruptly. "That is the monarch butterfly. The viceroy has the very dangerous habit of imitating the monarch. Am I making myself clear?'

"Sir?"

"I am the monarch, and you are the viceroy. You are the imposter, the inferior copy. If you always remember that you are the lesser butterfly, you will have nothing to fear from me."

"Of course, Excellency," he said silkily.

As the viceroy exited the count's study, Julian couldn't help noticing that instead of hunching in deference, he stood straight. It was as if he were an entirely different person than the Lucas he knew; much more self-assured and somehow . . . taller. Julian frowned. He would have to keep a close watch over his new second-in-command. It simply would not do for the servant to eclipse the master.

*

Viola put a hand over her mouth, trying in vain to hide a large yawn. "I can't believe your mother is still in bed. Maybe you should go and check on her."

"I'll save you the trouble," Megan said quietly, stepping into the doorway from the shadows where she'd been listening. Kaitlin's mouth dropped open in shock, cringing under her mother's look of disapproval.

"Megan, dear, how long have you been standing there?"

She finally raised her eyes to look into Viola's, sighing deeply. "Long enough to have my suspicions confirmed. Viola, I'm sorry, but I think you need to see a doctor."

Viola's eyes were small and tired, and she shook her head slowly. "I'm disappointed in you, Megan."

"If you'll excuse us for a minute, I need to have a chat with my daughter." Megan took Kaitlin by the arm, steering her toward their bedroom.

"Why didn't you tell me the truth about your grandma's story?" Megan demanded.

"I did. She told me about her family."

"Yes, but you conveniently left out the part about all the women being fairies!"

"I was going to tell you. . . ."

"I don't think you understand how serious this is, Kaitlin. If your grandma really thinks that fairy blood runs through her veins, then we have a big problem."

"It's just a story, Mom."

"Is it? Because if this all boils down to Viola having an overactive imagination, then everything is fine. But if she truly believes in fairies, then she's completely senile. We're going to have to take her to the doctor."

Kaitlin was horrified. "Mom, no! If she thinks we don't trust her, then she'll never tell me the rest of the story!"

"I don't have a choice. Your grandma might not be safe living by herself anymore, and your father would never forgive me if I knew she was crazy and didn't do anything about it."

"She isn't crazy," Kaitlin argued.

"Anyone who believes in fairies is certifiable. Next, you'll be telling me she has wings."

"No, but her grandmother did . . . before they caught her and cut them off."

Megan's eyes bulged. "See? This is what I'm talking about. It's not normal. There are no fairies except in stories."

"But, Mom, Grandma told me fairies are real, just like us."

"Kaitlin, just because she said it doesn't mean it's true."

"You think Grandma is a liar?" she challenged.

"Of course not. But sometimes when people get older, they get confused. Sometimes they remember things that didn't really happen, or can't remember things that really did happen. Everything gets jumbled in their heads. That must be what is happening to your grandmother."

"But what if it's true, Mom? What if there really were fairies?"

"It can't be true, Kaitlin."

"Why?"

"Because other people would know about them. There are plenty of people around who are older than Grandma. Why aren't any of them talking about fairies?"

"Grandma said it's because a lot of people who knew aren't alive anymore, and she said that some people would rather forget."

"She told you that? What else did she say?"

"She said it wasn't easy to be a fairy. She said that people were afraid of them and weren't very nice to them."

Megan took a deep breath, trying to summon what was left of her patience. "I think I understand why you didn't want to tell me, but you have to try to see this from my point of view. We need to get your grandma to a doctor to make sure that her mind is still working right."

"I think you're just jealous that she wanted to tell me the story instead of you."

"I'm sorry you feel that way, but you need to trust me on this one. I have to look after your grandma's best interests."

"You can't make her go, you know," she shot back.

"She won't have to," Viola said. She was standing in the doorway, speaking as calmly as if they were discussing dinner plans. "I'll go see whatever doctor she wants, Katie. I have nothing to hide because I'm not crazy."

* SIX *

The soft piano music playing in the waiting room did nothing to alleviate the tension between Megan and Viola. Kaitlin had come prepared with her iPod in an attempt to distance herself from the whole situation. She didn't actually turn her iPod on, since she only wanted to *appear* uninterested, keeping her ears open for any juicy tidbits of information. She wasn't too worried about getting caught because she knew her mother suspected her to be like any other kid; caught up in her own world most of the time.

Megan flipped nervously through a waiting room magazine that looked to be several years old. The cover was ripped, and there was something sticky spilled inside so that some of the pages were plastered together. Viola sat calmly, grasping the clipboard they gave her when she arrived. The receptionist said it was a brief medical history, but it was at least five pages. Kaitlin thought it was amusing that they gave someone who was supposed to be losing her mind a whole packet of papers to fill out about herself. Maybe it was a trick, and that was the whole examination: if Viola could answer all the questions, she was free to go with a certificate, proclaiming that all her marbles were intact. Her knobby knees made sharp peaks under the fabric of her skirt, which she smoothed unconsciously every few minutes.

A television in the corner was playing out the latest trials of a soap opera couple. Viola glanced at it every now and then but didn't appear to be paying attention. She filled out one page, laboriously completing every line with her spidery penmanship, only to turn it over and find an entirely new section.

Viola thrust it into Megan's hands as soon as she had finished filling it out. Megan took it to the desk and spoke briefly to the receptionist. Kaitlin took advantage of her mother's absence, tapping her grandmother on the shoulder.

"Do you like that show?" she whispered.

Viola shook her head, a look on her face as if she'd just tasted something rotten. "I used to watch it sometimes, since Fern liked it. If she was at my house playing cards, she insisted we take a break when her show came on. But I don't watch it anymore—too much trash." She pointed to a woman on the screen who was having a heated argument with a man in prison. "I swear that lady used to be a man!"

Kaitlin giggled, but the conversation ended abruptly as soon as Megan returned. She went back to pretending to be involved with her music until the door opened. A nurse with a cheery grin appeared, wearing scrubs covered with florescent penguins.

"Are you ready to go back now, Mrs. . . ." She checked the chart for verification. ". . . Patterson?"

"Do I have a choice?" Viola said, stone-faced.

The nurse gave a short, nervous laugh, obviously not sure whether her patient was making a joke or being serious. "And who is this lovely girl? I'm not sure whether she's your daughter or your sister!" she gushed.

"Megan is my daughter-in-law. And this is my granddaughter, Katie."

Kaitlin remember to look appropriately vacant until they pointed to her. She quickly pulled the headphones off and said hello.

Megan grabbed her purse from the chair. "Do you think she'll be okay waiting out here?"

The nurse gave her a critical look, hesitating only a few seconds. "I'm sure we'll get along just fine, won't we, Katie? Maybe I can find some coloring books for her."

Kaitlin looked on in amazement. She wasn't sure what was worse; that they were talking about her like she wasn't there or that the woman seemed to be under the impression that she was about five.

"Don't worry; I'm sure she won't cause you *any* trouble." Kaitlin knew her mother's remark was more of a veiled threat than an attempt to soothe the worries of the nurse. They left her in the waiting room, her only company the iPod and the soap opera. The lady who used to be a man was passionately kissing the prisoner through the iron bars, swearing that she would wait for him forever. Since there was no more information to glean, she snuggled down into her chair and turned up the music, hoping that if she behaved herself, the nosy nurse would leave her alone.

Megan and Viola were led to a small consulting room where the nurse checked Viola's vital signs. After this brief examination, she made a few notes in the chart and checked her watch. "The doctor will be in soon, ladies," she promised. She closed the door behind her, leaving them in an awkward silence.

"How good could this doctor be anyway, if he had an available appointment for the next day?" Viola demanded.

"I told them it was an emergency, and they very kindly managed to work you in."

She harrumphed. "In my day, an emergency was when you cut an artery at death's door. I hardly think this qualifies."

She glanced at her watch, trying to think of something to pass the time. She grinned suddenly. "I don't suppose you'd care to tell me some of the story while we're waiting."

Viola shot her a dagger look, and the smile died on Megan's lips.

"Look, I'm really sorry. I don't know what to say. I just have to be sure that you're okay. I would feel terrible if something happened to you, and Kevin would never forgive me."

"Let's not talk about it," she said briskly.

"But . . ."

"No buts! I'm only here to prove a point. I. Am. Not. Crazy," she said through clenched teeth, her eyes fiery.

"I never said you were. I just think that some of the things you've been telling Kaitlin don't exactly add up."

"So what you're saying is that if I told her some tame little story about rainbows and pussy willows, we wouldn't be here right now?"

Megan hesitated. Viola glared at her, watching her squirm. "You have to admit, it's a little hard to swallow."

"It's life! It's unfortunate and it's gritty. You might be on top of the world, and the next minute, you're as low as you've ever been. Not everything is sunshine and buttercups. I don't know what your life has been like, but I'm sure if you thought about it, you'd realize that there are some things you've seen that would sound pretty unbelievable. I know that if you were to tell me your story, there would be parts that would be hard to reconcile with the picture I have of you, but that doesn't mean they didn't happen. Do you think I chose the life I lived or the things that happened to me? Why do you imagine I've never told anyone else?"

Megan was silent.

"Exactly. Because they would think the same thing that you're thinking now. Believe me, I spent plenty of time wondering why something so horrible happened to me, just hoping that I would wake up and find it was all a dream. But you know what? The most raw and painful things in our paths make us the people we become, for better or worse, and I won't allow you to take that from me. I might not be any spring chicken, but I'm not a candidate for the nuthouse either. And if you try to make me go, I'll fight you every step of the way!"

Just then the door opened, and the doctor poked his head in. Viola was red faced and out of breath, while Megan could only stare at her feet like a naughty child. He discreetly ignored their apparent squabble. "Now, let me guess. Which of you is Mrs. Patterson?" he said jovially.

"We both are, actually. But I'll save you the trouble of buttering me up—I'm the Mrs. Patterson you want. The other Mrs. Patterson is my daughter-in-law; she's here visiting for a couple of weeks." Viola folded her arms across her chest, clearly setting her boundaries.

"How very nice to meet you, Mrs. Patterson, or should I say, both Mrs. Pattersons? I'm Dr. Grant," he said, ignoring her hostility.

"You might as well call me Viola—it's shorter. Otherwise, we'll be here all day."

"Of course, Viola." He opened her chart and scanned it briefly. "Now, it looks like you've been having a little trouble remembering things lately."

"I didn't write that."

"I'm sorry?"

"In that myriad of pages you gave me to fill out. I never said anything about having memory problems."

"But your daughter-in-law is very concerned about you. She's noticed that there are some problems with your memory."

"Megan knows that I don't have trouble remembering things. She just doesn't like the things I'm remembering."

The doctor had a confused look on his face but quickly wiped it off and replaced it with his signature grin. "How about we come back to that later? Right now, I just want to ask you a few questions. Is that okay with you?"

"Fire away," she said confidently.

"Do you know what month it is?"

"Well, that's just silly. Of course I know what month it is—it's July."

"Very good. Now, do you know what day of the week this is?"

"It's Friday. Do you know how I came to that conclusion?"

"Tell me."

"I could tell from the soap opera in the waiting room. All the really juicy things happen on Friday—that way, they can be sure that you'll tune in on Monday. You might want to change the channel in future when there's a child present. My granddaughter is probably out there glued to it right now, and I'm sure she's getting quite an education."

"I'll have the nurse check on her in just a minute. Now, do you know where you are, Viola?"

She glanced momentarily at Megan, as if to see if she really expected her to be subjected to such a ridiculous line of questioning. Megan merely gave her an encouraging look. "I'm in the doctor's office. By the way, if you want to make that question a little more challenging, you might try leaving the white coat outside the door. It's a dead giveaway."

"You're a funny lady, Viola. I can see that I'm going to have to come up with some more difficult questions if I want to stump you. How about this one? Who's the president of the United States?"

Viola looked blank. She cocked her head to one side, desperately trying to sift through her brain and find the needed information. Finally, she shrugged her shoulders. "His name has slipped my mind, but you can't really tell one from the next anyway; they're all crooks."

He laughed politely. "All right, let's try something different now. I'm going to name three things, and I want you to remember them, okay? Lighthouse, banana, and fork—have you got it?"

She nodded. He picked up a piece of paper and placed it on the table in front of her. "Now, I want you to pick up this paper with your right hand, fold it in half, and place it under your chair. Can you do that for me?"

"I can't believe I'm actually paying you for this," she grumbled, following the doctor's instructions exactly.

"That was perfect. I'm going to hold up some pictures, and you tell me what they are."

"Toothbrush."

"But I haven't shown you any pictures yet," he said slowly.

"I know. I'm just testing my latent psychic abilities," she deadpanned.

The doctor held up the first card.

"Elephant."

"Correct." He proceeded through the pile.

"Beach ball."

"Ice cream cone."

"Tree."

She hesitated on the last picture, squinting at it for a full minute.

"It's a football," he said finally.

"What? That doesn't look like a football to me. Who draws these cards, anyway? It's all blurry."

"I could tell it was a football," Megan piped up.

"Teacher's pet. I've never really followed sports anyway."

"We're almost finished, Viola. Do you remember what I said my name was?"

"Dr. Grant. Look on the bright side—if you're having trouble remembering, it's printed on your coat."

"So it is. And do you remember the three things I asked you to keep in mind earlier?"

"Banana, fork, and . . ."

"There's no rush. Just take your time," the doctor said gently.

"I can't think of the third thing, all right? Are you happy now?" she snapped.

"Lighthouse," Megan said in disbelief.

"Pardon?"

"You remembered banana and fork, and you forgot lighthouse! If your father was really a fisherman, why wouldn't you remember lighthouse?"

"Am I finished now?" Viola asked the doctor, doing her best to ignore Megan's question.

"Yes, and you did very well, Viola. Why don't you go see how your granddaughter is doing in the waiting room while I have a word with your daughter-in-law?"

She stood up stiffly. "Why not? I'll just go out there and wait like an obedient dog while you both talk about having me put down, shall I? It was lovely meeting you, Dr. Grant." She closed the door loudly behind her.

Megan put her head in her hands. "Well, that didn't go very well, did it?"

"Actually, she did better than average."

"Really?"

"The few things that she couldn't remember suggest that she might have some of the early stages of Alzheimer's, but it is nowhere near severe enough to be detectable in an everyday conversation. It's possible that the only reason you picked up on it is because you're visiting and happen to be spending an inordinate amount of time with her."

"Well, the thing that really started me worrying is this very strange story she's been telling my daughter lately. She says it's the story of her life, but it's pretty far-fetched."

"Maybe she just has a very good imagination. Your granddaughter should count her blessings. Every time I visited my grandmother, I was regaled with stories of her latest operation."

"I suppose the grass is always greener, right?" she said ruefully. "You said early stage Alzheimer's—does that mean she's going to get worse?"

"Only time will tell. It could be something as simple as age-related forgetfulness, or it could be more serious. Just keep an eye on her for signs that it might be progressing."

"Like what?"

"Oh, putting things in places where they don't belong; like a book in the refrigerator. The inability to come up with the right names for objects, forgetting what day it is, not being able to do things she normally did with ease, like following a recipe or balancing her checkbook."

"Most of the time, my checkbook doesn't make any sense at all. Maybe you should ask me those questions."

"Tragically, my wife has the same problem. I wouldn't worry too much about your mother-in-law if I were you. Just take her home and have a nice visit while you're here."

"I think I may have blown my chances for a nice visit when we walked through your door. I don't know her very well because we live so far away, but it seemed like we were really connecting before I insinuated she might be going around the bend," she said wistfully.

"She's a firecracker, but I think she'll come around. If she didn't care about you, she'd never have agreed to come here today."

"She didn't come because she cares about me; she came to prove me wrong."

"She does appear to be very strong-willed, and believe it or not, the sarcasm is actually a good sign. Her quick-witted retorts show that her brain is still fairly sharp. Trust me; I see a lot of blank faces in my office, people who can't remember their own names. Compared to them, she's in pretty good shape."

Viola sunk down into the chair next to Kaitlin, a satisfied smirk on her face.

"How did you do?" Kaitlin asked, turning off the music.

"Not too shabby, for an old woman."

"So you passed?"

"Of course I passed! I missed a few questions, but I'd say overall, I was pretty spectacular. What are you listening to on that contraption, anyway?"

"Music. Do you want to try it?"

Viola tentatively placed one tiny speaker in her ear. "I don't hear anything."

"I haven't switched it on yet." Kaitlin pushed a few buttons, and Viola nearly jumped out of her skin. She ripped it out and threw it back at her granddaughter.

"You've got the volume all the way up! Are you trying to kill me?"

"It's not up that far. I wanted you to be able to hear it."

"You'd better watch yourself. If you keep subjecting your poor ears to that, you'll be deaf long before you reach my age."

"Here, try it again. I'll turn it down."

Viola reluctantly placed it near her ear and waited. She listened for a moment, wrinkling up her nose. "Is that what music sounds like now?"

"It's just singing. Actually, it's called rapping," Kaitlin explained.

"I don't know where you've been getting your information, but that's not singing. I know—when I was young, I used to sing myself."

"You did?"

"My voice didn't always sound like this, you know."

"What happened?"

She shrugged. "Sometimes life has other plans for you."

Megan and Dr. Grant appeared in the doorway, laughing. Viola was tired of waiting. She stood up and walked over to them, with Kaitlin following close behind.

"Thank you for coming to visit with me today, Viola. I was just telling your daughter-in-law that this is probably the most fun I'll have all day."

"If that's true, then I'm very sorry for you. Can we go now?"

"Of course." He pointed to a basket on the counter. "Grab a handful of peppermints on your way out, for being such a good patient."

Viola's eyes darkened and narrowed, like a hurricane blowing across her features without warning. She stared at the doctor for what seemed like minutes in absolute silence. When she finally looked away, the air nearly crackled with tension. She stabbed one threatening finger at him. "I knew I was right to be suspicious of you. They should put you away," she said in her fiercest whisper. The words could not have been more pointed had she shouted them. Megan took her arm and started pulling her out of the waiting room. They didn't speak until they were all sitting in the car.

"What in the . . . ?" Megan wondered aloud as Viola turned the key in the engine.

"Language, dear. Someone might be l-i-s-t-e-n-i-n-g."

"I know how to spell, Grandma," Kaitlin added from the back seat.

"What did the doctor say?" Viola put the car into gear and started to back out.

"Oh, no. Do you think I'm going to ignore what just happened? I want to know why you came unglued back there."

"Tell me what the doctor said, and then I'll tell you about the peppermints."

Megan bit her tongue. "Okay, we'll do it your way. He said that, for the most part, your mind was very healthy."

"But?"

"He also said that you showed some of the signs of early stage Alzheimer's."

"Poppycock. There's no such thing as Alzheimer's."

"What are you talking about?"

"Alzheimer's isn't a real disease. It was created by the government."

"I don't believe I'm hearing this. As far as I'm concerned, your sanity is much more in question now than it was this morning."

"When people begin to get older, they realize that they're not going to be around forever," Viola said patiently. "They start thinking about how once they pass on, unless they were someone important, everything they lived and breathed and fought for will die with them. The idea of all your experiences and dreams just blinking out, like a burned up light bulb—it's frightening. So, what can you do to ensure that at least a little part of you continues to live on?"

"You share your story with someone else," Megan finished.

"Ah, but that's a big chance you're taking, entrusting all your secrets to someone. And what if they don't believe you? Or better yet, what if the person who is *secretly listening in* doesn't believe you? You did battle with the dragon and managed to escape with only your eyebrows singed! You lived to tell the tale! So what? Believe me, what you saw as your one shot at a tiny slice of immortality might just as well turn out to be a one way ticket to a nursing home."

"That's not fair. Besides, what does any of this have to do with Alzheimer's?"

"When old people mention things that don't fit into your frame of reference, you label it gibberish and nonsense. Suddenly, it's off to the doctor, who has a framed license on his wall that he thinks gives him the right to pass judgment on whether you are fit to continue existing. They should just give them two rubber stamps when they graduate—*Crazy* and *Sane*. On the way out, they can plant the appropriate one on your forehead."

"People get diagnosed with Alzheimer's because they are confused, not because they have a good imagination."

"And where do you think the confusion stems from?"

"I think they're starting to trace it to a specific gene."

"More government lies. That's where the peppermints come in."

Megan laughed, but there was no humor in it. "I can't wait to see how you're going to tie all this together."

"All across the country, in doctor's offices and senior centers and nursing homes, there are bowls of peppermints, and all the old people sneak handfuls and fill their pockets and purses. Before you know it, they're actually buying them in the store. They're addicted, and they don't even know it!"

Megan gave her a blank stare.

"Don't you see? The peppermints are causing the confusion! The government has engineered the peppermints to create a haze—it's their cunning plan to silence anyone who might want to pass on the fairy lore, or any other part of history that they view as dangerous. That's why I never eat peppermints. I watched too many of my friends end up not even knowing who I was. But that's not going to happen to me. As long as I stay away from them, my mind will continue to be crystal clear."

"So you're saying that there is no Alzheimer's, and that most of the elderly population is suffering from peppermint-induced dementia?" Megan said incredulously.

"Think about it—do you ever see children eating them?"

"I don't like peppermints," Kaitlin said, out of the blue. Megan rolled her eyes. She was hoping that the omnipresent iPod had been blasting away. She could just imagine the calls she would get from other parents when her daughter started telling all her friends at school about the Great Peppermint Conspiracy.

"See! If you gave a child a bowl filled with gumdrops and peppermints, which one do you think they will choose?"

Kaitlin made a disgusted face. "Eeew. I don't like gumdrops either. They stick in your teeth."

"What kind of candy do kids eat now, anyway?" Viola questioned, turning around in her seat to face her granddaughter.

"Skittles."

"All right. So you give a child a bowl filled with Skitters and peppermints . . ."

"Skittles," Kaitlin corrected.

"Whatever. Which one will they choose?"

"Being an authority on candy, I would have to go with Skittles."

"Exactly! Children would never pick the peppermints, whereas old people can't seem to get enough of them! So, you see, there's nothing for you to worry about. I'm perfectly capable."

"Your mother's name," Megan said quietly.

"What?"

"You said your mother's name was Claire, but when I talked to Kevin on the phone, he called her Francis."

"Her name was Francis Claire. Everyone called her Francis when she got older, but she was Claire when she was a girl, and since I just called her Mother, it didn't really make much of a difference to me. Is there anything else you'd like to accuse me of?"

"I'm sorry. Kevin had to hang up before I had a chance to ask him about her name. I guess I just thought . . ."

"Yes, I know. You thought I was a lunatic who couldn't even remember her own mother's name." She pulled into the driveway and took off her seatbelt. "I'm going to bed."

"It's three o'clock in the afternoon."

"Well, I'm very tired. It's quite exhausting, trying to prove you're not crazy."

"What about the story?" Kaitlin asked.

"That, my dear, is entirely up to your mother. But I'm afraid she's already made up her mind."

* Seven *

"Do you think she's ever going to forgive me?"

The question hung in the air, trapped in the heated haze over Kaitlin and Megan's bed. Kaitlin rolled over onto her side, facing her mother and propping up her head on her hand. "Why can't you just believe her?"

"It's complicated," Megan hedged.

"Why?"

"Because even though I want to believe it for her sake, it can't be true."

"Why?"

"Because it's impossible."

"Why?"

"Because there are no fairies!"

"How do you know?"

"Because I've never seen any. No one has."

"Grandma has. And what about God?"

Megan studied her quizzically. "What about God?"

"Well, plenty of people believe in him without ever actually seeing him."

"Have you been watching the evangelist channel on TV again?"

"You know what I mean. Some things you just have to take on faith," she said solemnly.

"I'm not very good at faith. I'm one of those people who need solid proof. I want to be able to know something is true, not just hope that it might be. It's fiction; it has to be."

"Okay, I don't get it. If you don't believe the story, then why do you want to hear the rest of it? Why do you even care?"

Megan shrugged. "It's good fiction."

There was a sharp rap at the door. "Come in," Megan said eagerly.

Viola opened the door, fully dressed with her purse resting on her arm. "Good morning."

"How did you sleep, Grandma?"

"I had a dream that I was thrown into an ocean filled with hungry piranhas. Do you think that's significant?"

"You look nice. Are you going somewhere?" Megan said smiling, neatly sidestepping the question.

"Yes, I have some errands to run, and I thought you might like me to drop you and Katie off at the library while I'm out."

"I need some new books. I never thought I'd be saying this, but you can only spend so much time in the pool."

Viola nodded. "Very wise. The mind needs cultivation as well as the body. Well, this train leaves the station in twenty minutes, so you'll have to hurry."

"We'll be quick!" Kaitlin promised, hopping out of bed.

Viola retreated into the kitchen. "See, that wasn't so bad. She doesn't seem mad at all," Kaitlin whispered.

"No, not mad; just a little short."

"She looks the same height to me," Kaitlin said, a puzzled expression on her face.

Megan rolled her eyes. "I mean with me. She was a little short *with me*." She flopped back onto the bed, staring at the ceiling hopelessly. "If she's going to forget something, why can't it be this?"

"You just hurt her feelings. She'll get over it."

"I'm not sure about that," she said doubtfully. "Telling someone you don't believe them is like saying you don't trust them, and I went a step further than that. Not only did I say I didn't believe her, I dragged her to the doctor because I thought she was crazy!"

"Thought? As in, you *thought* she was crazy, but now you've changed your mind?"

"I don't know what to think."

"Why couldn't you just say you believe her, even if you don't?

It would be like a teeny white lie."

"She won't buy it. It's not like apologizing for forgetting to take the garbage out; it's something much bigger."

"All you have to do is say you're sorry. She'll believe you. Maybe she'll even tell *both* of us the rest of the story!"

Megan smiled at her daughter and the simplicity of the world she lived in. "I wish it were that easy, sweetie." She grabbed the bag with her laptop, slinging the strap over her shoulder.

"Why are you bringing the laptop with you?"

"While you're getting books, I want to look some stuff up."

"What kind of stuff?"

"Oh, just a little detective work."

"Why not just look it up here later? You're going to have plenty of free time, now that Grandma isn't telling the story anymore. Maybe you can actually clean the windows!"

"Very funny. No, it will be easier if your grandma isn't around."

"Why? Are you trying to prove her wrong?" Kaitlin asked suspiciously.

"No, I'm trying to prove her right."

Kaitlin loved libraries—aisles of books as far as the eye could see, and all of them arranged neatly in endless rows. Kaitlin enjoyed reading books so much that she thought she might want to write her own one day. And when that day came, she would come to the library to write it. Something told her that it would be the perfect place. It was quiet and organized, and what could be more conducive toward bringing a new book into the world than the encouraging whispers of thousands of others?

This library wasn't as large as the one near her house, but the same wonderful smell greeted her when she walked through the door; the comforting smell of paper and ink. She loved to sniff new books, and when you filled a whole building with them, the scent multiplied. It was like going to an old friend's house to visit, only this was where the books lived. People walked the aisles with stacks of books, while others lounged in soft chairs, caught up in their individual stories. The only place Kaitlin liked better than a library was a bookstore, because instead of just borrowing a book, she knew it would be hers forever.

Megan took a breath and sighed blissfully. Kaitlin knew her mother wasn't much of a reader but thought for a moment that she understood the appeal. Perhaps she was a closet library fan as well.

"Can you feel that?" Megan asked finally.

"Mmmmm," Kaitlin said, the vibrating hum of thousands of books beckoning to her, murmuring in her ears.

"Air conditioning! Why didn't we think of this sooner? We could have been coming here every day!"

So much for the idea that her mother was in tune with the spirit of the library—she was just glad to cool off. Megan sat down at a table and set up her laptop. "I'll be here while you look around, so come get me when you're done. And don't get a whole stack, okay—we're only going to be here another week. Besides, if you run out of books again, that would be a good excuse to come back here and take advantage of the cool air."

Kaitlin nodded, eager to be turned loose. She wandered off in the direction of the children's section to please her mother. Once she was out of sight, she went to the computer and looked up *Fairies*. This brought up a whole page of books, and she wrote down a few that looked promising to check out.

To her dismay, none of them were really what she was looking for. There were a few novels with the word *fairy* in the title that she thumbed through, but as far as she could tell, there wasn't one book about actual fairies. She found a book of fairy tales and looked through the titles, but as it turned out, there didn't have to be a fairy in your story to qualify. And then there were the few stories with fairies; Cinderella had a fairy godmother, and Sleeping Beauty lived with three fairies that did their best to protect her. But none of them seemed right. Either they were no bigger than a thimble, or spent the whole time flying around and making mischief.

She grabbed a few non-fairy related books that looked interesting and returned to find her mother bent over her laptop, her head resting in her hands with her eyes closed. Kaitlin dropped the books on the table with a thud, and Megan jumped.

"Sorry. I didn't realize you were asleep."

"I wasn't asleep. I was just . . . concentrating."

"Right."

"I have a headache. I seem to be getting nowhere fast."

"What are you looking for?"

"Castles."

"It works better if you narrow it down," Kaitlin said.

"Where were you twenty minutes ago?" Megan googled *Castles + Spain,* and her hopeful expression changed to one of grim desperation. "Well, instead of having twenty-four million sites to investigate, now we have just over three hundred thousand. If we have your grandmother come back in time to pick us up and take us to the airport, we might just make it through."

She went through the first few pages of hits but was quickly losing patience. "This is hopeless."

"What about the count? Did you google him?" Kaitlin asked.

Megan thought for a minute, and then typed in *Castle + Spain + Count Diavolo.* There were twenty-five thousand hits. "Getting closer," she said, her eyes narrowed in concentration. She played around for a minute with different search combinations.

"Let me try something," Kaitlin interrupted. Megan surrendered the keyboard and watched as her daughter typed in *Count Diavolo + Spanish castles.* The total hits were 3,210.

"Nice," Megan said appreciatively.

"Thank you."

"But I'm afraid that it's still more than we have time to sift through. Megan clicked on the first link; it was some sort of advertisement in Spanish. The second one led to a page that wasn't there anymore. She went to the next link, which was nothing more than a tiny newspaper clipping. As she quickly scanned the contents, her eyes widened and her mouth dropped open. "This is incredible," she said finally.

"What is it?" Kaitlin asked, her voice full of excitement.

Megan finally blinked, coming out of her trance. "I think your grandmother might not be crazy after all." She glanced at the clock. "I need to send a quick email to your dad. Will you go look in the parking lot and see if she's waiting?"

Kaitlin vanished, and Megan typed out a quick message.

Kevin,

Call me as soon as you get a chance. I wanted to tell you what the doctor said about your mother, but there's something else. I said before that I thought she might be losing it, but I found something on the Internet, and now I'm more confused than ever. It looks like there might be some truth in the story she's been telling. And if part of it's true, it might all be true!

I realize this doesn't make any sense. I need to hear your voice. I'm starting to feel like *I'm* the one who's going off the deep end.

Love,

Megan

*

"That was delicious," Megan said, wiping her mouth with a napkin. "Where did you get your recipe?"

"My mother had the best recipe for spaghetti sauce, and I've never made it any other way."

"Maybe you'd let me copy it down later?"

"Oh, it isn't written anywhere. It's all in my head . . . where it's safe." Viola smiled and took a sip from her water glass.

They sat in silence for a minute. Kaitlin pushed the rest of the green beans around her plate with a fork, eyeing the last breadstick in the basket.

"Maybe tomorrow night I could make dinner," Megan said brightly.

"Nonsense, you're a guest. Doing the windows was bad enough."

"I can make SpaghettiO's," Kaitlin said proudly.

"What are SpaghettiO's, dear?" Viola inquired.

"They're circle-y noodles in sauce. They come from a can, and you heat them in the microwave. But you can't put the can in the microwave," she said, her reddened face revealing that she had obviously learned this lesson from experience.

"I guess you have to start somewhere. Maybe I could teach you to make this sauce. If you practiced, you could make it for your dad when he gets home . . . unless your mom thought it was too scary."

"That would be so cool!"

Megan gave Viola a hard look, which she simply ignored. "Now, who wants brownies for dessert?"

The phone rang, and Kaitlin reached it before the second ring. "Hello?" she said eagerly. Her face was neutral for a moment before breaking into a wide grin. "It's Dad!" she whispered loudly, covering the receiver with her fingers. "Do you want to talk to him first, Grandma?"

"Go ahead, I don't mind waiting."

Kaitlin turned her full attention back to the phone. She had to strain to hear what her father was saying.

"Are you having a good time with Grandma?"

"We're having a great time! Grandma can't keep me out of the pool."

Her father guffawed. "I knew you'd be impressed."

"You should have told me about it before we came. I don't know how you kept it a secret," she said sweetly.

"I couldn't resist. When I called your grandma to let her know we'd booked the flight, she was so excited. She said that she was going to go to Wal-Mart that afternoon to buy a little swimming pool for you. I think she was under the impression that you were still a toddler. I tried to explain that you were big now, but she was just positive that you would love it. I hope you didn't hurt her feelings—she meant well."

"No, I've been swimming in it a lot."

"You're a sweet girl. How's everything else going?"

"Okay, I guess. How hot is it there?"

"It got up to 119 degrees yesterday."

"Wow. I'll let you talk to Grandma now. Make sure you put on your sunscreen!"

"Love you, Kaitlin."

She handed the phone to her grandmother. "Hello?" she rasped.

"Hi, Mom! How are you?"

"Kevin? Is that you?"

He laughed. "Who did you think it was?"

"You just sound so different; I hardly recognized your voice. Are you taking care of yourself? Are they feeding you enough?"

"They feed me plenty, but it's not in the same league as your cooking."

She smiled. "I made the spaghetti you like for dinner tonight. I wish I could send you some, but I'm afraid it would be spoiled by the time it got to you."

"When I get home we'll come and visit again, and you can stuff me with all the spaghetti you want." He hesitated a minute. "Megan said she was going to take you to the doctor."

Viola flashed Megan a biting look, but her voice was all sweetness. "Yes, isn't she a dear?"

"I'm sorry, Mom. I'm having a hard time hearing you."

"I said you're very lucky to have found Megan. She's a lovely girl." She locked eyes with Megan again, raising her voice as much as she was able. "But she *worries* too much."

"She's just concerned about you. What did the doctor say?"

"He said I'm fit as a fiddle. I might forget where I parked the car every now and then, but so does everyone else. There's nothing wrong with me."

"I'm glad to hear it."

"Well, I'd better let you go. I'm sure you want to talk to Megan before you have to hang up."

"Thanks for taking such good care of my girls, Mom. You're the best."

"I love you, Kevin."

She handed the phone to Megan. "Come on, Katie, we need

some lemons." She grabbed her granddaughter by the hand and started pulling her to the back door.

"But I want to talk to Dad again," she whined.

"Everybody gets a turn, and now it's your mother's. Besides, I always say you can't make a good pound cake without lemons."

"What's a pound cake? Is it better than brownies?" Megan heard Kaitlin's voice fade until she couldn't make out the words anymore.

"So, what did the doctor really say?" Kevin asked.

She sighed. "Pretty much what your mother said. He did say that she showed some signs of early-stage Alzheimer's, but that her reasoning and memory were basically sound."

"I'll bet she threw a fit when they mentioned Alzheimer's."

"There isn't enough time to explain it to you now. Let's just say that your mother has some very creative ideas about candy and government conspiracies."

"I'm sorry; the connection on my end isn't very good. I thought you said candy and government conspiracies."

"Yeah. Don't even try to make sense of it—it will only make your brain hurt."

"Never mind, then. How are you doing?"

"I was doing fine, until I took it upon myself to diagnose your mother. We were getting along great, and now she hates me."

"She doesn't hate you. She just said you were a lovely girl."

"Please, that was strictly for your benefit."

"Honey, whatever she's been telling you, can't you just pretend you believe it? You'd be doing something nice for an old woman."

"I might not have to. I found something on my laptop that might prove at least part of it."

"See? What did you find, you clever girl?"

"Do you remember me mentioning Julian, the guy she told Kaitlin about? The mean one?"

"That sounds familiar."

"Well, to make a long story short, he took a position as a servant at a castle where a family lived by the name of Diavolo; the count and countess, and their three children."

"Already I can understand why you're having a hard time swallowing this. It sounds like a fairy tale. What does any of this have to do with her?"

"She hasn't explained how she fits into the story yet."

"Go on."

"Julian was jealous of the count—he wanted the castle and the title for himself. So he poisoned the entire family, took the count's ring with the family crest, completely changed his appearance, and showed up at the funeral claiming to be the younger brother of the count; the last surviving heir of the family Diavolo."

"And?"

"That's it. Well, that's as far as she got, anyway. I'm sure there's more."

"I can't imagine what you found on the Internet that makes any of that seem plausible."

"You're not going to believe this. There was a tiny newspaper clipping; I almost missed it, it was so small. Apparently in the 1920s, there was a Count Diavolo who lived in a castle in Spain. His entire family perished suddenly from a mystery illness, and the story said that his younger brother showed up to claim the property, with no proof of his identity other than a ring with the Diavolo family crest."

"Your entire belief in my mother's sanity hinges on this one newspaper clipping you stumbled onto online?"

"Don't you see? It makes perfect sense. The stories are practically identical!" Megan said triumphantly.

"Did it ever occur to you that she might have read the same thing you did and just repeated it to Kaitlin?'

"Can you really picture your mother surfing the Net?" she said in disbelief.

"No, but she might have read the original newspaper."

"She couldn't have. She wasn't even born then."

"Maybe her parents told her about it."

"Aren't you reaching a little?"

"Says the woman who believes my mother when she says that she knew a count who lived in Spain."

"It could be true. You said yourself that you don't know very much about her. How else would she know so many details about an event that happened before she was born and was reduced to a three-inch column in the newspaper?"

"I think you need to hear the rest of the story before you go jumping to any conclusions."

"That's the problem. She was upset that I eavesdropped in the first place, and then I insulted her further by saying I didn't believe her. I don't think she'll tell me the rest."

"But you have the perfect solution already."

"I'm not following you."

"You just made a very compelling case for the validity of her claim. All you have to do is explain it to her like you did to me."

"I don't know if it's going to be that easy," she said slowly. "I think it's safe to say that there is going to have to be some fairly serious groveling involved."

"Well, you're running out of time. There's only a week left, so you'd best get groveling!"

"It seems so simple when you say it. You sound like Kaitlin."

"It won't be as hard as you think. She's never been one to hold a grudge. I hate to say it, but I have to go now."

"I love you, husband."

"I love you too, wife."

Viola carefully pushed the pound cakes onto the rack, and Megan stifled the urge to flee when the massive rush of heat escaped from the oven.

"How long does it take for the pound cake to cook?" Kaitlin asked.

"About an hour."

"And when do we get to eat it?"

"Tomorrow."

"Awww, can't I stay up another hour?"

"It wouldn't do you any good, because the cake has to have

time to cool before we can cut it. Otherwise, it will fall apart."

"I don't care if it falls apart."

"Well, I do."

Megan rubbed Kaitlin's back until she slumped forward playfully onto the kitchen table, pretending to be asleep. "Why don't you go get in bed, and you can read for a minute?"

"How many minutes?"

"You can read fifteen pages, and I expect you to be asleep when I come in."

"How about thirty pages?"

"Your eyes are tired. You'll never last thirty pages."

"I'm not tired at all," she protested, but was unable to suppress a wide yawn.

Megan grinned. "See?"

"Promise you won't talk about anything important without me?"

"Cross my heart and hope to die," Megan said solemnly.

"Good night, Mom. Good night, Grandma."

"I'll see you in the morning, Katie."

Kaitlin trudged down the hall, and they heard the squeak of the door closing.

"She probably won't last five pages," Megan said, trying to make conversation.

"But I'm sure she won't go past fifteen. That's one of the great things about Katie—she's very loyal, and you know you can trust her."

"Viola," Megan said wearily.

"No, it's okay. I understand why you don't believe me. I'm sure that my story sounds very farfetched to you, and since I have no actual proof, I wouldn't expect you to put any stock in it."

"I found some."

"Found some what?"

"Actual proof," Megan said sheepishly.

"What kind of proof?"

"A newspaper article on the Internet, confirming the deaths of Count Diavolo and his family in Spain in the 1920s, and the unexpected arrival of a younger brother no one knew even existed."

"Really?" Viola breathed.

Megan nodded. "It was really short, but it happened just like you said it did. What I want to know is, how did you know so much about it when it happened before you were born?"

"The count, well, Julian, told me part of it. He boasted about it, really. The rest I got secondhand from people who knew. I'm sure part of it was lost or embellished over the years, but I think the main parts are true. I had no idea that any documented trace existed anywhere. I guess it's true what they say."

"What is?"

"You really can find anything on the Internet. I always thought it was just a newfangled nuisance."

Megan giggled, but the sound got stuck in her throat when she noticed that Viola still had a stern look on her face. "I'm afraid there's still the issue of you not trusting me."

"But I just said . . ."

"I know what you said. But the fact remains that it took an outside source to convince you that I was telling the truth. And I guarantee you, there are parts of this story for which absolutely no physical proof exists." She shrugged her shoulders. "At least Katie believed me. I just don't feel comfortable telling you about my life when I know that you're not taking it seriously. You thought it was just some fantasy that only existed in my head."

"I do believe you! All I needed was one little bit of proof I could actually see, and the whole time you were telling it, I wanted it to be true!"

"How much of it did you actually hear, anyway?" Viola asked, unable to wipe the wry grin from her face.

"Everything except the part about your grandmother; Kaitlin filled me in on that. Why do you think it's taking me so long to finish the windows?"

Viola sat back in her chair thoughtfully. "I don't know. You certainly were in a big hurry to label me as a loony and cart me off to the doctor . . ."

"Just a precaution," she said reassuringly. "How could I ever look Kevin in the eye again if I didn't follow up on a suspicion I had about his mother's health?"

"Well, I suppose you might have the tiniest bit of a valid point . . ."

"So, you'll finish the story?"

"On one condition."

"Name it."

She paused. "I'll only agree to finish the story if both you and Kaitlin still want to hear it."

"Well, I can't speak for Kaitlin, but . . ."

"Are you *kidding?*" a voice yelled from around the corner.

"I'll take that as a yes," Viola said.

* EIGHT *

Megan's eyes popped open in the middle of the night, and she could hear Kaitlin snoring evenly beside her. She eased out of bed and wandered into the kitchen, hoping to find a snack. The kitchen was dark and empty, and the only sign of habitation was the shapes of the pound cakes, cooling on a rack under a tea towel. She touched the towel lightly with her palm, noting with satisfaction that they were cool. She got a knife from the drawer, cut a thin slice from one of the ends, and took a bite. The buttery cake nearly melted on her tongue. Megan admired her mother-in-law's cooking ability—heaven knew she herself was no chef. In fact, she and Kaitlin were about equal in the food prep department, hovering somewhere in the SpaghettiO's skill level. Before she knew what she was doing, she was trimming off a slightly larger piece before heading back to bed.

When Megan woke up again, the sun was high in the sky and Kaitlin's side of the bed was empty. She was surprised to see the flashing red numbers on the alarm clock next to her. Some time between when she'd come back to bed and now, the power must have gone out. The heat in the room was making her a little nauseated, so she stumbled out of bed and went in search of her daughter. She found her at the kitchen table, hacking into the pound cake.

"Morning, Mom. Or should I say . . . good afternoon?"

"What time is it, anyway? The alarm clock was flashing and I couldn't find my watch." She pulled up a chair and sat down, watching Kaitlin consume a piece of cake at an alarming rate.

"This is such good cake," she mumbled with her mouth full. A stray crumb was nestled on her lip, and Megan brushed it away.

"Honestly, you're eating like an animal! The cake isn't going anywhere—do you think you could slow down a little?" She examined the significantly diminished loaf. "How many pieces have you had?"

"This is my fourth," she said, pausing to take a gulp from her glass of milk.

"Kaitlin Marie!"

"What? Grandma said to help ourselves. See?" She held up a note, and Megan squinted at the contents.

Girls,

I have gone to church. I will be back around noon. Help yourselves to pound cake for breakfast. (Apparently, one of you already did—you know who you are.)

Love,

Grandma

P.S. Don't spoil your appetite—save room for lunch!

"She said to help yourself, not make a pig of yourself. Do you really think you're going to be able to eat lunch now?"

"Probably not."

"Well, you'll just have to make room. Hopefully, by the time your grandma gets back, you'll be hungry again."

"I doubt it—it's 11:30."

"11:30! Why did you let me sleep so late?"

"I figured you must have been worn out from your midnight pound cake raid."

"What makes you think it was me?"

"Well, it wasn't me. Unless I'm a sleepwalker! Wouldn't that be cool?"

"I have to go get dressed. I don't want to be lazing around in my pajamas when your grandma gets back." She jumped out of her chair and dashed down the hall. Kaitlin waited a second, then quietly picked up the knife and closed in on the cake.

"Don't even *think* of cutting another slice!" Megan's voice threatened from the bedroom.

"Would you like another, Katie?" Viola held out a plate of chicken salad sandwiches. She'd sheared off the crusts before cutting them into triangles and stacking them neatly.

Kaitlin groaned, slumped over in her chair. "I don't think I could eat another bite, Grandma. I'd have saved more room if I knew you were going to cut off the crusts. Mom always makes me eat the crusts," she whispered.

Viola wrinkled her nose. "I've never understood that. Why fill up on crusts when what you really want is the soft white part?"

She shrugged. "She says that's where all the vitamins are."

Megan's face turned red instantly.

"Now that's just silly. The crust is made of the same dough as the rest of the bread." She turned to Megan. "I know you don't know much about cooking, but you're a smart girl. Do you really think all the nutrients magically rise to the surface when you bake it?"

The light switched on in Kaitlin's brain. She faced her mother indignantly. "Is that true? Have you been making up stories about vitamins?"

"My mother told me the same thing when I was a little girl, and if it makes you feel any better, I was much older than you when I figured it out. Just wait until you're a mother—you'll be making things up too," Megan said dryly.

"It makes me wonder what else you've been making up . . ."

Megan flashed her a knowing grin. "Won't it be fun finding out?"

Kaitlin rubbed her belly uncomfortably. "I don't feel so great. I think I'd better go lie down for a while."

"Oh, that's too bad. I was going to start telling you my part of the story today."

"Or I could just sit here and let the food settle while you tell the story," Kaitlin said smoothly.

"I thought you might like that idea."

"There's one thing I have to know. Does your story have a happy ending?" Megan asked urgently.

Viola's smile cast a bittersweet shadow in the sun-filled kitchen. "I'm afraid there are no happy endings, not really."

"Of course there are!" Kaitlin said.

"It's all about perspective, dear, but make no mistake; happy endings in this life are very scarce indeed. Happiness is a choice you make. You can choose to be happy or unhappy—it's as simple as that."

Kaitlin looked troubled. "But everything turns out okay at the end, right?"

"You're not listening! Happily ever after only exists in books. When you're safe at home in a comfortable chair, it's easy to imagine yourself as the hero of your own story. But when you're actually out there living it, that's when you discover who you really are, and sometimes it's disappointing. You might not be nearly as brave as you prided yourself on being, or you might surprise yourself by rising to the occasion."

Kaitlin and Megan looked even more confused now.

"I think someone might be worried that I'll disappoint them. Maybe this isn't the proud tale of a warrior, but a deathbed confession instead? Hmmm?"

"I'm sure that no matter what happened, I could never be disappointed," Megan said.

"We all have our cowardly moments, Megan. The person who says they were never afraid and has no regrets is a liar. Are you both positive you want to hear the rest?"

"I don't scare that easily, and I certainly haven't come this far to quit now."

"Yeah," Kaitlin added, nodding. "What she said."

VIOLA

Viola loved the beach, but not the sea. She didn't mind the waves that lapped against her toes or even the bolder water that washed up past her ankles. But she never went into the sea much further than that. Once it crept up to her knees, she was filled with a sort of nameless dread. It was a fear that went beyond anything else she knew, and nothing could make it go away until she found herself safely on dry land again.

She spent many happy hours walking on the sand, up and down the shoreline, waiting for her father's boat to return. Her father was a fisherman, drawn to the deep water as much as she was frightened by it. And while she roamed among the sand and rocks, she sang.

From the time she was old enough to speak, Viola sang. She had a very unique voice—sweet and clear, yet at the same time, quietly powerful. Even when she wasn't old enough to comprehend the meaning of the words, they poured out as if she understood not only the vocabulary but also the feeling behind them. When Viola sang, it was as if an invisible bell was ringing, and everyone stopped to see where the hypnotic sound was coming from. When you heard the notes, whether the song was sad or joyous, you couldn't help feeling a tremendous lift, like you were somehow better for having been there.

There was a line of trees that dotted the far end of the coast, melting into thicker trees and meadows and patches of wildflowers. When Viola came near, the trees bent down from their lofty position in the clouds to hear her better. The flowers stretched, standing tiptoe on their roots so as not to miss a single word. She felt comfortable singing in the trees where no one could hear her, or near the water, where her voice disappeared into the pounding waves. But she was terrified of singing in front of people—only her mother and father ever heard her true voice, and even that made her want to duck her head and hide.

On this particular early spring day there was a new wind stirring the branches into a frenzied madness and breaking the necks of the tallest flowers. Unbeknownst to Viola, who was rambling across the sand, the wind also brought a carriage to their cottage. The carriage door opened to reveal an impeccably dressed, thin man of medium height. Everything about him seemed polished—the carriage, his boots, even the slight balding spot on his head he wore with distinction. His gray eyes and gray suit completed the illusion of genteel sophistication.

Although he did not hurry, all his movements suggested a destination. Motion was reserved until deemed necessary, and not a twitch of a muscle was wasted. He descended from the carriage and strolled to the cottage door, rapping it smartly with his gloved knuckles and frowning slightly. He gave the impression of barely concealed annoyance, as though he should have his own servants for menial chores of this nature. When the door opened, he wasted little time with pleasantries.

"Good afternoon. I am here to retrieve the cloak I left to be mended."

"Yes, good afternoon," she said, bowing her head slightly in deference. "It is a great pleasure to see you again—"

"Is it finished?" he said curtly, cutting her off.

"I will go and fetch it. Would you like to come in?"

"That will not be necessary."

Claire disappeared into her sewing room, picking up the cloak and brushing off an errant thread. Claire was one of the most gifted seamstresses within several hundred miles. Still, she'd never had a client as important as this one before. She was eager to please him as she knew he was wealthy and well-connected, and it would bring additional business her way. She was already quite busy, but a few members of the upper class wearing her work would really make a difference. She carried it carefully to the door, and handed it across to him. He inspected the seams, testing their strength and finally nodded.

"This appears to be satisfactory." He reached into a pocket in his suit, handing her a small white envelope. She tried not to openly gape when she saw how much money was inside. "I hope you will find the payment compensatory," he said dryly.

"Sir, you are too generous," she protested.

He nodded in absent agreement. "It is difficult to find an adequate seamstress. I am certain that I will have some additional, more substantial work for you in the future."

"Thank you very much, sir." She had to raise her voice so that he could hear her over the wind.

He was nearly halfway to his carriage, his mind already switching gears to his next errand. He moved fluidly into his seat, opening the window a little so that he could still feel the brisk wind against his face. There was something about this new wind that made him feel alert and efficient, and he relished it.

He motioned to the driver to go, and allowed himself a moment to relax. He leaned back against the cushion, trying to retain some semblance of dignity as the carriage jolted down the bumpy road, tossing him about as if he weighed no more than a feather. He closed his eyes, trying in vain to catch a minute's rest when an unfamiliar sound met his ears. He sat up at once, trying to trace the origin of the unusual noise. He rapped on the roof of the carriage with the silver handle of his cane, a signal to his driver to stop. Peering through the window, his curiosity was enough to make him willing to break precedence and be tardy for his next appointment.

The mournful, almost ghostly sound appeared to be coming from the beach. He opened the door and crept toward the noise, which he identified as singing. As he crouched down, hiding himself from sight, the wind carried the melancholy song directly to him, presenting it at his feet as if delivering a ritual sacrifice. He could not see the owner of such a voice, but he imagined her to be a young woman, her heart quite recently broken. It was not a showy voice, yet it somehow commanded his undivided attention.

Her voice traveled to notes that he'd never heard before; he wasn't even sure they existed. Surely there were no songs written for these sounds—she was creating them as she saw fit. It was different than anything he'd ever heard. He knew very little of vocal quality or tone, but even he could recognize that the strength and range in her voice would have been sought after and prized, even in a seasoned vocal veteran. He was unable to retain his composure when she finally appeared to his view.

She was only a child! She could not have been ten years old, probably six or seven. But the wrenching despair in her voice was unmistakable. She paused suddenly, stopping to look around, as if she could sense that she was being watched. She was so near to him, he could have reached through the tall reeds where he crouched and grabbed her arm. When she abruptly cut off her song, something peculiar happened. He felt as though something inside him was tearing apart, writhing and separating until he was short of breath. He didn't recognize the sensation, but if he'd had to put a label on it, he would have described it as a sort of exquisite pain. His heart pressed against his rib cage violently, until he thought the bones would shatter.

Once satisfied that she was alone, she began to sing again, and the expanding feeling in his chest eased. Her powerful voice belted out endless strings of notes with effortless precision, as if it was no more taxing than a lazy gossip over a cup of tea. He found the whole experience incredibly unsettling. He had no use for little girls or singing, and he did not like being controlled by an outside force. He, who had always prided himself on holding the reins, was completely helpless under the spell of this . . . this dangerous child. He did not enjoy being manipulated, however bewitching or novel the experience.

But he knew someone who did—someone who was willing to submit himself to any torture in exchange for reaching a new height, someone who constantly sought the beautiful within the unusual, someone who was always in search of a new possession to top his last acquisition, a true connoisseur of unexplainable perfection.

He watched the girl slowly make her way down the sandy path until he could no longer hear her, and he noticed with satisfaction that the painful and strange phenomenon of before did not return. Perhaps the pain in his chest had been a mere coincidence, or indigestion from the piece of fish he had for lunch. His mouth twisted into the grim line that passed for his smile. Someone would pay handsomely for a chance to sample this particular novelty.

The only beautiful time of year at Castle Diavolo was in the spring. Ten years had passed since Julian had poisoned the family and taken possession, and he hadn't taken much interest in the grounds keeping. The moat was clogged and overgrown with plants that rippled when the fish squeezed through the convoluted pathways. Most of the flowers had been choked out by weeds. The countess's priceless tulips were reduced to masses of thick green leaves. The bulbs had never been separated, so they grew out of control, larger and larger, until the flowers vanished completely. The carefully sculpted bushes grew in every direction, so wild that it was impossible now to distinguish what their original shape had been. The vines that covered the castle had pushed their way through the stone, twisting and crawling until some of the rooms on the south end looked as if they'd been wallpapered with foliage.

But the one thing that made the wilderness lovely was the fruit trees in blossom. When spring came and the weather turned slightly warmer, the buds swelled and began to open, the grounds erupting into a rainbow of color. White, pink, blue, violet, yellow, green—every color you could imagine, including some that didn't belong on trees. Although the pruning was sadly neglected, over the years the trees mingled, producing different shades of blossoms and new strains of fruit. In the spring, with the foreboding, crumbling castle as their backdrop, they had the look of garish, inappropriate relatives intruding on a somber funeral to which they had received no invitation.

Most of the original servants fled soon after the tragedy. The personal maid of the countess claimed that she saw her ghost walking up and down the halls at night, wringing her hands and moaning that she couldn't find her children. After that, several others also came forward and said they saw the incandescent apparitions of Frankie and his father, both of whom appeared to be trying to communicate with the terrified witnesses. Their mouths moved, but no sound accompanied the spectacle.

Julian dismissed the tales as the superstitious ramblings of uneducated, lower-class servants. But secretly, when he was alone in his room at night, he was frightened. In the light of day, he scoffed at the idea of the so-called ghostly visitors, but there were plenty of nights when he left candles burning in his room to help him fall asleep. He woke in the morning to cold, spent piles of wax, a testament to his dread. And as much as he scorned the local superstitions, he did have a terrible fear of mirrors. When he was a child, Henri had told him a story about one of his friends who was lured through a mirror by a spirit and was never seen again. He never got over that terror, and even in adulthood, he flinched whenever he saw a mirror. When he became the new count, he ordered all of the mirrors to be removed from the castle. If he ever wanted to look at himself, he filled a basin and surveyed his reflection in the still water instead.

Even more than mirrors, the count was afraid of somehow being deprived of his treasures. Over the years, he'd painstakingly created new collections, hoarding his rare finds in glass display cases. There were whole rooms of the castle that were off limits, to ensure that his groupings remained undisturbed. There was one room that was completely filled with random stacks of keys; some shiny and new, and some rusting with age. Julian was fascinated by the idea that all those keys fit an unknown door or cupboard or chest somewhere—it gave him an odd sense of ownership, even though he had no idea where their locks were or what they guarded. Ironically, he hadn't actually been inside the room for years—the door was locked, and somehow, the key had been mislaid. Perhaps it was inside the room, jumbled together with all the others. That thought always made him chuckle. Without warning, he would be suddenly overtaken by a new obsession, pursuing it relentlessly until just as inexplicably the desire faded and his interest turned to something new.

On the walls of the main hall, he displayed his sword collection. Polished until they gleamed, the swords looked particularly lethal whenever they caught the light from the huge fireplace. He had the floor in the grand ballroom torn out and replaced with millions of tons of crushed seashells, so that it glittered like the whitest sandy beach imaginable. He also had several locked trunks filled with jewels and precious stones. On occasion, he opened them and admired his brilliant acquisitions. Among the most impressive was a blue diamond as big as his fist and an unpolished ruby that would fetch enough at auction for Julian to buy his own island. But his most prized collection peppered the walls of his massive study—thousands of butterflies under glass. When he wanted to relax, he poured himself a drink and sat in his leather armchair amongst the butterflies, imagining that he could hear them fluttering and whispering.

It wasn't long before all but his most stalwart servants fled and stories of the haunted castle and its eccentric master spread through the town. After a while, the count stopped interviewing for a new groundskeeper; most took the job out of curiosity, and none of them lasted very long. Besides, he found that he liked the look of the overgrown trees and vines—they added to the untamed atmosphere, like the castle was reverting back to its true self.

In order to protect his wealth, the count hired guards to patrol the grounds. He also bought several large fish to stock the moat. They were supposed to be vicious, but when they were delivered, they looked more like something you might find on your dinner plate. He complained that they were not threatening enough to keep strangers out and demanded that their price be reduced. The deliveryman barked out a hard laugh, telling him these fish were worth every penny; just wait and see. The men dropped them into their new home, collected his fee, and left, leaving Julian feeling that he'd been swindled. Six months later, he happened to catch a glimpse of one of the fish, just under the surface. It was the size of a canoe, with disturbingly large teeth that could tear a grown man to pieces. Somehow, it gave him comfort to know that the fish weren't particular: if he accidentally fell into the moat, they would devour him just as certainly as if he were an intruder. He didn't like having to rely on loyalty—he found it much easier to put his trust in nature.

Nearly everyone in the town was indebted to the count for some service he had performed for them. He did these favors, not out of the kindness of his heart, but in order to ensure that he kept all his subjects in a permanent state of obligation. When he first arrived, the townspeople commented that he was very generous—he did not ignore them as his predecessor had. But all too soon, it became apparent that there was much to be said for invisibility. It was no light matter to owe the count a favor, and people lived in fear of the moment he might choose to collect his due. Wealthy and poor alike were on his list—the poor did their best to avoid him, and the wealthy flocked to him in crowds, hoping that there was safety in numbers.

On this spring night he sat in the study, surrounded by his butterflies, trying to recover from the nasty scene he'd been subjected to that very morning. A poor couple in the village had been unable to repay the money he loaned to them. He'd given them a reasonable due date and a rate of interest that was more than fair, compared to what others were offering. They begged for more time when the final notice was delivered, but as far as the count was concerned, they had reached the end of his patience and goodwill. He ordered his carriage readied and went into town, determined to see the situation remedied.

He leaned back into the cool leather, trying to soothe his harried nerves. If people would only live by the rules, he would not be compelled to enforce them. All unpleasantness could be avoided, but people, as he had learned, were notoriously impatient. They wanted what they wanted immediately, and were generally willing to commit to whatever terms were offered to make it happen. They quite gullibly believed that when the time came to pay, fate would somehow step in and pick up the bill.

Julian got out of his chair and paced restlessly, compulsively straightening the books on the shelves. The couple that morning was shabbily dressed and visibly frightened. They knew all too well who he was and why he was on their doorstep. They protested that business had been slow lately. If the count could only give them two more months, they were positive they would be able to repay the balance of the money owed. He'd sniffed delicately while holding a handkerchief to his nose, as if poverty were something contagious.

He spied a child, one eye visible peering from behind a corner.

"Send the boy out," he said finally, his voice low and unyielding.

The woman's eyes widened in panic, but the child came slowly of his own volition. He was thin and wiry, his skin pinched with hunger. His height made his age impossible to determine—he could have been a gangly seven-year old, or stunted at sixteen. Either way, he was old enough to work.

"Consider your debt repaid," he said grimly. He grabbed the boy's shoulder, pulling him out into the street and pushing him into the carriage. Over the clattering of the horse's hooves, he could still hear the shrill scream of the boy's mother. The boy said nothing during the carriage ride back to the castle. When they arrived, he placed the boy under the charge of another servant and sent them to work in the stables.

Why couldn't people understand that this was the way the world operated? This awful turn of events was just as upsetting to him as everyone else, but there must be justice, and there was no mercy in justice.

The count crossed wearily to the gramophone in the study. Perhaps his favorite opera would help him relax. The familiar notes began to play, and he felt the first tinge of comfort steal over him. He refilled his glass and sunk into his chair, closing his eyes and waiting for the soprano to begin. The power in her voice was so unexpected that, no matter how many times he heard it, it always took him by surprise. By the time she was several bars into her aria, Julian realized that the stress was gone from his limbs. He melted into the chair as if his bones had mysteriously dissolved, and he felt the tension of the day dissipating.

A timid knock on his door interrupted his reverie. He sighed in annoyance; only one person would dare disturb him while the music was playing. "Come," he said abruptly, not bothering to move from his chair or even open his eyes. He heard the door open, and footsteps that came nearer until they stopped in front of him.

"With respect, sir, I don't know why you bother with opera.

The screeching is bad enough, but they could at least pick a language that is understandable," the viceroy commented.

"It's Italian, and some of us with a little culture can understand it," he said in a clipped tone. "What do you want?"

"I heard a girl singing on the seashore today, Your Excellency."

The count tried to concentrate on the soprano instead of the unimportant news from the viceroy.

"Dicon ch'oltre mare se cade in man dell'uom,
ogni farfalla,
da uno spillo e'trafitta ed in tavola infitta!"

The viceroy continued, undaunted by the lack of response from the count. "She must be the daughter of the seamstress and the fisherman."

"I advise you to consider your next words very carefully. If you bothered me in the middle of the opera for village gossip, I assure you, there will be consequences."

"She had such a powerful voice. I was sure she must be a young woman . . ."

The count interrupted him, raising his hand to stop the flow of words. His eyes remained closed; now the tenor would answer the soprano.

"Un po' di vero c'e.
E tu lo sai perche?
Perche non fugga piu.
Io t'ho ghermita . . .
Ti serro palpitante. Sei mia."

". . . but to my surprise, she was only seven, maybe eight," he finished, taking a chance with his unauthorized intrusion.

The count finally opened his eyes, his annoyance immediately changing to mild interest. "You say she is young?"

"Yes," he purred. "Still a girl—an oddity to be sure, and I know how you adore unusual things."

"What do you know of singing? I will almost certainly be disappointed."

"Her voice is extraordinary; absolute perfection. You will

see—once you've heard her, you will not be willing to part with her for any price. You will be the envy of the whole world when she belongs to you."

The count smiled briefly, a grimace that put you in the mind of someone finding great amusement in pulling the legs from grasshoppers. He closed his eyes again, settling back into his chair and surrendering himself once more to the demanding soprano.

"Just one more thing, sir; may I ask what opera this is?"

"*Madame Butterfly.*"

"I should have known." He cocked his head quizzically. "Why do you like it?"

The count opened his eyes, fixing them on the viceroy until they would have seared the skin of a less determined man. "It is about a man who takes what he wants from the world at his convenience, and cares nothing for the people he hurts along the way. It is about possession without consequences."

The viceroy filed away his answer to consider later. Having planted his idea, he wisely exited without saying another word, leaving his employer to his solitary pleasures.

. . . ✶ . . .

June 1, 1942
Conservatory Vocal Academy

Dear Headmaster,

It has been brought to my attention that a child of tremendous musical ability is being neglected. Her name is Viola Connelly, and she lives in the village of Navia. She is very young, but already she shows promise for a shining vocal career. Her parents surely cannot afford to forward her education, but I am willing to pay her tuition and any other fees she may accrue. My only condition is that I remain anonymous. I wish for you to send a letter to her parents, conveying my offer. This brilliant child will bring your school more notoriety and fame than you can possibly comprehend; all I ask in return is that my identity remain secret. I realize that your school has very stringent entrance requirements and a long waiting list for new students, but if you are willing to waive them for this child, I will see that you are richly compensated.

I look forward to hearing from you.

Sincerely,

Count Diavolo

. . . * . . .

July 6, 1942
Dear Mr. and Mrs. Connelly,

It is our great pleasure to notify you that we have reserved a place in our vocal school for your daughter, Viola. Although she is slightly younger than our other pupils, we have been persuaded to make an exception by someone who has praised her very highly as a child with a voice that is mature beyond her years. Our upcoming term begins in two weeks' time, and we are very excited to welcome her and feel that she will be a valuable addition to our school.

It is also my duty to inform you that Viola's tuition will be paid by a benefactor who wishes to remain anonymous. We anticipate a positive reply from you soon, and we will send a carriage for her in two weeks.

Sincerely,

Professor Gallegos
Headmaster, Conservatory Vocal Academy

. . . * . . .

Claire pricked her finger with her sewing needle, wincing painfully. She was not clumsy, but this was the third time today. She couldn't stop worrying about the letter she had found in the mail that morning, an invitation for Viola to attend a prestigious vocal school. She knew how gifted her daughter was and what an incredible opportunity this would be for her. But she was still so young. Viola would be turning nine soon, but she was still very small for her age, probably because of her fairy blood. That was another thing that Claire didn't want to think about.

If only it were a few years down the road, she could feel better about sending her child into the big world. But she couldn't exactly write back and tell them to ask again next year, and certainly they could never afford a school of this stature on their own. Who could this mysterious benefactor be, and how had he managed to hear Viola sing? Claire could count on one hand the number of times she'd actually heard her daughter's angelic voice, and heaven knew she was too shy to sing for anyone else.

Claire knew that she and Ian couldn't make the decision for Viola, yet it seemed ridiculous and cruel to expect her to choose on her own. She even considered destroying the letter before showing it to her—then life could simply go on as before. But she knew how much singing meant to her daughter, and she couldn't bring herself to deny her outright what might be her one chance to cultivate her talent. She spoke with Ian, and they agreed that they would leave the decision up to Viola.

Her thoughts were interrupted as Viola poked her head around the corner, a bunch of wildflowers clutched in her hand. "Hello, Mum!"

Claire jabbed her finger with the needle for the fourth time. She sighed, putting her sewing aside. "Let us have a little chat, hmm?" She patted the chair next to her and tried to push away the legion of butterflies that were bouncing around in her stomach.

Viola bounded to the table and sat next to her. "What did you want to talk about?"

"A letter I got in the mail today."

"What sort of letter?"

"A very important one. What do you love, more than anything in the world?"

"You. And Dad. And Midnight."

Claire smiled at her answer. At least she and Ian ranked above the cat.

"Okay, besides that. What is the thing that makes you the happiest?"

"Singing, I guess."

"I thought you might say that. Sweetheart, the letter I got is from a vocal school. They want you to go live there for a while, so that they can teach you how to sing."

"But I already know how to sing, Mum."

"Yes, but they can help you learn to use your voice, so that you can sing even better. Maybe they could teach you not to be so shy as well. You could even sing on stage someday, in front of all sorts of important people. Would you like that?"

"I *guess* so," she said hesitantly.

Claire shook her head. "That is not good enough. We do not want to send you if you are feeling uncertain about it. You know that everyone is blessed with a gift, right?"

"Like your sewing?"

"Exactly. I did not start out making beautiful dresses; I only knew one stitch to begin with. But I practiced and practiced, and I learned whatever I could from people who were more skilled than I was. Now I can sew all sorts of things, but there are still stitches that I do not know. If I keep practicing, maybe someday I will know them all. Sewing is my gift, and I would find it hard to live if I woke up one morning and found it was taken away from me."

"Sewing is different than singing, Mum. You never have to perform. I love to sing to myself, but my voice disappears in front of other people. All those eyes, looking at me . . . ."

"What good do you think my talent would be if I kept it hidden? I could sew the most incredible dresses in the universe, and what difference would it make if I kept them tucked away in a drawer? What if, when people came to drop off their mending, I told them I could not fix their clothing because I was afraid they would not be pleased with my work, or they might laugh at me?" She paused, pushing a strand of red hair from her daughter's face.

"Your voice is a gift, Viola; it was given to you for a reason. It seems a shame not to share it. When you are blessed with a talent, you should improve it. But if this is not what you want, if the thought frightens you, your father and I will not push you into it. We would never want you to go away if you were unsure about it."

"But how will I know if it is the right thing to do?"

"You must decide how badly you want it. You must ask yourself, will I always wonder what I could have been? Will I be happy living out my life in a more common way, or will I regret not trying to be something more extraordinary?"

"I am only eight, Mum. I never think about things like that."

"I know it is unfair but you have to, darling, because you might not get a chance like this again."

. . . ✶ . . .

Viola felt sick inside, but she wasn't sure if it was with fear or excitement. She checked her bag one more time before closing the clasp. She didn't know why she kept opening it. Nearly everything she owned was inside, which wasn't much. She wore her favorite seashell necklace from her father, the spiral on the gold chain. It was a strange feeling, knowing that all her worldly possessions fit in one satchel, small enough to be lifted by a little girl such as herself. She felt like a turtle with her home on her back. She took one last look at her room before closing the door behind her and dragging the heavy bag to the front door.

Her father and mother were waiting: her mother with a trail of tears on her cheeks, and her father nervously clearing his throat. He took her bag and placed it by the door, kneeling down to hug his child. He wrapped his arms around her carefully, as if she were a piece of fine porcelain that could shatter under too much pressure. "Write us as soon as you are settled, so we know that you are safe."

"I will." She kissed his cheek, and he cleared his throat again, busying himself with her bag so that she wouldn't see the emotion in his eyes.

Claire squeezed Viola as tightly as she dared, brushing away the tears that fell freely now. "I want you to know how proud we are of you. But it is not too late to change your mind, if you are having any doubts at all," she said, her voice unsteady.

"It is all right, Mum; I have made my decision. Everything is going to be fine."

Her mother nodded, taking a deep, shaky breath. "Good girl. Off you go, then. The carriage is waiting for you."

Ian helped her into the carriage, placing her bag on the empty seat across from her. He rejoined Claire on the front step, and they waved to their only daughter as her carriage disappeared in a cloud of dust.

Viola waved back until she couldn't see them anymore. She fell into her seat and began to weep, violent sobs shaking her body until sleep mercifully took her.

The Conservatory Vocal Academy was a prestigious school that had seen better days. The count observed his surroundings as he passed the time in the dingy waiting room. Dark, heavy curtains hung limply at the windows, blocking out any rays of sunlight that might have attempted to break through. The only source of light in the room was a kerosene lamp that was perched on a small table near his chair. The carpets were threadbare, swimming with mold and silverfish. The spines of the numerous books on the shelves were covered in a thick layer of dust, and judging from the general state of disrepair of the room, no one had bothered with it in years.

Finally, a tall, silent man showed him into another room; the office of the Headmaster, which was only in slightly better condition than the waiting room. The Headmaster rose, shaking his hand wearily, as if the gloom hanging in the air around him made it a supreme effort to even lift his arm.

"Count Diavolo, this is a surprise. To what do I owe this great pleasure?" His voice was flat, giving no hint of any pleasure, great or otherwise.

"Headmaster, I come here today with a proposition for you."

"I am at your service."

"The girl that I wrote to you of . . . Viola."

"She is not yet with us, but she should be arriving shortly. We sent a carriage for her this morning. We are anxious to see if her gift is as great as you claim. She will be a most advantageous addition . . ."

"I want her," the count said, interrupting the seemingly endless stream of meaningless words.

The Headmaster's eyes widened, as though he had been asleep until this moment. "I beg your pardon?"

"I never intended for her to be left at this third-rate firetrap. Her acceptance was only a means to an end. When she arrives, she will be transported to Castle Diavolo, where she will live as my guest."

"And why, pray tell, would I just give her to you?"

The count surveyed the room with a practiced eye, giving the headmaster a measured look. "Because if my assumptions are correct, the future of this school is hanging by a thread. You are obviously in desperate need of funding, which I am only too capable of providing. You will go down in history as the headmaster who restored the school to its former glory, and all I ask in return is for you to give me one child. I think that anyone would say that the terms I am offering are more than generous. Do we have a deal?"

"Even if I did agree to your monstrous plan, there are the girl's parents to consider. Do you really think that they would not notice if she simply disappeared?"

"I have dealt with that particular problem." The count pulled an unsealed envelope from the pocket inside his suit. "You will send this letter to the parents. I think you will find that it ties everything up quite neatly. All you have to do is sign the bottom, and I will give you this handsome check in return." He handed the envelope to the headmaster.

As he scanned the brief letter, the color vanished from his cheeks, leaving a sickly gray color in its place. He took a pen from his desk, hurriedly scribbling his signature before he could change his mind. He looked at the count with disdain, as if he loathed even having to breathe the same air as this creature, even though it was painfully necessary for his own survival. His eyes burned with fury, but his tired soul had already admitted defeat. He placed the letter on his desk, pushing it toward the count.

He sighed. "When she arrives, I will have her transported to your carriage. I trust that since our . . . transaction is concluded, we shall never have the misfortune of meeting again."

The count took the letter before pushing the check across the desk. He rose from his chair, the rare smile on his face conveying his enjoyment at the other man's impossible choice. "You may depend on it, headmaster. The next time you and I meet will be on the day when we shake hands in hell. Good day."

. . . ✶ . . .

July 27, 1942

Dear Mr. and Mrs. Connelly,

We regret to inform you that soon after your daughter Viola arrived, a plague of fever passed through our students. Viola was, regrettably, among those affected. She succumbed to her illness yesterday and was buried with the five other students who perished.

The fever progressed at such a rapid rate that we had no warning, and there was no opportunity to contact the parents of the ill children. Your daughter died a quick death and did not suffer. We return to you this necklace, which was in her possession when she passed away. The short time that she was with us was enough to catch a glimpse of her enormous potential, and we offer you our sincerest condolences for your loss.

Sincerely,

Professor Gallegos
Headmaster, Conservatory Vocal Academy

. . . ✶ . . .

There were two carriages at the Conservatory Vocal Academy

that day. The count left immediately in his carriage, leaving the viceroy with the other to bring Viola back to the castle when she arrived. He hadn't had time yet to contemplate how he wished their initial meeting to take place, but he was certain that the long carriage ride home would not be the best way to make her acquaintance. He wanted to be able to properly savor the idea of hearing her voice for the first time.

The count spent the rest of the afternoon in his study, answering his mail. He had one particularly interesting letter from his solicitor, informing him of the upcoming liquidation of a large estate in Austria, owned by a Lord Ellis until his recent passing. As Lord Ellis left behind no heirs, the instructions in his will were that the contents of the estate were all to be sold at auction. Count Diavolo had never met Lord Ellis, but knew him to be an avid butterfly collector by reputation. The idea of bidding on his marvelous collection made the count salivate with delight. The only inconvenience was that if he wanted to arrive in time for the auction, he would need to leave early in the morning. This necessitated a certain waiting period before he could be introduced to the newest item in his collection.

He heard the creaking sounds of the bridge being lowered across the moat and carriage wheels, crunching through the loose rocks in the entry. He frowned. Although he wanted additional time to contemplate meeting Viola, it would take weeks if not months to make the trip to Austria, attend the auction, and arrange for the butterflies to be transported back to Spain. And with the war raging in most of Europe, months might be a conservative estimate. After going through so much trouble to secure his little songbird, he wasn't certain that he could sustain a delay of that magnitude. Still, the chance of making such a monumental addition to his butterfly collection could not be ignored.

He heard the steps of heavy boots echoing in the hall, along with the muted sounds of a child's whimpering. He leaned back in his chair and closed his eyes, listening as the tiny cries vanished into the distance. He knew that the viceroy would be installing her in her new quarters momentarily, from which there could be no hope of escape. Yes, the trip to Austria was definitely unavoidable. For now, just knowing that she was finally his would have to be enough. He could not risk rushing their meeting, and after all, there was something to be said for anticipation.

. . . * . . .

The viceroy led a wide-eyed, teary Viola down a long, winding stone staircase. When they reached the bottom, he unlocked the massive wooden door, revealing a small round room. It took a moment for her eyes to adjust to the near darkness. The room was about twice as large in diameter as the only item it contained: a large metal cage. He steered Viola through the entry wordlessly, unlocking the door of the cage and pushing her inside. She had no time to protest or struggle—she didn't think it necessary. Surely this was some awful nightmare and any moment now, she would awaken to find herself safe at home in her own bed, listening to the sound of the water lapping against the sand.

When the cage was firmly locked, the viceroy left her, pausing outside the door just long enough to ensure that it was locked as well. Viola looked around her, waiting for her eyes to adjust to the dimness and cautiously examining her prison. The room made up in height what it lacked in width, extending so far into the sky that she could not see the ceiling. There was one tiny window, but it was so high that it the only thing she could see through it was sky. Out of the corner of her eye, she saw something dart across the floor, disappearing before she could identify it. The only thing she could say for certain was that it had too many legs to be friendly. She shivered, curling up on the cold floor and squeezing her eyes shut tightly. Her tears dripped onto the stone floor, and her last thought before falling into an uneasy sleep was that perhaps she was better off not having enough light to see her fellow occupants.

"I thought we might take a break for a little while, maybe go for a walk. Some fresh air might do you good, Katie." Viola's voice was barely a whisper, and Megan realized that she was much nearer to her mother-in-law than when they started. Sometime during the story, she must have migrated closer so that the precious words would not escape her hearing. Megan blinked.

"Now? You want to stop now?! I have to know what happens! Tell me about when you finally met the count," Megan said.

Kaitlin nodded eagerly.

"Actually, it was two years before the count returned."

"Two years! Did he get lost?" Kaitlin asked.

"Well, travel in those days was quite different. There wasn't the convenience of just hopping on a plane at a moment's notice and, to make matters worse, the war made crossing into other countries even more difficult. To tell you the truth, I think that the count forgot about me."

"So you're saying that you spent two years in a cage by yourself, and no one remembered you were there?" Megan said incredulously.

"Well, obviously someone remembered, or I would have been nothing more than a pile of bones by the time he returned. For two years, I saw no one but the viceroy, and not once did he speak to me. I think the only way I managed to retain my sanity was by singing. Even though they confiscated all my possessions and locked me away, I still had my voice. That was the one thing they couldn't take from me."

"So, what happened when the count came back?" Kaitlin asked.

"Later, dear. Tomorrow I will tell you all about the count's return and his great plans for me. Right now, I think we should take advantage of this nice summer afternoon."

"I think we should stay here, Grandma. I'm pretty sure it's going to rain."

"Katie?" she rasped.

"Yes?"

"Don't press your luck."

Kaitlin shrugged. "You can't blame a girl for trying."

* NINE *

Dear Kevin,

Well, I'm back in your mother's good graces. She agreed to tell the rest of the story to Kaitlin and me both, as long as I promise to show a little more faith in her. So far, she's told us that when she was a little girl, she loved to sing but was very shy. She had an amazing voice, and one day, her mother and father received a letter inviting her to attend a prestigious voice school at the expense of an anonymous benefactor. Anyway, to make a long story short, her generous admirer was none other than Count Diavolo. He bribed the school with money, and in exchange they sent a letter to her parents, informing them that she had died of a fever. Meanwhile, she was whisked away to the Castle Diavolo, where she was kept locked in a cage in a dungeon room for two years—that's where she left off yesterday.

I know this sounds ridiculous, but the more I hear, the more I think it really could be true. Maybe she just never mentioned her childhood to you because it was too painful for her to relive. One part of me keeps saying how impossible it all is, but another part can't imagine that she's making it up. Could your mother really have been kidnapped?

Email me back with any information as soon as you can. I wish that I could say I hope you are getting settled, but that would mean that I have come to terms with the fact that you are there to stay. I am so very proud of what you are doing, but my mind refuses to accept that you won't be there when we get home. It's funny the little things you take for granted. I am counting the days until you are home again. Please be careful.

Love,

Megan

Megan quickly reread the email before sending it. With any luck, some part of the story might stir Kevin's memory. She conveniently left out anything having to do with fairies, since she was having enough difficulty trying to get her husband to accept the tamer version. If she wasn't careful, she had the feeling she might end up tossed in the care facility along with Viola, taking antipsychotic drugs and playing bingo all afternoon.

Kaitlin came through the door, flopping down on the bed next to her. She was wearing an apron that was spattered with spaghetti sauce, as though she'd had a narrow escape in a cooking-related battle. She sighed loudly. "Cooking is hard work. I can see why you don't make dinner more often."

Megan swatted her playfully on the bottom. "Well, not all of us were cut out for domestic greatness. My special talents lie elsewhere."

"Like Claire with her sewing?" Kaitlin said.

"Exactly."

"What is your special talent exactly, because I'm pretty sure you can't sew either."

"Do you want me to taste this sauce or not?" Megan demanded.

Kaitlin grabbed her arm and dragged her into the kitchen, where they found Viola scrubbing spaghetti sauce off the wall behind the stovetop.

"Good heavens, it looks like something was slaughtered in here!"

Viola smiled. "Well, there is a bit of a learning curve, I'm afraid. Just think; the next time Katie makes sauce, it will be at your house."

"Great. I feel much better now." Megan took a spoon from the drawer and dipped it into the simmering tomato sauce. "I'm so impressed," she pronounced. "It tastes just like Grandma's!"

Kaitlin frowned. "That is Grandma's. Mine is over here."

Megan took a spoonful of Kaitlin's sauce as well, mulling it across her tongue like a fine wine. It had a slightly burnt flavor and needed salt, but she didn't want her daughter to lose heart. "Very good, especially for your first try. By the time Dad gets home, you'll be an old pro."

Kaitlin beamed.

Megan walked around the kitchen, peeking into corners and surveying the countertop casually.

"Are you looking for something, dear?" Viola asked.

"I thought I might have a slice of pound cake. I was hoping that my darling daughter left a crumb trail to lead me to it."

"I'm afraid the pound cake is long gone, although I can't figure out for the life of me when Katie ate it."

"Maybe I really am a sleepwalker!" Kaitlin chimed in.

"Never mind; I don't really need it anyway. My pants are starting to get tight. I'm not used to being around all this delicious food. It seems that I lose all self-control the moment I enter this kitchen."

"I'm glad to hear it," Viola said, her lips curling in satisfaction. "So, are you two ready to hear about the boy?"

"What boy?"

"You know, the boy; in the story."

"I'm afraid you've lost me," Megan said.

Viola sighed impatiently. "The boy the count took from his parents as a servant, to repay their debt."

"Haven't we already done that part?" Kaitlin asked.

"Of course, but that wasn't the end of the boy's story. When the count returned, he suddenly became thrust into my life."

"The count did?"

"No, the boy."

"Maybe if you just called him by his name, it wouldn't be so confusing," Kaitlin added helpfully.

"But he didn't have a name."

"You mean, you don't remember his name," Megan said.

Viola's eyes narrowed into dangerous slits. "Are you questioning my memory?"

"Of course not," Megan stammered. "It's just, everyone has a name."

"Well, *he* didn't. Now, who's telling this story, you or me?"

"You are," she said meekly.

"As long as we're both on the same page."

The Boy

A note hung in the air, clear and sad. The boy heard the singing every night. Sometimes it reminded him of the keening wail of an animal in a trap, sometimes of the rhythmic sound of waves scratching on sand. He had only seen her a few times from a distance, being taken into the woods by the viceroy, covered in a heavy cloak. Once, she turned in his direction unexpectedly as she was being spirited away, and he could see a glimpse of her face under the hood. He thought she was a ghost, pretty and pale. But she was also dirty, and who ever heard of a dirty ghost?

Then there was the cage to consider. Because the boy never spoke, people had no fear of conversing around him. They assumed that their secrets were safe with him. When the count left for Austria and the singing began, so did the gossiping. Whispers of rumors began to circulate that the hauntingly beautiful voice came from a little girl the count was keeping in the bowels of the castle. They said she was in a cage in a locked room so that she couldn't escape. The boy concluded that she must not be a ghost. Why would anyone bother locking up a ghost when it could just walk through the bars or the walls?

Sometimes when everyone was sleeping, the boy would creep from the pile of hay where he slept in the stables to a spot near the castle, where he could hear her voice better. Over time, he became bolder. He learned the schedule of the guards and knew when they would be out on patrol. He waited until they passed, allowing himself to get closer and closer to the castle each night until finally, he sat crouched with his back against the stone wall, his breath lingering before him in icy puffs.

It was a chilly night, and the caress of her voice seemed to warm him in a way he couldn't describe. When he shifted to find a more comfortable position against the wall, he noticed something odd. The stones behind him were warm; he wasn't aware of it until he realized that he'd stopped shivering. He skimmed his hand across the stones until he reached a spot that was icy cold. He could tell exactly where her room began and ended, because of the wave of heat breathing through the wall.

Besides the warmth, he noticed a slight vibration against his palm when he touched the stones, like the friendly hum of insects. He wondered in awe at the strange power of the girl on the other side of the wall. Maybe that's why she was in a cage; because her gift evoked fear. Still, it was difficult to imagine the count being afraid of anything.

The castle was in turmoil. There were servants rushing in all directions like crazed ants whose home had been stomped on by a destructive child. Everywhere you looked, there was activity—cooking, sweeping, polishing, tidying. For two years, the castle had been dormant. The dust had gathered as the staff had sleepwalked through the absolute minimum duties necessary.

No one in the castle had slept through the night since Viola had arrived. When her singing reverberated through the halls after dark, not one person could get any rest. So when the sun climbed over the mountains in the morning, the servants went to work just as Viola was finally drifting off to sleep. Everywhere the viceroy looked, he found servants asleep in odd places; curled up on the cold stone floor or sometimes even standing up. They dared not sleep during the day and work at night, for they never knew what moment the count would choose to reappear, and they shuddered at the thought of being caught unaware.

A thick scum rested on all the furniture and trinkets, coating them with a dull layer of neglect. Everything seemed to be decaying at an alarming rate. But today, the servants hurried from room to room. They dusted with rags, polishing furiously until their fingertips bled, watching as the years dropped away. This sudden chaotic spell of cleaning could mean only one thing—the count was coming home.

The viceroy had received a letter from the count that very morning, announcing that they should be expecting him to arrive any day. Although it was beneath his station, the viceroy was doing a little tidying of his own. He had been living almost exclusively in the count's quarters while he was away, and it wouldn't do for him to return and find that his servant had taken up residence. He hardly thought His Excellency would look kindly on such an intrusion. He gathered all his possessions, careful to leave no trace of himself that might betray his uninvited presence.

The viceroy would miss lounging in the count's plush rooms, which were the most comfortable the castle had to offer, and he knew this from experience. He had tried sleeping in every room in the castle, but there was no refuge from that voice. There was no room far enough and no walls thick enough to protect him. He finally gave up, disturbed by the thought that there was no spot on the castle grounds where that voice could not find him. He hid motionless beneath the blankets, holding his breath and waiting in dread for that moment when his chest felt as if it would explode. While Viola was the one in the cage, it would be difficult to say which of them felt more like a prisoner.

The count arrived around dinnertime the next day. He looked well-fed, yet strong and fit at the same time. His skin was tan with the glow of travel, and he appeared to be in good spirits. He took his dinner with the viceroy, who he noticed sipped his wine prudently and delicately, as though each glass could be his last. This filled the count with glee, as it was evidence of the power he exercised over the viceroy. Even better was the knowledge that he knew the other man knew it as well.

The viceroy watched enviously as the count finished the last slice of blackberry pie swimming in fresh cream. He used his spoon to scoop up every last bit of sticky purple juice, smacking his lips in ecstasy. "Is there anything else you require, Excellency?" the viceroy asked, his tone carrying a barely hidden note of sarcasm.

"Not at the moment." His eyes scanned the room carefully. "Everything seems to be in good condition. Is there anything I should know about?"

"No, Excellency. Everything is as you left it. Except the girl—I am afraid she has grown a little taller, but I am certain you will agree that that was something I had very little control over."

He paused, searching his memory. "The girl?"

"Viola? The child with the amazing voice who you left locked in a cage in your dungeon?"

A look of surprise mixed with pleasure stole across his features. "Do you know I had almost forgotten about my little songbird? How inconsiderate of me to leave her languishing in the basement while I was enjoying myself. And to think, you have had the exclusive pleasure of her company for two whole years."

"Yes, Excellency, I have been hoping to speak to you about that. Delivering her meals is becoming quite a drain on my time. And then there are the weekly walks, which are not only inconvenient, but also humiliating."

"In what way?"

"All the precautions you asked me to take—it is ridiculous. I know that the servants are whispering about me, saying that I am afraid of a harmless child. Having her hand manacled to mine, hiding her in a hooded cloak in case we happen to be seen. Excellency, surely you must see, it is like wearing a thick leather glove to handle a canary!"

"Are you saying that you think watching over my pet songbird is beneath you?" the count said, his voice dangerously calm.

"Of course not. I just thought that perhaps my vast resources could be put to better use. Perhaps the boy could take care of her instead?" he suggested hopefully.

The count was silent, staring at the viceroy like a snake preparing to strike.

"You know, the boy in the stables? The one you took from his parents?" he rambled. "He is very efficient at his job. I am certain that he could handle the task of delivering her food and taking her for walks."

Still the count did not say anything, and the viceroy began to worry that he'd overstepped his bounds. His face was hot, and a drop of sweat beaded at his hairline.

"I want to see the boy," he said finally. "If he is suitable, I will agree to him taking her food, but not the walks. She is the crown jewel of my collection, and I cannot take the chance of her escaping. I am certain that a ramble in the woods once a week will not interfere with your busy schedule," he said dryly.

"Of course, Excellency. You know best," he said, his words dripping in relief. "Shall I bring the boy to you now?"

. . . ✶ . . .

The only person in the castle who wasn't rushing around in a frenzied state was Viola, who had no idea that the count had returned or, for that matter, that he even existed. To her, this day was exactly the same as every one that preceded it since she arrived. With the exception of her weekly walk in the forest, the days ran one into the next with mind-numbing monotony. She spent her days sleeping and trying to forget the life she left behind. But at night, when the creatures in the dark came out and she dared not close her eyes, she sang. It may have been only her imagination, but it seemed that when the first notes of her song pierced the night, the monsters receded into the shadows. She sang without stopping until the first sliver of light appeared in her tiny, high window. Only then did she allow herself to rest.

Sometimes when she couldn't sleep, her thoughts wandered. She thought of her mum and dad. She pictured them, scouring the world for their lost child who had simply vanished, hidden in a place where no one would think to look. In her dreams, she imagined her father, fighting the cloaked man who kept her locked away and rescuing her. In her prayers, she hoped that they were safe and that somehow they would have the strength to keep looking for her. But in her darkest moments, a mocking voice in her head questioned if her parents might have known where she was really going. She wondered if the school had ever really wanted her. Was her voice really as unique as the letter had implied, or was it all just part of the plan to lure her away? She tried to push those thoughts aside when they appeared, but occasionally they lingered, causing her to doubt the people she loved most in the world.

. . . ✶ . . .

The boy had never been in this part of the castle before. He tried not to stray too far behind the viceroy, but there were so many things to see that it was hard to know where to look first. He gazed in awe at the sword collection and wondered if he would be able to use one in a fight, in the event that he managed to escape and had to defend himself. A few of the blades looked ancient and rusted, but most looked shiny and sharp enough to slice neatly through a man. He swallowed hard, trying to ignore the sudden lump in his throat.

The viceroy led the boy into the count's study, where he was surrounded by thousands of butterflies, forever caught in flight. The boy had only ever heard about the spectacle. When he stepped into the room, they made him feel trapped as well. For all the freedom he had, he was effectively under glass himself, if only figuratively.

There was a servant in the study hanging some of the count's new specimens from his expedition to Austria, which appeared to have been very successful. The count himself was sitting in his armchair, uncorking a bottle of wine. His voice was so deep and unexpected that the boy jumped when he spoke.

"What do you think of my butterflies? Are they not the most magnificent thing you have ever witnessed?"

The boy nodded cautiously, afraid that any answer he gave would be wrong. The count poured himself a glass of the deep red liquid. The wine was thick, and the boy found himself unnerved. It was as if he were seeing the count pour himself a glass of blood.

The count watched the boy watching him and saw his face turning white. "You know, it is very rude not to offer a guest a drink. Would you like to try this? It is a lovely Cabernet Sauvignon

I picked up while I was in Krems."

He swirled the inky red-purple wine in the glass, and the boy found himself hypnotized by the way the syrupy liquid coated the crystal. The count finally raised the glass to his lips, taking a sip and releasing the boy from its dizzying effects. He shook his head.

"It would probably be wasted on you anyway," he said, shrugging. "Well, I am told that you are a hard worker and do an excellent job in my stables. I have decided that you will be rewarded. Would you like that?"

The boy stared at him blankly.

"The boy does not speak, Excellency."

"Yes, I can see that, thank you," he said curtly. "That makes you the perfect choice for the new job I have for you. Do you know about the girl in the dungeon—the girl with the beautiful voice?"

He nodded hesitantly.

"I need someone to take her meals to her. That will be your new responsibility, in addition to your other duties." He paused, a cold smile spreading until his eyes glittered like ice. "I was going to tell you that you must never speak to her, but since you cannot speak, I will have no cause to worry. Take the food and leave it; that is all. Do not try to communicate with or befriend her, and never believe her, whatever she may tell you. I am not a cruel man. I had an excellent reason for locking her in that cage. She is the most dangerous girl you will ever meet, and she will bewitch you if you let your guard down."

The boy listened to this speech impassively, his face showing none of his thoughts or emotions. Obviously he had been mistaken—the count was either very afraid of this girl, or lying through his teeth.

"I seem to remember now. The day that I took you from your parents, you never spoke then either," he mused.

The boy flinched slightly, but his eyes never left the count's.

"I assumed it was because you were in shock. Are you certain that you cannot speak?" he goaded.

The boy remained silent.

"I hope that you would never play games with me, thinking that you were smart enough to get away with it. My eyes are everywhere, and trust me when I say that there is no secret you could keep from me, if I wanted it exposed." He rose from his armchair, strolling purposefully around the study. "I suppose I could always torture you until you cried out for mercy . . . or until I was satisfied that you were truly unable to cry out."

The boy's legs were shaking, but he did his best to hide it, standing as tall as he could.

"But perhaps I give you too much credit. I suppose it is possible that out of all the people who owed me money, I managed to choose the parents of the village idiot to make an example of. Never mind—luckily for you, it does not matter to me how intelligent you are. The only thing I care about is that you can work and follow instructions. Are we clear?"

He nodded, almost imperceptibly.

As an afterthought, the count added, "It is probably best that you cannot speak after all. You are so coarse and common that if you tried to talk to Viola, she would certainly laugh at you and mock you. Why would a girl with a gift like hers bother with someone like you?"

It was finally more than the boy could take. He broke eye contact, hanging his head and staring at the floor.

"I am so glad we had this little discussion. I trust that you will not disappoint me," the count said, waving his hand in dismissal. The viceroy grabbed the boy's arm and steered him out of the room.

The count sat in his chair, waiting for the viceroy to return. He drained the last sip from his cup, feeling the delicious warm haze of the wine as it spread through his body, leaving him feeling pleasantly buzzed yet sleepy. The boy seemed convincing enough, but the count wasn't entirely persuaded that he was mute. Not yet, anyway. Still, there was no need to hurry—he would have plenty of time to pry out any secrets he might be hiding. He was just considering putting on a little music before bed when he heard the footsteps of the viceroy returning.

"I led the boy to the kitchen. He is taking the girl's dinner to the dungeon as we speak. Do you want me to have her brought to you now, Excellency?"

"No. It is late, and I am suddenly very tired. I suppose the fatigue of the journey is finally catching up with me. I am not feeling up to meeting her this evening, but I am certain that I will feel better once I have bathed and rested. In the morning after breakfast, I will be in the study. Bring her to me then."

"Of course. I will see if I can find something suitable for her to wear."

"That will not be necessary. I want to see her as she is—there is no need to clean her up."

"If you say so, Excellency. Is there anything else you require this evening?"

"Not tonight. But I do have one chore for you tomorrow."

"Yes?"

"After I have spoken with the girl, I want you to drive into town and buy me some new bedding."

"Certainly, Excellency, but . . ."

"Did you think I would not notice you have been sleeping in my bed?"

The viceroy's face colored. "There was a good reason . . ."

"I am not interested in your excuses," he snapped. "Perhaps you were not listening to the lecture I gave the boy. It is very good advice and I will only tell you once, so you would do well to pay attention. My eyes are everywhere. Nothing happens in this castle that escapes my notice. The next time we have this exchange, you might find yourself sharing a room in the dungeon . . . with Viola."

"What sort of sheets do you require?"

The count looked mystified. This was the part where the viceroy was supposed to cower in shame and beg his forgiveness, not ask questions about sheets. "What did you say?"

"The sheets, Excellency." The viceroy wandered toward the door. "The sheets on your bed now are of the highest quality. I wondered if you were willing to spend the money to replace them, or if you might want to settle for something cheaper. I seem to recall that there was a time you slept covered in any obliging hay bale—perhaps the very best is not necessary. After all, I believe you inherited that bedding from your poor . . . dead . . . brother." He said the last words so softly that the count had to strain to hear them, yet punctuated them in such a way that it was impossible to escape their meaning.

"You had better watch your tongue, or you and the stable boy might suddenly have more in common than you think. The two of you could have a great deal to talk about . . . or not."

"Excellency, I was merely asking a question," he said, his voice now placating and innocent. "I would hate to buy the wrong thing. I apologize for any offense I may have given; it was unintended."

"What you are referring to is in the past. How many people are left that would show any interest in your wild tale? Whose word do you think would be more widely accepted—yours or mine?"

"You have it all wrong. I am not one to spread gossip, nor do I think that I am asking for much. All I want is a little respect and dignity. And I am certain that the day will never come when I have to test your theory."

The count looked relieved. "Perhaps since I am getting new bedding, you might like to have the things from my bed. I am sure you will find them quite comfortable," he said generously.

"Thank you, Excellency, for the kind gift."

"I like to reward those who are loyal servants. And when you go into town tomorrow, rest assured that I have no qualms about paying for the very best sheets they carry."

"As you wish." The viceroy did not smile, but his eyes sparkled with merriment as he bowed to the count. His master would simply have to learn that, even though he was the wealthiest man in the county, there was still someone who could put him in his place, someone who knew what he really was.

The count snarled as the viceroy closed the door behind him. He threw his empty wine glass at the fireplace, watching with satisfaction as it shattered into tiny shards. The viceroy might think he was clever, baiting him into submission. But unfortunate accidents and strange illnesses had been known to occur at Castle Diavolo before, and he would not hesitate to orchestrate a fitting demise for the viceroy, should it become necessary. For such a confident man, he could be remarkably stupid. The viceroy had no idea what a dangerous game he was playing.

When the door creaked open that night, Viola knew that it must be the silent, cloaked man who brought her food—he was the only person who ever came down here. But, to her surprise, a young man peered around the corner at her instead, carrying a silver tray that contained her meager dinner. She rose as far as she could, not being able to stand completely straight without hitting her head on the top of the cage.

"Do you know who I am?" she asked frantically.

The boy did not make eye contact with her, or even acknowledge her presence.

"My name is Viola. I have been here for two years now. I was kidnapped from school and brought here."

He raised his eyes to hers, but they were as blank as a clean sheet of paper.

"Surely it must have been in the newspapers! You have to go to the police and tell them where I am," she hissed.

The boy took the bread and water from the tray and reached through the bars to set them carefully inside the cage. Viola grabbed his hand, holding it more tightly as he struggled to get away.

"Do you understand what I am saying? They are holding me prisoner here! My name is Viola Connelly," she repeated, her voice shaking. "My parents are Claire and Ian Connelly, and you have to go to them and tell them where they can find me. Please!"

Her grip was surprisingly strong, but the boy gave his arm a good tug, catching her unaware. There were marks on his hand where her fingernails cut during his escape, bloody half moons carved into his flesh. He clutched his hand to his chest protectively, his face full of pain and confusion, like a naïve animal that doesn't have the capacity to understand why someone would want to hurt him.

"Oh, I am so sorry!" she said, putting a hand to her mouth, horrified at the blood. "I did not mean to hurt you, but you pulled away. Let me see your hand."

He held his hand tighter, backing toward the door, away from the cage. He kept his eyes on Viola the entire time.

"It was an accident! Please, do not go," she pleaded.

When the boy reached the door, he took one last look at her before turning around. He opened the door quickly, pulling it closed behind him and locking it again.

Viola collapsed into a heap at the bottom of the cage, sobbing. The first person she'd seen besides the silent man in the cloak in two years, and she'd alienated him in a matter of minutes. Her one chance to get out of here, and he stared at her as if she were a monster. Maybe she really did belong in this cage.

She cried until there were no more tears, her sobs turning into hiccups. For the first time since she'd arrived, the darkness closed in around her, and she didn't care. While she slept, the rest of the castle closed their eyes and dreamed. There were only two people who sat awake: the boy, who licked his wounds in the hay loft, and the count, who was looking forward to a concert, as the viceroy told him that Viola sang all night. Both were bitterly disappointed.

Viola was awakened from a dream by the sound of the key clicking in the heavy lock on the dungeon door. The silent man appeared, not bothering with the hooded cloak or the manacles.

"Come; it is time for you to meet the Master."

"You are talking to me! Why have you never spoken to me before?" she asked eagerly.

"Before today, there was never a reason for us to speak." When she didn't move, he snapped, "Hurry—he does not like to be kept waiting."

"I thought you were the Master."

"No, I am merely the caretaker of his most important treasures."

"What should I call you?"

"You may call me viceroy."

She wrinkled her nose. "That is a strange name."

"It is a title."

"But what is your real name?" she pressed.

"My name is irrelevant, and I am not here to play games with you. Now, come!"

Viola followed him up the stone steps into the main halls of the castle. Her arms were covered in goose bumps, and the cold rose from the floor, settling into her feet. "How far are we going?"

The viceroy stopped abruptly, turning to face her. "I think I liked you better when we never spoke," he said threateningly. They continued down the hall, both of them quiet. The creaking of the wind through the branches of the trees outside was the only sound.

Viola heard the faint strains of opera music before they entered the room. When she left her cage for her weekly walk, it took a long time for her eyes to adjust to the light. She could barely open them to begin with, and she never remembered the world from her childhood as so unnaturally bright. She unconsciously straightened her tattered dress. The skirt was too short now, hanging in shredded ribbons with numerous spots where the fabric had completely disintegrated. Her feet were bare, and her hair hung around her face in limp clumps. She blinked rapidly, still fighting for focus of the shapes blurry and hazy, the light grating like sandpaper against her eyes.

The sounds of the opera were closer now, and she thought in bleak disappointment of how the voice might have been hers someday. She'd lost so much time already—not just with her voice, but with her family. She wished there was some way she could let them know she was okay. She thought that she could almost bear to stay here locked away in solitude, if only she knew they weren't worrying about her.

"The count is waiting," the viceroy said, a catch in his voice revealing his impatience. He held the door open for her, and she cautiously crept forward, peeking around the corner.

The first thing she saw was the enormous fireplace with its cheerfully crackling flames. There were bookcases stuffed with books extending to the ceiling, with a ladder to reach the books at the top. This was a room Viola would have loved to explore, had she not been so terrified of meeting the man inside. He stood, facing the fireplace so that she could not see his face.

The viceroy cleared his throat. "Excellency, may I present the girl?"

All the hours the count spent planning this moment could not prepare him for the petite, bit-of-nothing girl standing in the doorway. There was not an ounce of fat on her skinny frame, and he was painfully reminded of himself on the fateful day that he arrived at the castle. He wished now that he had left instructions for the viceroy to take better care of her, but he had been in such a rush, his mind filled with nothing but butterflies. The timing of her arrival had been terrible.

He groaned quietly to himself. Surely her voice could have no real power, not in such a small package. He felt hot anger bubbling up inside; he never should have trusted the judgment of the viceroy without actually hearing her. What would he do with her if she truly couldn't sing? It wasn't as if he could just take her back where he got her—she knew too much. So now, he would be saddled with a child to look after. These were the thoughts that ran through his mind as she stared at the small girl, coupled with his hopes which, even when presented with the physical evidence, still refused to die. He couldn't help fantasizing that she might really be as perfect as the viceroy claimed she was.

"Viola," he said finally. His voice was neither welcoming nor distant; it was simply a confirmation that he knew her name. "We have not been properly introduced. I am Count Diavolo. I must apologize for my extended absence. I fully intended to meet you the day after you arrived, but my business took me abroad for longer than I expected." She remained frozen in the doorway. "You must be cold in that thin dress. Come in and warm yourself by the fire."

She didn't want to go any closer, but found herself too tempted by the orange fingers of warmth radiating in her direction. Warily, she stepped softly into the room until she was directly in front of the flames. She reveled in the heat, warming her hands until all the stiffness dissolved. She wiggled her fingers in delight, feeling the blood returning to them. Suddenly she remembered where she was, sneaking a look at the count, who was watching her with interest.

"I'm afraid it is very cold in the dungeon, even during the warmest months of the year. Can I get you something hot to drink?" he said pleasantly.

"What I would really like is to go home." Her voice came out sterner than she felt, and she was quite pleased with herself.

The count was very amused by her tone. "This is your home now. The sooner you realize that and accept it, the better your life will be."

"Please, sir, no one ever has to know what happened. I will never say a word. I could even tell my parents I ran away from school, if you wish it."

"I am afraid you do not understand me. What you are suggesting is impossible," he said flatly.

"You cannot keep me here forever," she said sharply.

"I can do exactly that, and I will. You are mine now. I own you."

"No matter where you hide me, my mum and dad will never stop looking for me!"

"Ah, yes—your parents. Life is so tragic and unpredictable, is it not? Even the most loving and devoted parents generally are not searching for children who are dead."

Viola gasped. "What did you say?" she whispered.

"I arranged for the school to send a letter to your parents, telling them that you fell ill with a fever and succumbed soon after you arrived; deepest sympathy, sorry for your loss . . . that sort of thing. So you see, my little songbird, no one is looking for you. No one even knows you are alive."

Viola wanted to cry, but she felt too numb. It was as if everything inside her had turned to stone, even the tears that were threatening to fall only moments ago. The polished grandfather clock in the corner was still ticking as loudly as when she entered the room, but for her, the last scrap of hope she'd been clinging to was dashed to pieces.

"Now that we have dispensed with the preliminaries, we can get down to business. I went to a great deal of trouble and expense to obtain you, and I have been waiting a very long time to reap the rewards. I am not one to purchase items before determining their worth, but in your case, I was willing to make an exception. So . . . whenever you are ready, my dear." He turned off the gramophone, sat in his armchair, and waited.

"Ready for what?"

"To sing, of course. You can choose whatever song you like—it makes no difference to me."

"I cannot sing in front of you," she stammered.

"Why?"

"I am afraid. I never sing in front of other people."

"You have been singing to a crowd every night for years."

"What do you mean? I sing only when I am alone."

"My dear, no one in this castle has slept since you arrived. Your lovely voice echoes through the halls and keeps them awake all night."

Viola felt as though the room were getting smaller, the walls ready to topple down around her. She never worried about singing in her cage because she thought that since she could never hear anyone else, they would not be able to hear her. Never in her wildest dreams did she imagine that her voice would carry past the rough stones. The idea of other people intruding on her singing made it difficult for her to breathe.

"Neither of us is getting any younger. Your best effort, if you please."

"Since you have heard me sing already, why do I have to sing now?" she pleaded.

"This is different. I want you to sing . . . for me." His bloodless lips formed a humorless smile.

"I cannot," she said calmly, shaking her head.

"What if I were to tell you that I have a nice room waiting for you upstairs? The fluffy blankets on the bed are turned down, there is a cozy fire, a hot bath, and you will have your own personal servant to do whatever you might fancy. Since you have to stay here anyway, would you not rather be my guest than my prisoner? I can make life so much easier for you, if you give me this one thing in return," he coaxed.

When she looked into his eyes, hers were tired. But her gaze was immovable. "You have taken so much from me already. I refuse to give you the last thing of worth that is mine."

"Very well." He stood from his chair, walking in circles around her, as if taking inventory. "You are not particularly beautiful to look at, although I imagine when you are cleaned up, you could be quite presentable. I can see the potential," he leered. "But I already have plenty of pretty things, and as far as I know, you have no other special talents. I am not a patient man, but I am willing to give you another chance." He grabbed her chin, his fingers pressing into her neck, forcing her to look at him. "Find your voice by the next time I send for you, because if you cannot sing, you are of no use to me."

He pushed her away, turning once again toward the fire. "Viceroy, please escort my songbird back to her . . . quarters."

"With pleasure, Excellency."

* Ten *

"Katie, I think you have more jam than bread!"

"That reminds me! I had a dream about you last night, Grandma. You were trying to cross a river of milk on a piece of toast, but the bread was falling apart. I was afraid you were going to drown." She continued to slather more homemade raspberry jam on the toast. Her knuckles were red and sticky where she'd buried her fist in the jar.

"Oh dear, I hope you're not psychic. Psychic dreams do run in the family, you know."

"Really? Are you psychic?"

"Well, not on a regular basis. But while I was in the cage, I had a very peculiar dream. I found out later that it actually happened."

"What did you see in your dream?"

"As soon as your mother gets out of the shower, I'll tell you both. Ah, right on cue! Megan, did you have enough hot water, dear?"

"Yes, thank you." She had a towel wrapped around her head, and her skin was scrubbed pink. She eyed them suspiciously. "You two were deep in conversation when I came in. You weren't telling Kaitlin the story without me, were you?"

"Of course not. Katie was telling me about a dream she had last night."

Megan put a slice of bread in the toaster, watching as her daughter dove yet again into the jam. "Kaitlin, you've got enough jam on that bread for four slices. You might as well just eat it with a spoon straight from the jar."

"Can I?"

Megan gave her a dry look. "Viola, there's something I've been meaning to ask you. What happened to your parents?"

"What do you mean, dear?"

"I just wondered what happened to them after you disappeared. I mean, they thought you were dead. I can't imagine what that must have done to them."

"My mother was a true example to me in facing adversity. If I learned nothing else from her, she taught me that when life deals you a rough hand, you just have to keep playing. She was the bravest woman I ever knew, and I am proud to say that you, Megan, are a lot like her in many ways."

Megan shrank back. "Me? I'm not brave."

"Of course you are. For one thing, you came here without your husband to stay with a person you've only met enough times to count on one hand."

"But I'm afraid all the time!"

"You're afraid?" Kaitlin said in awe. "I didn't think grown-ups were afraid of anything."

"Everyone is afraid of something, but being afraid is different than being cowardly. As far as I'm concerned, the only really cowardly action is giving up."

"So, your mom was brave, but what about your dad? Was he a coward?" Kaitlin asked.

Viola sighed. "I loved my father very much. I used to see him coming home from sea, waving from his ship. He cut such a dashing figure. I couldn't imagine a more courageous man than my father. But when my mother needed him the most, he fell apart. Are you sure you want to hear about my parents?"

"Well, I want to hear the whole story," Kaitlin said decisively. "Even if your dad was a coward."

"I choose to remember him fondly. I will leave it to you to make your own decision."

Ian

Claire sat by the window, listening to the sounds of the outside world. The birds twittered noisily, the mad chirping at times getting very near, only to eventually drift off into the distance. The bees droned in the fragrant flower bed, humming and buzzing their industrious songs.

She licked the end of her string before expertly threading her needle. She tied a tidy knot at the end of the string, and began the job of basting the hem of a dress, brought to her by one of the women in town. She worked quickly, making tiny, even stitches. Claire never paid much attention when she was sewing—she didn't need to. Stitching was in her blood, the way some people have perfect pitch or can paint a beautiful sunset. She sewed a straight seam without even trying, never needing to go back to unpick anything crooked. Her needlework was highly respected, and her gowns were commissioned by wealthy women in places she'd only heard of.

Her creations had come to be even more sought after lately. She wasn't sure if it was the two new stitches she'd recently mastered, or if people pitied her because her only daughter had taken ill suddenly and passed away without so much as a goodbye, at a well-reputed but distant school no one had ever been to. It probably wasn't either of those things. Most of the people who had enough money to buy Claire's dresses were not low enough in society to be included in her small circle of friends, and therefore would be unaware of the tragic circumstances surrounding her daughter's death. And they didn't know enough about needlework to see that her knowledge of advanced stitches was what made her gowns so immaculate and different. No, probably the reason that Claire now had a waiting list of women desperate to be seen in one of her dresses was that for the last one year, eleven months, and three days, Claire had been completely blind.

Going blind was easy, maybe the easiest thing she'd ever done. The day they received the letter telling them that Viola was dead, Claire was completely distraught. She vaguely remembered everything going dark. She assumed that it was Ian picking her up off the floor, but she couldn't see him. She babbled to him about how when she was little, her family went to see a film, and halfway through, the filmstrip accidentally got pulled from the projector. It was like she was the projector now, and everything had suddenly gone blank.

Ian got one of the neighbors to sit with Claire while he fetched the doctor. She thought this was odd—why didn't he send the neighbor so that he could stay with her? But then, he'd just sustained a massive shock himself; perhaps he wasn't thinking clearly. When they returned, the doctor startled her by patting her arm. He apologized, telling her in a low, reassuring tone that everything would be okay. She'd had some distressing news and her body was compensating, trying to cushion the blow and minimize the damage by shutting down temporarily.

She felt a sharp prick in her arm, and immediately she began to feel woozy, a fog settling over her mind. The last thing she remembered was Ian holding her hand and the doctor promising her that when she woke up tomorrow, everything would be back to normal. But nothing was ever normal again.

When she opened her eyes she felt rested, but the room was still dark. She had just decided to go back to sleep for a while when she noticed something strange. Her arm seemed very warm. She slept on the side of the bed nearest the window, and she could feel the sun shining on her bare skin. It wasn't the world outside that was dark—only she was trapped in solitary blackness. Then she remembered: the letter, her vision disappearing; all of it seemed like a bad dream, but it must be true. She felt blindly for her husband, but the sheets on his side were empty.

Claire stumbled out of bed, stubbing her toe on the groove in the hard wood floor. She ran carelessly down the hall, calling out for Ian and receiving nothing in answer but the echo of her own voice. In her desperation to find him she ran straight into a wall, bumping her head. She was stunned for a few seconds, finally reaching to feel the fat lump that was already beginning to form on her bruised forehead. The door opened and Ian came to her, touching her head tentatively.

"Claire, what do you think you're doing?"

"I was trying to find you. I woke up, and you were gone. I still can't see anything. I guess I got scared," she said feebly.

"You cannot just rush around, plowing into the furniture. You are going to have to learn that there are things you cannot do anymore."

Claire felt like a disobedient child. She wanted Ian to take her in his arms and comfort her. She wanted him to swear that he would take care of her and make sure she didn't get hurt. She felt for his shoulders, grabbing him in a tight hug. She could feel his heart beating into her chest, but there was something different about his embrace. It was cold and hesitant, as if she were a complete stranger. She tried to relax against his body, but it was unnaturally stiff. He broke away at the first opportunity, and she could hear a weak smile in his voice. "I did not mean to scold you, but you have to be more careful now; you are all I have left."

Ian guided her back to bed. "Stay here and I will bring you some tea." His voice was a little less critical than before. She nodded. As she heard his steps disappearing down the hall, she had the impression that he was incredibly relieved to have a task; anything that would take him away from her. It was like he couldn't even bear to be in the same room. That was the moment when she knew nothing would ever be the same. Her child was gone, her sight was gone, and her husband, she felt sure, would soon be going himself.

When Ian returned, he placed the cup carefully in her outstretched hands. He quickly made his excuses and fled, leaving her alone in the dark with only her tea for company. She took a sip, but her stomach threatened to send it back. So she sat motionless, waiting as the cup grew colder.

She didn't know how many days she passed in this state of oblivion, but one day, it was like Claire finally woke up. She felt like she'd been far away, watching everything happen to herself as a detached, impartial observer. One morning as she lay in bed, she came back to earth and she knew that this was not the way she wanted to live the rest of her days. She had two choices: she could surrender and spend the rest of her life in bed, lamenting her losses, or she could choose to move forward, accepting her limitations while acknowledging that there were still things she could accomplish.

She learned to cook simple food so that when Ian came home, she could have dinner waiting. She did the washing and worked in her small garden. She even decided to try sewing again. There were still unfinished projects she had taken before Viola's death. She knew that no one expected her to complete them—after all, how could a blind woman be expected to continue producing the beautiful dresses she made when she had eyes? But she was determined to try. She knew she had no chance of making gowns to be worn by great ladies any longer, but surely simple repairs could be relearned.

During her spare time, she was secretly working on a dress she had been making for Viola when she left for school. She wanted to test herself, to see if she could still manage anything intricate. She didn't dare experiment on a client's dress, for fear of damaging the expensive fabric. Claire planned to give it to her neighbor, Olive. Olive had a daughter about Viola's age, and even if the dress wasn't perfect, she knew that they couldn't afford to be picky because they had a very large family and not much money for clothing.

When the last stitch was in place, she wrapped the dress in brown paper and took it to Olive's house. Claire knew exactly how many steps it was from one house to another, so she could walk around the village. She didn't go too far by herself, but it was nice to know that she could visit her friends, if she wanted. She took a deep breath and knocked on the door, waiting anxiously.

"Claire! What a nice surprise—it is so good to see you. Please come in." Olive liked it when Claire visited, because she didn't have to be embarrassed or worried that her friend would judge her by the disarray of her household. At least if the house was a mess, Claire couldn't tell. Olive took her arm gently and led her into the kitchen, showing her to a chair. It was hot inside the house, and Olive wiped a thin sheen of perspiration from her upper lip. She tried in vain to brush away the streaks of cocoa powder on her apron, somehow managing to rub the stain even deeper into the fabric instead. She sighed in frustration. "Would you care for some cider?"

"Mmm, please." Claire was pleasantly overwhelmed by the smell of something chocolaty baking in the oven.

"You are just in time; the brownies are almost finished."

"What a treat. I have tried a lot of recipes, but I never seem to find one that I like. They either come out as hard as a rock or completely raw in the middle."

"If you like these, I will write down the recipe for you."

"I might have a little trouble reading it," Claire quipped.

"Well, I can teach you then. They are so simple they practically bake themselves."

"You let me know when you have some free time, and we will make an afternoon of it. It would be a good laugh." She paused. "Speaking of a good laugh, I brought you something." Claire placed the package on the chair next to her. "I know that it is not much, but I thought you might be able to get some use out of it." She heard the sound of paper rustling as Olive peeked inside, followed by a gasp.

"Claire, I could not possibly take it."

Her face colored, and even though she didn't have to worry about meeting Olive's gaze, she lowered her eyes out of habit. "Is it that bad?" she asked quietly.

Olive was flabbergasted. "It is the most amazing dress I have ever seen! My girls would have no place to wear such a fancy frock. Between doing their chores and playing, I am afraid they would ruin it. You know how children are."

Claire turned her face away, but not before her friend could see the twinge of pain flit across her features.

"I cannot believe I said that. I am so sorry."

"It is nothing," she said, pushing her sadness away. "You must take the dress—I insist."

"But why would you give me something so elaborate? It must have been hours of work. Did someone change their mind after they had already ordered it? Because if they did, you should charge them anyway. It is not as if you did not complete your end of the bargain; no one could ask for a lovelier dress."

"Actually, I was making it for Viola, when she . . ."

Olive was uncomfortable. No one had known what to say to poor Claire since she had lost her only child and her vision in rapid succession.

". . . but I decided to finish it. I wanted to see if I could still make a presentable dress, and I knew that if I ruined this one, I would not be losing anything."

Realization dawned on Olive's face. "You do not mean . . . surely you did not finish this dress after you went blind?" she mumbled in astonishment.

Viola nodded.

"How did you know where to sew? How could you tell your seams were straight?"

Viola shrugged. "It was like my fingers just took over. But it is good to know I can still make a decent dress."

"Decent? It is miraculous. You were the most polished seamstress I knew, but now, I think your work is even more detailed. I would not have dreamed it possible."

Claire got a whiff of something and wrinkled her nose. "What is that smell?"

"The brownies!" Olive rushed to the oven, flinging the door open and filling the room with an acrid black smoke. "I got so excited about your gift that I completely forgot to check them," she said, choking. "That is what I get for singing my own praises."

Claire laughed. "Well, I hope Anabelle likes the dress," she said, standing from her chair to go home. "I had better get back—I have some dough rising."

"I cannot wait to tell everyone that you made that dress. At least you will not be at a loss for customers. When word gets out that a blind woman made such an incredible dress, I think you'll have more orders than you can keep up with. Plus, you are such a novelty that you can practically name your price; anyone who is anyone will want to own one of your creations. And I will be able to say I had the first one—imagine that."

. . . ✶ . . .

As soon as he dared leave Claire, Ian made the long, arduous journey to the school. He waited to speak to the headmaster, who he found to be very kind but also rather vague.

"The children were buried up in the hills, to reduce the chance of anyone else being infected," he said apologetically.

"I think you could at least have the courtesy to take me to the site."

"I am so sorry, but the groundskeeper who was responsible for ensuring that the children were properly buried has recently left our employ. As it turns out, he alone knew where their final resting spot was."

Ian jumped out of his chair and began pacing around the room. "I promised my wife! I told her that I would bring our daughter's remains home, to be near her family!"

"If only there was something I could do. We did not want the fever to spread, and we were not afforded the luxury of time."

"But what will I tell my wife? Her grief has made her blind. If I return without Viola's body, she will be inconsolable."

"Perhaps I might be of some assistance to you after all."

"I do not understand," Ian said slowly.

"I could give you some ashes from the fireplace. You could tell her that we had to burn the bodies, to minimize the risk of the disease spreading."

"I could not lie to her about something so important; it would be incredibly cruel. How could you even suggest such a thing?" His expression was indignant, but his eyes were thoughtful.

"Forgive me if I offended you, sir. I was only trying to protect your wife from any further unnecessary pain. I am very sorry for your loss, but I am afraid I have other matters to attend to, if you will excuse me. Please let us know if there is any way we can be of assistance to you or your wife."

Ian strode quickly to the door. "You have been most helpful," he muttered, slamming the door shut behind him. He began walking into the hills, in the general direction the headmaster said he sent the groundskeeper. He knew that the chances of him finding the burial site were not good. The earth would have begun to settle again, especially if there had been any significant rain. But he had to try; he could at least give Claire that. Even if he came back empty-handed, he could look straight into her eyes and tell her he did everything humanly possible.

He wandered around in the hills for hours, looking for any signs of digging or spots where the ground had been recently disturbed. But there was nothing. As night came on, the air began to turn very cold. He started to shiver, finding it impossible to keep his teeth from chattering. He decided that he would have to camp somewhere for the night and try to make a fire. He wouldn't be much help to Claire if he froze to death.

Summer had come to an abrupt and unexpected end much earlier than usual. The chill in the air seemed to come from nowhere, an unwelcome guest as people tried to hold onto those last, bittersweet warm days for as long as possible. He found a spot he thought looked promising, gathering any twigs and branches he could use to start a small fire. He made a bed of dry leaves, rubbing two sticks furiously together until they struck a spark. Slowly, the leaves began to smoke, then glow. He patiently added tiny twigs at first, building up to bigger and bigger branches as the fire grew hungry enough to consume them. Soon he had a halfway decent fire, large enough that it should have kept him toasty warm, at least for an hour or two. But he still felt cold and empty inside.

He gathered anything he could find that would burn, throwing it onto the blazing heap. When he could no longer locate any dry sticks and dead leaves, he started tearing live branches from the trees. He pulled at them viciously, snarling and making shouts of pain, like a wild animal. There were no words for these feelings, only primal grunts. The noises had no written translation, but their meaning was universal and unmistakable.

Soon, the flames leaped into the sky, taller than he himself stood. He watched as the fire consumed everything he threw onto it, yet was still ready to accept more offerings. No matter what he fed it, it was never enough. When he had finally exhausted his strength, he collapsed on the ground, his breath coming in raspy sobs as his chest heaved, trying to expel the overwhelming emptiness that had taken possession of his soul.

Ian awoke the next day feeling completely drained. The ground was covered in black sooty ashes, spread over a much wider area than he remembered. The fire must have continued to grow after he fell asleep. He knew what must be done now. He scooped up some of the fine, white-grey ashes. When he touched them, they scattered and floated on the breeze like the paper thin wings of insects. He dumped some into his empty thermos, filling it as full as he could before screwing down the lid tightly.

He felt nothing as he performed this task—not grief, nor sadness, nor guilt. It was as if his insides had been scooped out, emotions and feelings and organs together, and burned in the fire. He felt strangely as if he were carrying his own ashes back to his wife. It was a means to an end. It would give Claire some closure, and perhaps she could find a way to move on. It was his fault that Viola had come to this untimely end, buried in an unmarked grave. He should have never allowed his young daughter out of his sight. And if he had to lie in order for Claire to survive, he was willing to pay the price, whatever it was.

Shortly after Ian returned home, he went into the pub for a drink and happened upon an old friend. Michael had once worked regularly on the big fishing boats, but Ian hadn't seen him for months. Michael told him how he'd sunk every penny he had into buying his own boat. He boasted that he was now earning ten times what he made before, taking affluent tourists on fishing expeditions.

"I have a small group arriving in a few days. You should come out with us."

"I am supposed to be leaving on a boat tomorrow," Ian said glumly.

"Postpone it, then."

"I cannot just stay here and go on a pleasure cruise with you!

It is my job—we need the money."

"Are you daft? I just told you that you could be making a fortune, and you still want to keep doing the same backbreaking work for pennies? I am offering to give you a chance at something better."

"I am not sure," he hedged. "It may be hard work and long hours, but at least it is steady."

"You only need to impress one client, and you will be set. They all move in the same circles, and they all have more money than they could spend in a lifetime. Trust me—come out on my boat, be my apprentice, help one of them catch something huge. They will love you. With a little luck, you could be taking out your own boat by this time next week."

Ian still looked doubtful.

"Listen, I have so many trips lined up that I cannot manage any more, and still there are loads of rich men just begging to give me their money. There is plenty of business to go around. Come try it once before you make up your mind. I guarantee you'll be hooked," Michael said, laughing heartily at his own pun.

Ian chuckled himself, taking a gulp of his beer. "Well, never let it be said that I turned down handfuls of money just for the sake of it. What have I got to lose?"

His friend clapped him on the back. "You will not regret it."

. . . * . . .

Claire was sewing in her chair by the window when she heard the door slam. "Ian, is that you?" she called.

He grunted an answer from the kitchen, but she couldn't decipher it.

"I cannot hear you," she yelled back.

She heard the sound of boots in the hallway, coming closer until they stopped in front of her chair. "Of course it is me." His tone confirmed the annoyance she'd detected in the petulant way he'd stomped into the room.

"I thought you'd gone. Should you not be at the dock already?"

"I should, yes. But they cannot exactly leave without me, can they?"

"So you came home to see me before you left?" she said hopefully.

"I forgot a few things that I needed, so I had to leave the boat and come back to fetch them."

"You were going to leave without saying goodbye?"

"Claire, could we talk about this later? I have kept the man waiting long enough as it is."

"I hardly ever see you anymore. You come home in the middle of the night after I am asleep, and you are gone again before I wake in the morning. You take unnecessary risks."

"What risks?" he demanded. He couldn't find the words to explain to his wife that the reason he'd been keeping such odd hours was because whenever he was near her, he could feel the blame radiating from her in waves, and it was unbearable.

"Last week, you knew it was going to storm, but you agreed to take those two men out anyway. You never would have considered going out in a storm before."

"They understood the risks. In fact, they wanted to go when the weather was bad."

"Why?"

"I provide a service, and I am willing to do whatever it takes to make the men with the money happy. They wanted a certain sort of experience; a story to tell. And I made sure that they got it."

"Listen to yourself! I know you are not this foolish."

"I am not foolish," he snapped. "I have been doing this for years now, and I happen to be very good at what I do."

"You could have lost the boat. You could have lost your life! My daughter was already taken from me—I do not want you to be next!"

"She was my daughter too."

"I know. But you act as if you would just as soon join her." She stood from her chair and used her hand to caress his face, trying to judge his emotions without the aid of her eyes. "I am still here, you know. I still need you." Her fingertips rested on his lips.

He removed her hand from his face, placing it at her side. "I really must go. Is there anything that you need before I leave?"

She walked across the room with her head held high, like a distant, regal queen. "When should I expect you back?" she asked, ignoring his question.

"I will be back when the man who is paying the bills catches a fish large enough to satisfy his ego," he said bitterly.

"I worry about you out alone, on that rickety boat . . ."

"I am not alone. I always have at least one or two men with me."

"Trophy fishermen—what good are they? They have no idea how to run a ship. What use would they be if a storm suddenly came up?"

"I have never feared the sea, and I see no reason to start now."

"Could you not go back to fishing on the big boats, with people you trusted?" she persisted.

"The money I was making before is nothing compared with what I bring home now."

"It is not about the money. We are not wealthy, but we have always had enough, and that was enough for you. No, I think you like the danger. I think the rush you get from knowing your life is constantly at risk is the only way you can feel anything anymore. You're not afraid of dying; you're afraid to live."

Ian said nothing, but tears burned the corners of his eyes and his throat felt constricted, as if a tight fist was squeezing until he feared it would snap.

"One of these days, you will press your luck too far and you will not come back. They will come into my house and tell me that my husband is never coming home, and then where will I be?"

The room was so quiet that Claire couldn't even hear Ian breathing. "I know that you are sad about Viola," she continued. "Losing her has almost destroyed us both. I am sure it would be easier to just lay in my bed with my sightless eyes and wait for death. But we cannot give up. *You* cannot give up. There are things left worth living for. We still have each other." Her eyes were bright and earnest, animated with raw emotion.

Still Ian stood, motionless and silent. He knew that whatever his wife said, she held him responsible for what happened to their daughter. He could have stopped her from going, and he should have. It wasn't right for a girl that young to be on her own in the world. She belonged here, with her family. He never should have left the decision up to Viola—how could she possibly know what she wanted at that age? He could have refused, put his foot down, and Claire would have honored his wishes. He would do anything for another chance, but it was too late. He had let their family down. How could she feel anything but disgust for him now?

Ian knew that he should make peace with his wife, but the truth was she would be better off without him, even if she refused to see it. He was too weary to argue anymore, so he swallowed his tears and said the first thing that came into his head. "What is it you want from me?" The hard words dropped at her feet like sharp stones.

"I want you to try," she cried desperately. "I want you to learn how to live again. I want to believe that you still love me."

"I am doing the best I can," he said flatly.

She paused, her cheeks covered with tracks of hot tears. "I know your heart is broken, but it is up to you whether or not it is terminal. You told me that once. Do you remember?"

There was a long pause, the only noise in the room the sound of his footsteps getting farther away. She heard the door open, and he stopped momentarily in the doorway. "I do not think that I can be that person anymore."

Ian steered the boat out onto the sea, the wind stirring the water up until it was rough and choppy. The skies were darkening, and he felt the first rain drops spattering his face. Occasionally, he could hear the ominous rumbling of thunder, but he didn't mind—the low, threatening growl matched his mood.

When he finally arrived at the dock, there was a distinguished looking man waiting for him. He made his apologies, saying that his master had unfortunately been called away on urgent business and would be unable to make the trip after all. He would, of course, pay half his fee for the inconvenience of the last-minute cancellation.

Ian was quite relieved to accept the money, since he didn't really feel capable of trying to be subservient and pleasant. But he also knew that there was no way he could turn around and go home right now either, since he couldn't face Claire. So he decided to take the boat out anyway, sail around on his own for a few days and try to figure out what he was going to do. The weather was worsening by the minute, and he took a sort of juvenile satisfaction in the idea that he was acting in open defiance of his wife's wishes.

He didn't really have any specific destination in mind—he only wanted to be left alone. Once the boat was safely in open waters he let the sea take control, trusting it to know where to take him. He opened a bottle of beer, drinking half of it in one sustained draft. The rain was coming down much harder now, and he found himself mesmerized by the millions of pockmarks the drops were making on the surface of the sea. He finished his drink and started on another. With every gulp he tried desperately to fill the hollow place inside, all the while knowing that it would never be enough. He didn't know whether it was the alcohol or the escalating wind, but it was becoming more difficult to tell which was the sky and which was the sea, as both seemed to be made of water.

The boat was being tossed around wildly, and lightning was starting to tear through the blackness, an indiscriminate show of the seniority of nature and his own insignificance. It struck like a white spear, dancing ever nearer to the boat. A particularly deafening crack of thunder cut through the water, the lightning illuminating the area directly in front of Ian. The sight that met his eyes was enough to bring him out of the fog he was in; a tall line of rocks had appeared on the horizon. If he didn't change his course soon, he would run straight into them, tearing the boat to pieces.

He stumbled to the wheel and began the arduous process of

fighting the waves, in an effort to turn the craft. The muscles in his arms strained, the veins bulging like blue cords, but Ian was no match for the storm. With every flash of lightning, he saw that he was getting nearer to the range of jagged rocks. He pushed his entire weight against the wheel, willing the winds to change and carry him away from his own imminent destruction.

A sudden wave came over the side of the boat, hitting him with the force of a hundred men and knocking him onto his back. As he lay on the bottom of the boat, watching the catastrophic beauty erupting on all sides, his mind was suddenly clear. Why was he fighting so hard against his fate, when the likely outcome would probably be best for everyone involved? He knew now that he could never be the man Claire needed him to be. He'd failed her when she needed him most; every breath he took while his daughter slept in the ground only added insult to injury.

But there was a part of him that still loved Claire. He remembered the first time he saw her, a mere girl withering away from unrequited love, and how he'd been both entranced and amused at the same time. He loved her naivety and stubbornness. He was tied to her, and he knew in his heart that he would never have the courage to leave her, even if it was in her best interest. But if there were to be an accident . . . that would be different. It would be out of his control.

Ian remained where he was, being pelted by rain and waves at the bottom of the boat. All his life he had trusted the sea, and he would put his fate into its hands one last time. Either the winds would change and he would drift away from the rocks, or he would crash. As the unearthly cataclysm of splintering wood exploded in his ears, in his last thoughts, he took great comfort in the idea that the outcome had nothing whatever to do with him.

✶

Viola let out a ragged sigh. She pushed back her chair and stood, wincing a little as the blood began to circulate through her legs again.

"You can't stop there," Kaitlin said in disbelief.

"I haven't really much choice. You see, that was the end of my father's story."

"That doesn't sound like the end. It's more like the part at the end of the TV show where they flash, 'To Be Continued . . .' across the screen," Megan said.

"I *hate* when they do that!" Kaitlin said vehemently.

"My father was lost at sea. He must have perished in the storm, because he was never seen or heard from again. They never found a body or his boat; he simply vanished."

"Wait a second," Kaitlin said, the wheels whirring in her brain. "If he was the only one on the boat, how do you know he crashed?"

"That was the strangest part. While I was being held prisoner in the Castle Diavolo, I dreamed the whole thing."

"What do you mean, you dreamed it?" Megan asked.

"I had a dream that my mother went blind, and my father disappeared at sea."

"You're joking."

"I swear on a stack of Bibles. It was incredibly detailed, and since my mother's part of the story turned out to be true, I have no reason to believe otherwise where my father is concerned. Of course, I didn't put much stock in it at the time, since I also had a dream one night that I turned into a tiny fairy and flew out the window."

Megan shook her head, smiling ruefully. "What about your mother?"

"Her part of the story isn't finished yet, but first I have to tell you about how I tried to get the boy to help me escape."

"By the way, I was wondering if you might be willing to watch K-a-i-t-l-i-n for a while tomorrow. Do you know if there's anywhere around here that I could buy a c-a-k-e?" Megan asked.

"You're going to get a store-bought c-a-k-e? For my granddaughter's b-i-r-t-h-d-a-y?" she said incredulously.

"Why are you guys talking about me like I'm not here? And how many times do I have to tell you? I can spell!"

"Of course I wasn't going to buy one."

"I didn't think so," Viola sniffed. "You just leave it to me."

"Hello? Can anybody see me?!" Kaitlin shouted.

Megan and Viola grinned.

"Now, I'm going to go check my email, and I am leaving you with strict instructions not to continue the story until I get back," Megan said.

"Grandma and I will just have to talk about something else; like this c-a-k-e she's going to make for me," Kaitlin said slyly.

"Don't count your chickens before they're hatched, Katie," Viola warned.

"Who said anything about chickens?"

* Eleven *

Dear Meg,

It sounds like my mother still knows how to weave a fascinating story, although I must say that this makes the ones she told us when we were kids look tame in comparison. I'm glad now that you took her to see a doctor, because I'm not sure I'd believe she was sane if you hadn't. I suppose your theory about not telling me about her childhood because it was too painful is possible, but I think it's more likely that it was just dull and she didn't think it would hold my interest.

I can tell you what I actually know about my mother's life in less than one page. She spent the first part of it somewhere in Europe, but she was always vague about exactly where; something about not really being old enough to remember it very well. Her mother, Francis, liked to sew things, which I always thought was pretty amazing because she was blind. I hardly knew her or Grandpa Leo, but they were the only grandparents I ever had. Leo wasn't actually my mother's father—Francis married Leo once my mother was already grown herself. Her real father was a fisherman, and he was lost at sea in a storm. My mother hardly ever talked about him, and when I tried to ask her questions about her father, it only made her sad. It sounds silly, but I don't even know his name.

Well, that's it, really. I don't know anything about her talent for singing or being kidnapped by an evil count, and she certainly never mentioned being kept in the dungeon of a castle in a cage. If I had to guess, I would say that my mother has been lonely for a long time, and she's probably enjoyed having someone around to listen to her talk. She must have taken parts of isolated incidents from her life and built a story around it; something just crazy enough to ensure that she keeps you and Kaitlin interested. But unless she's been very good over the years at concealing an almost unbelievable past, I would have to say that most of her so-called life story is fiction.

I'm planning to call on Kaitlin's birthday. I feel really bad about not being there—I hope she isn't too disappointed.

Love,

Kevin

P.S You're a very sweet girl to listen to my mother's ramblings for two whole weeks. I'll have to find a way to make it up to you. ☺

"Mom, come over here and roast marshmallows with us!"

Megan sat at the table, the light reflecting from her laptop giving her a faintly bluish tinge. She was lost in thought, considering the email from her husband. She couldn't believe how much of the story was the same as the one Viola had been telling them, only it seemed that Kevin had heard the edited version.

"MOMMMMM!" Kaitlin said impatiently.

"I'm almost finished, okay?"

A sudden clap of thunder made them all jump, and Kaitlin and Viola giggled like little girls. The skies outside, which would normally be reddish-pink with the fading sunset, were crowded with black foreboding clouds. The small light in the kitchen didn't do much to brighten the room. Kaitlin and Viola were huddled near the open oven door, toasting marshmallows on some long metal rods Viola produced from a drawer. Although the thunder and lightning made it seem cozy in the little kitchen, the air still felt dry and hot, and the heat pouring out of the oven wasn't helping.

"Careful, Katie—you don't want to burn yourself."

"Aren't these great?" Kaitlin said as she eased her third marshmallow onto the stick. "Mom, can we buy some marshmallow roasting thingies when we get home?"

"I've never seen 'marshmallow roasting thingies' in the store before. Where did you buy them, Viola?"

"Actually, I got them at a garage sale. I love garage sales—you never know what you're going to find."

"I think they're supposed to be for shish kebabs," Megan commented.

"No, the man at the garage sale was very specific. He said they were marshmallow roasters, and they were one of a kind; handcrafted," Viola argued.

Megan smiled tightly, telling herself that this definitely wasn't worth arguing over. "Well, we don't get out to many garage sales, but maybe I'll run into some when I'm out browsing one day. They could be a sort of late birthday present."

Viola's face lit up. "That's right, Katie, tomorrow you'll be the birthday girl! Are you excited to be ten?"

Kaitlin nodded. "When is your birthday, Grandma?"

"My birthday is coming up in October."

"How old will you be?"

"Kaitlin!" Megan exclaimed. "It's rude to ask people their age, especially your elders."

"Why?"

"Because . . . sometimes people don't like to talk about it," she stammered.

"I don't get it. I didn't mind when Grandma said my age."

"There's a big difference between being ten and being . . . well, older," Megan replied.

"I can't wait until I'm older. I'm going to do anything I want," Kaitlin mumbled around a mouthful of hot, gooey marshmallow. Viola was in the process of wedging her perfectly browned marshmallow between two graham crackers and a square of chocolate. She passed it across to Kaitlin, who took it with wide eyes.

"I remember being ten. I had a hard time keeping track of the days, but I'm quite certain that I spent my tenth birthday in the cage," Viola said dreamily.

"That sounds like the worst birthday ever," Kaitlin said.

"As much as those were terrible years in my life, it wasn't all bad. There was definitely something magical about it—sometimes I miss that. And I made a friend."

"I bet it was the boy," Kaitlin said confidently.

"Now, you're jumping ahead. You'll just have to wait until we get to that part."

"We're listening."

"I suppose now is as good a time as any, but not until you eat this," she said severely, passing Megan one of the s'mores. "You're too skinny."

Megan took a huge bite out of her s'more. "Yes, ma'am," she mumbled with marshmallow on her lips.

The Dress

"You sent for me, Excellency?" the viceroy inquired, issuing his customary bow.

"Yes. Go and fetch my songbird from her quarters, as there is someone here waiting to measure her for a dress." The count inclined his head toward a scrawny woman, standing at a window. She eyed the viceroy nervously, as though she might bolt at any moment. The viceroy raised his eyebrows in surprise but did as he was asked, retrieving a sleepy Viola and presenting her to the count.

"Good afternoon, my dear. I hope I was not disturbing your rest," he said, his voice weighted with false concern.

"Why have you brought me here? I believe I already told you that I have nothing to give you," she said tiredly.

"Ah, but I am going to give you something." He pointed to the woman near the window. "This is Miss Hastings, and she has come all the way here to measure you for a dress."

The woman gave her a feeble smile, but it quickly faded under Viola's scrutiny. "Why?"

"Why?" he repeated. "What a silly question! Look at yourself! The dress you are wearing is three sizes too small and practically in shreds. It would not do for you to be wandering around looking like a ragamuffin. I thought you would be pleased," he pouted.

"Wandering around?" she said incredulously. "I do not know what sort of game you are playing, but a new dress is not going to change my mind."

"Poor girl," he said, shaking his head. "She has a beautiful voice, but her mind is quite unhinged." He motioned to Miss Hastings, who crept up to Viola cautiously, the measuring tape shaking a little in her hands. She made the required measurements as quickly as possible, scribbling down a few lines in a battered notebook before scrambling toward the door.

"Just a minute," the count said, halting her hasty retreat.

"Sir?" she quavered.

"You will have ten days to complete this dress. That should be more than enough time, and I do not tolerate lateness. In ten days, I expect you to return for the final fitting. I am certain I do not need to outline the consequences of failure. Are we clear?"

"Yes, sir." The viceroy appeared to show Miss Hastings to the door, but he had a difficult time keeping up with her, such was her hurry to get as far away from the count as possible.

"Why did you have to frighten that poor woman? What has she done to deserve such treatment?"

"Fear is a useful tool, and it has helped me obtain many of the things I have coveted over the years. If this is a concept that is unfamiliar to you, I would be delighted to instruct you in its virtues."

"Why are you dressing me up?" Viola repeated. "I doubt that your intentions are selfless, and I do not think the spiders really care about my current attire."

The count laughed politely. "The spiders might not be particular, but when you sing for my guests, I want your gown to match the splendor of your voice."

Viola's stomach lurched unpleasantly, but she managed to look calm. "What guests?"

"You are going to be making your singing premiere to the world in about two weeks' time, and that is all you need know at present." The viceroy appeared behind her, taking her arm and pulling her toward the door.

"Are you going to ask me to sing?" she asked.

He smiled coldly. "Not this time. I have just finished listening to a new opera, and I am afraid your thin, reedy voice would pale in comparison." He hoped that she might rise to his bait, but she merely returned his icy, condescending smile and allowed herself to be taken back to her cage.

When the viceroy returned, he had a curious smile on his face. "Am I to understand that we are expecting guests, Excellency?"

"That is correct. I made many important acquaintances during my time abroad, all of whom spared no expense to entertain me. Now, I have the opportunity to play host myself. I am afraid that you are going to be very busy assisting with the preparations because in two weeks, when the cream of European society arrives, there is going to be a gala the likes of which you can only imagine. There will be orchestra music for dancing, exquisite food, and of course, Viola's vocal debut. It will be the highlight of the evening."

"That explains the dress."

The count nodded. "Now," he said briskly, "I have a list of things that need to be done. You may distribute tasks to the other servants however you see fit. As long as the end result is perfect, I do not care how you attain it."

"I will make the success of the evening my first priority, Excellency."

The boy continued to bring Viola her meals, and Viola continued trying to communicate with him. After their unfortunate first meeting, it took a few days before there was anything in his eyes but terror when he came near her cage. After this initial period of him being frightened of her, his mood changed to one of mild curiosity. It was difficult for her to tell whether he could even understand what she was saying. At first she thought that maybe he spoke another language because there was never any spark of recognition when she spoke to him. But surely he would at least attempt to say something in his own words, if he were able.

Viola was convinced that despite the blank stare, his personality might still be trapped inside somewhere. Right now, her only hope of escape was with his help. And so she kept on chattering from the moment the door opened until he shut it again behind him. She tried spouting out lists of words, strings of numbers, bits of stories she remembered from her father. She told him about her parents; how she lived by the ocean, and how she liked to sing while she walked along the sand. She even told him a joke one day, and although she couldn't be sure, she could swear she saw a faint glimmer of laughter in his otherwise vacant eyes. Viola seemed to have an endless amount of patience, and she was never discouraged by her apparent lack of progress. That is, until the day she was measured for the dress.

Viola sat cross-legged in her cage with her back to the door, staring at the stone wall. What a fool she'd been, thinking that she could talk the boy into helping her escape when it was obvious that he either couldn't understand her or didn't care. And even if she could somehow get through to him, what chance did the two of them have against the count? What use was it trying to outsmart your opponent and win the game when he was playing by his own set of rules? It was all so unfair, she thought bitterly. She could see the rest of her life stretched out in front of her, possibly not a very long one if she refused to give in and sing for her captor. She sighed miserably, sinking lower as she pitied herself even more. What had she ever done to deserve it?

When the boy brought in her small supper, she heard the hinges on the heavy door groan, announcing his arrival. But she didn't even bother to turn around. He walked quietly to her cage, depositing the stale bread, small chunk of cheese, and flask of water. The boy stood, watching her and wondering why she was not babbling at him in the strange way she always did. Instead, she was motionless, slumped against the cage. The cold metal bars pressed into her cheek, leaving their mark of ownership. He studied her, waiting patiently for her to say something, but this was different. The only sound that came from Viola was an enormous sigh. Something had changed; it was the sigh of someone who had given up.

After what seemed like an eternity, the boy realized he had other chores to do and turned to go. His hand on the doorknob, a tiny murmur stopped him cold. "Do you know what I really miss?"

He went back to the cage, eager to listen. "Apples," she continued, but did not turn around. "I really love apples. At my house, there was an apple tree with twisted branches that made it easy to climb. I was always so impatient, waiting for those hard, little green apples to ripen. Finally, when I could not wait any longer, I would pick the biggest ones I could find, hide somewhere, and eat them all. They were sour and not very juicy because they were not ready yet, but I could not stop eating them. I always regretted it after; I got such a terrible stomachache. You think I would have learned my lesson, but I never did. Once they finally got ripe, I would climb the tree and pick three or four of the prettiest ones near the top, and I would sit in the tree and eat them," she said, a smile spreading across her face at the memory. "I just really love apples. I started thinking about how I would never climb that tree again—it made me sad, you know?"

The boy was absolutely silent, and Viola turned to look at him. He was facing her, but there was no emotion in his face. He might have been a marble statue, solid and unmoved. He was no different than he had always been, but for some reason, this blankness suddenly infuriated Viola.

"But you do not know, do you?" she shouted. The boy blinked at this outburst, but did not budge. "You cannot understand at all, and I am tired of pretending that you ever will! So, if it is not too much to ask, I would like you to please go away and leave me alone."

He remained where he was, a confused and hesitant look clouding his features. All of the anger and helplessness she'd been feeling built up inside Viola until she couldn't restrain it any longer.

"GO!" she shrieked in frustration, her eyes squeezed shut.

The loud yelp seemed to force the boy into action. He ran out the door before she had the opportunity to make that inhuman noise again. When Viola opened her eyes, the boy was gone, and she was astonished to see that the bars of her cage were covered in thick ice. Her breath hung misty in the air, as if the area directly surrounding her was a good deal colder than the rest of the room.

She sat down dumbfounded, watching the ice slowly begin to melt, while trying to figure out exactly how it had happened. She tried shouting again, but her voice was too hoarse to achieve the same sound. Besides, it wasn't as if she really imagined she had done anything in the first place. Perhaps it was just a very cold night. Maybe the ice had been there all along, and she hadn't noticed it before. Then again, if it was so chilly, why was it suddenly melting now? It made her nervous to think about it and she was exhausted, so she curled up in the center of the cage, away from the rapidly thawing ice, and immediately fell asleep.

. . . ✶ . . .

In the middle of the night, when the boy knew that everyone would be in bed, he slunk quietly down the corridors, silent as a shadow. He made his way to the staircase that led to Viola's dungeon room. He knew that she would be sleeping, so he could just slip in the room and out again without being detected. He felt sorry for her, but at the same time he still was unable to decide whether he could trust her. He knew for certain that the count was a wicked man, but then again, even liars tell the truth when it suits their purpose. He'd seen what happened when Viola yelled, how for a moment, her voice was somehow . . . visible. It appeared in the air before her with a physical presence; an icy yell that somehow instantly solidified. Maybe the count was right—maybe she was dangerous, but that still didn't keep him from wishing that there was something he could do to cheer her up.

The door creaked when he pushed it open, and he cringed in the semi-darkness, waiting to see if he had woken her. When he finally dared peer around the corner, he noticed with relief that she was still asleep, lying in a large puddle of water at the bottom of the cage where the ice had melted. Her thin, wet dress clung to her, and she shivered in her sleep. He held his breath as he moved toward the cage, not wanting to disturb her uneasy rest.

The boy took something from his pocket and set it gingerly next to her, where she couldn't miss it in the morning. He'd stolen it earlier from the count's own table. He knew the implications of his gift—that Viola could no longer be in any doubt that he understood at least some of what she was saying. But he was willing to accept the risk; he couldn't resist giving her such a perfect, shiny green apple.

The next day, preparations for the gala were in full swing. Deliveries began to arrive, along with the first of the count's distinguished guests. The count himself happened to be in the stables when Lord Elliott's carriage arrived, and although he was perturbed because the castle was not yet in a fit state to be seen, he managed to cover his annoyance in smiles.

"Welcome, Your Lordship, and may I say what an honor it is to receive you in my home." The count spied the boy out of the corner of his eye, trying to hide behind some hay bales. "If you will excuse me for just a moment, there is someone I must have a word with."

When the count started in his direction, the boy knew he'd been spotted. He crouched down further, pretending he was looking for something. The count grabbed his arm and dragged him to a standing position. "I have a job for the viceroy—do you know where he is?" he demanded

The boy could only stare.

"What a surprise. He never seems to be here when I need him. He is no doubt off flitting around, enjoying himself under the guise of making preparations for the gala. It is becoming apparent to me that he is taking advantage of my generous nature—I suppose we will have to have a little chat about that."

The boy continued to watch him speak, but it was clear to the count that although he appeared to be focused on every word, his brain was not lucid enough to attach a meaning to all of them. As far as he could tell, the boy seemed capable of understanding and completing simple commands, but nothing beyond that.

"In his absence, I'm afraid you will have to do." The count reached inside his shirt, pulling out a chain on which dangled a tarnished silver key. He pulled it over his head and handed it to the boy. "You will get Viola and bring her to my study where I will be waiting with my guest. Do you understand?"

He nodded.

"And be quick about it. I do not want to keep His Lordship waiting."

The boy watched as the count rejoined his friend, apologizing for the interruption. "If you will come with me, I think there is something that you will find most intriguing . . ." he said mysteriously, as his voice faded into the distance.

. . . * . . .

The boy took a deep breath before turning the key in the lock to Viola's room. After their last meeting, he really didn't know what to expect. He needn't have worried—Viola was ecstatic.

"I am so happy to see you! I just knew you understood what I was saying. Something inside me knew that something inside you . . . knew. I am not sure if I am making any sense, but there it is. Everything is going to be all right now. You will help me escape and we can run away from here, where he can never find us. Of course, it will be tricky, but I am certain that between the two of us, we can come up with a good plan. Now, let me see . . . maybe if you could smuggle me some tools, I could dig my way out! Then again, if the entire castle could hear me sing, someone would be bound to hear me chipping away at the wall. Never mind, we will think of something."

She suddenly stopped, and the boy assumed it was because she had to breathe or she might pass out. Her eyes were riveted to the second key in his hand, and she looked even more excited than when he first came in, if that was possible.

"But, this is perfect! See how clever you are! Here I am, babbling on and on about making detailed escape plans, and I see you have already beat me to it. What need is there to tunnel out when we can just stroll through the front door? Now, all we have to do is figure out how to get there undetected, and just slip away," she said triumphantly.

The boy shook his head slowly.

"Oh? Well, if you have a different idea, I am more than willing to do it your way. After all, you are the one with the key."

The boy shook his head again.

Her happy mood vanished. "You are not here to help me escape, are you?" He looked away, unable to meet her eyes, as all of the joy had gone out of them. "Let me guess—you have been sent here because I have been summoned to appear before the master."

The boy nodded his head solemnly.

"I refuse to go," she said, folding her arms firmly across her chest. "I will not be rushed back and forth like a parcel at his every whim. If he wants to see me, he can come and get me himself."

The boy unlocked the cage, opened the door, and motioned for Viola to follow him.

"No," she said stubbornly.

The boy closed his eyes, concentrating his energy and quieting his mind. He still wasn't entirely sure that he could trust Viola, and he really didn't have time for this now, but he knew she wouldn't go with him otherwise. He opened his mouth, his lips working desperately, but no words came. He paused for a moment, wet his lips with his tongue, and then tried again. After all this time, if was more difficult than he imagined transferring thoughts into sounds. Viola waited expectantly, not realizing that she was holding her breath. The word finally tumbled out, lingering heavily in the silence.

"Please?"

Viola broke into a huge grin, and the boy looked pleasantly

surprised, as if he was never completely sure that he was capable of such a feat.

"Well, since you said please . . ." she said wryly.

. . . ✶ . . .

The door to the count's study was almost closed, so that only a glint of light showed through the crack, painting a narrow swath across the floor. The boy hesitated. He looked at Viola, who nodded in support. He knocked loudly.

"Enter."

Viola appeared in the doorway, followed by the boy. She squinted a little, unaccustomed to the light after being in the dungeon. She took a few steps into the room, but the boy kept his place near the door. The count stood near the bookshelves with a man Viola had never seen before.

"And how are you settling in, my dear? Is everything to your liking?"

Viola looked confused, but before she could respond, the count continued. "I think the poor child is still in shock. I found her on the streets and took her in as my ward. She had nothing in the world and no one to care for her, but she has a beautiful voice; absolutely sublime. I must say, I have never heard anything like it, especially not in a girl her age."

If she was baffled before, this newest confession rendered her speechless. She could only listen in what must have appeared to be a silent confirmation of the count's tale. When he found his story was not contradicted, he continued, addressing Viola as if they were great friends.

"Viola, this is Lord Elliott, a very distinguished friend of mine and a great connoisseur of all things musical. I have been telling him of your impressive gift, and he is most eager to experience your talent firsthand. I know that this is putting you on the spot, but would you mind favoring us with something?" he said innocently.

"Now?" she squeaked.

"The count has talked of nothing since I arrived but your angel voice," Lord Elliott said reverently, a look of open admiration on his grandfatherly face. "I have heard all the operas in my time, seen the best performers sing the greatest arias ever written. But you, child, are something entirely different. If you have even a fraction of the talent the count says you have, you could be the most important voice of your generation. How I would love to hear you sing," he said fervently, his wrinkled hands clasped in rapture. He seemed genuine, and Viola wondered how he had been unfortunate enough to be taken in by the count's charade. He looked at her as if he saw more than a dirty girl in a tattered dress. For a moment she was tempted to sing, and amazingly enough, she actually wanted to, if for no other reason than to fulfill this kindly man's wishes. But when she saw the count leering at her in triumph, she knew that she couldn't give in, even if she wished to.

"As much as it would please me to sing for you both, I am afraid my voice is still weak . . . from my recent illness. I have been resting it, just as you said I should," she said, gazing with admiration at the count. Two could play at this game.

He frowned. "But, my sweet, I thought that you were feeling much better."

"Yes, I did feel almost back to normal. But when I woke this morning, my throat was quite sore. I think there must have been a draft in my room last night," she said, forcing a look of concern onto her face even though she desperately wanted to laugh.

The count gave her a tight smile. "You know best, my dear." He turned to Lord Elliott apologetically. "I am afraid that you will have to wait a little longer, my Lord. We must be sure that Viola is in prime condition for her performance at the gala. I had hoped that you would be the first to be serenaded by my songbird, but we must respect her wishes."

"Of course, I would not wish to do anything that might damage her precious voice."

"I agree with you wholeheartedly," he said icily. "Boy, would you escort Miss Viola back to her room and make certain she has everything she needs?"

"You are too kind," she declared in a saccharine tone. She went to the door, turning before she left. She spoke softly, fixing her gaze on Lord Elliott only. "I am sorry, sir. It would have been my great pleasure to sing for you," she said sincerely.

He beamed, obviously touched by her words. As a final gesture, she curtsied politely to her master before following the boy out.

Lord Elliott sighed. "You were right. She is enchanting."

The count fought the urge to throw something.

. . . ✶ . . .

Once back in her cell, Viola couldn't help crowing a little over the small victory. "That was the most fun I have had since I arrived here! Did you see the look on the count's face?"

"Exactly," the boy pronounced, the word rolling easily from his lips.

"What do you mean, exactly?"

"I mean . . . for someone who should be focusing on . . . getting into the count's good graces, you are going about it all wrong."

"I see someone has found his tongue. I always suspected you could speak," she said in a singsong voice.

"Be quiet! Do you want everyone to know?"

"Your secret is safe with me," she whispered. "You speak very well, for a . . ."

"For a what? For a servant?" he said, his eyes dancing with amusement.

Her face turned bright red. "For someone who pretends he cannot speak. And why should I care about what the count thinks of me, anyway?"

"Because if you give him what he wants, he might loosen your leash a little. Do you want to spend the rest of your life down here?"

"Of course not," she huffed.

"Well, use your brain then. Start thinking about what you can do to please the count; that is the first step to escaping."

She rolled her eyes. "He wants me to sing at his gala."

"Brilliant. Easy as pie."

"But I refuse," she added.

"You just said it is what he wants."

"I cannot do it."

"Cannot or will not?"

"I am . . . unable to sing in front of people."

"Not even for your freedom?" he persisted.

"I would not give him the satisfaction."

"Ah, now we are getting somewhere. I have work to do, but I suggest that you give some careful consideration to his request, because right now, it is your best chance."

"He said if I could not sing, I would be of no use to him," she said lamely, as if realizing her perilous situation for the first time.

The boy gave her a sad smile. "Believe me when I say that this is not a man who makes idle threats."

"My voice is the one thing I have left, and he cannot force me to surrender it."

"I hope you change your mind."

"What is your name?" she asked the boy softly.

He thought for a moment. "I cannot tell you."

"Why?"

"Because it is the one thing left that is mine, and you cannot force me to surrender it," he said smugly.

"Well, if you want to be childish . . ." she sniffed.

"Oh, so it is all right for you to use that argument, but when I use it, it is childish?"

"It is completely different!"

"You are going to have to learn that sometimes, we must all make sacrifices for the greater good—"

"Please tell me your name," she interrupted.

"On the night that you sing at the count's gala, I will tell you my name." The boy closed Viola in her cage and locked it. "I will return later with your dinner."

. . . ✶ . . .

"What is this?" The count wrinkled up his nose in distaste. He held the dress between a thumb and finger away from himself, as if it were a second-hand shroud.

Miss Hastings legs quavered uncontrollably. "You asked for a dress," she whimpered. "This is a very good dress. I am certain it will fit the girl."

"I see. Obviously, the error is mine. I neglected to explain that I would not accept just any old rag simply because it was the right size! Did you really think that this would be good enough?" he roared.

"It is much better than what she was wearing when I saw her. At least there are not any holes in it."

"That is hardly the point. Even I could probably sew something better than what she is wearing now. I wanted something stunning—something to make her . . . shine. I would not put this down for my dog to sleep on."

Miss Hastings looked as though she would burst into tears at any minute, which only infuriated the count more. She had been hired to do a job, and she'd barely managed to cross the line into mediocre. Crying certainly wouldn't make him feel sorry for her. On the contrary, her pitiful tears only served as a reminder of her incompetence. He grabbed her by the shoulders and shook her violently. "I wanted the best!"

Her eyes were wide, and she stared at him as though he were a wolf she'd stumbled onto, ripping apart his unfortunate rabbit dinner. "Sir," she pleaded, "I swear, that is the most elegant dress I ever sewed."

He released her shoulders, pushing her away from him disgustedly. "Then it is clear that I have no further need for your services. You are dismissed."

"But sir, about my wages . . ."

"You would be wise to leave now, before I come up with a better way to punish you than simply refusing to pay your bill." His dark eyes glittered dangerously, and Miss Hastings backed out of the room, not eager to be on the receiving end of the count's reputed favorite methods of punishment.

With only two days left until the gala, this was serious indeed. As one by one his guests began to arrive he'd relished his job as host, and the two weeks disappeared through his fingers like sand. Until the viceroy announced the arrival of Miss Hastings, the count had completely forgotten about the dress, and now it was too late to hire anyone else. Of all the preparations for his important night, the only one that was really essential was Viola, and now her performance would be imperfect. No matter how ethereal her voice, her shabby clothing would still be a distraction.

"So, what do you think of the dress? Miss Hastings has truly outdone herself," the viceroy sneered. The offending garment remained where it had been discarded, strewn across the couch, and he fingered the fabric thoughtfully.

"Do not be absurd. I should have known better than to hire some second-rate nobody without a waiting list. The mere fact that she was available should have been a clue as to her mediocrity," he grumbled. However, his countenance went from resentful to devious pleasure in an instant. "I've just had an idea, so perfectly ironic that I cannot imagine why I never thought of it before. Could we not get Viola's mother to create the dress? You said yourself that she was the best."

"I also said it would be three months before she could even see us," he said, giggling.

"What precisely about that do you find funny?"

"You know, three months before she can see us, as in meet with us. Except she is blind, so she will never really be able to see us in the literal sense."

The count found no humor in the viceroy's play on words. He took a cigar from the drawer in his desk and twirled it in his hand. "Pity; you would think she could make time to sew a dress for her own daughter."

His eyes widened. "Certainly you are not thinking of . . ."

"Of course I am not going to tell her," he snapped. "Do you think I am insane?"

The viceroy looked relieved, but it didn't last long.

The count shrugged, striking a match and puffing on the cigar until the end glowed a fiery red. "I want you to get her for me; whatever the price."

"But, Excellency, she is blind. True, she makes spectacular dresses, but not overnight. Perhaps if we had hired her in the first place . . ."

"I do not care what you have to do. Offer her a small fortune, bribe her, or threaten her; just convince her that she has to accept."

. . . ✶ . . .

"What sort of a dress did you have in mind, sir?" Claire had not spoken with the viceroy since the day he picked up his cloak. Although he suggested that he would need her services more regularly in the future, he hadn't returned, and she fretted that he was somehow displeased with her work. She was quite relieved when he knocked on her door, and regretted that her schedule was so full.

"A dress fit for a princess—something to make the moon and stars pale with envy."

"Goodness, that sounds like quite a gown. She must be a very important woman. I only wish that I could help you, but unless you can wait a few months . . ."

"I need the dress in two days," he said brusquely.

"Two days?" she repeated. "Why, sir, even if I started this instant, I would never be able to complete such a dress so quickly."

"But I have seen your dresses—luminous creations that could make the most homely creature come to life," he said, his voice smooth as butter. "I can settle for nothing less."

"You are too free with your praise," she demurred. "But not even a magician could do what you are asking."

"It is not me who is asking; it is Count Diavolo."

Claire gasped.

"He sent me here today, not to ask, but to inform you that

he expects the dress to be ready in two days, at which time I will return to collect it."

"It is impossible, sir. I am very sorry."

"As far as the count is concerned, nothing is impossible. I would not want to be the person who tried to convince him otherwise."

Claire felt trapped. Never since she was first blind had she felt so out of control. She'd prided herself on not only surviving, but doing it on her own terms. She'd heard stories about the count, how unreasonable he could be when things didn't go his way. She straightened her skirt, as if smoothing the outward ruffles could calm the waves inside. "I will do my best, sir," she said finally.

"The last seamstress the count hired did her best. I hope your best is better."

Two hours later, the floor of Claire's house was covered with boxes. She opened them feverishly, using her fingers as her eyes to try to decipher their contents. Even though she hadn't seen the item she was looking for since just before she was married, she was positive she would recognize it when she found it. Without her sight, she had no idea what most of the random shapes were. She remembered packing them in scraps of paper with such care. How strange it was that all these things had been so important to her, only to end up relegated into dusty boxes she hadn't needed in years. In the end, that's all they were—things.

Claire reached the bottom of a box of papers she'd been sifting through, and it didn't appear to be in that box either. Worry created a whirlwind in her gut; what if she couldn't find it? She was running out of places to look, and with the clock ticking, she didn't really have the time to tear the house apart anyway. Her hands groped blindly, sweeping into the corners and out of the way places where things could hide. She poked through drawers and cupboards until her fingertips brushed against a small, cold vial. She closed her hand around it, feeling it immediately warm on contact. It scared her as much as it had the first time.

She filled a pot with water and placed it on the stovetop. While it was heating, she rummaged through her sewing basket until she found the thread she was looking for at the very bottom. Even though she couldn't see it, she knew from the oblong shaped spool that it was a rather nondescript shade of beige. Her mother gave it to her along with the vial, admitting that she had been determined to throw them out, but decided at the last minute to give them to Claire and let her decide their fate. When Claire asked her what they were for, she said that her mother told her years ago that in case of an emergency, she would know what to do with them. She remembered thinking at the time how ridiculous it all was—who had ever heard of a sewing emergency? She put them away and forgot all about them, until now. If this wasn't an emergency, she didn't know what was.

She could tell the water was hot from the steam that beaded on her face. As expertly as if she'd done it a thousand times, she uncorked the vial, sprinkling the contents into the boiling pot. Claire unraveled some of the thread, cutting it into sections and feeding it slowly into the water. She worked completely on instinct, not knowing where the instruction came from or why. She let the thread simmer until the water had almost evaporated before removing it and hanging it across a rack to dry.

As she threaded her needle, she considered briefly what would probably happen to her if this didn't work. She pushed the needle through the fabric, pulling it smartly through the other side. She completed several stitches before she noticed something odd: although she could not see the needle or her hands or the room, she could see the thread. It wasn't much, only a few stitches that gleamed in the permanent darkness that surrounded her.

She smiled grimly. Fairy dust was an almost non-existent commodity; she only hoped the recipient of this dress would appreciate it, since there would likely never be another. It appeared that the count would get her best work after all.

. . . * . . .

"Tomorrow is the big day. Are you ready to sing?" The boy pushed Viola's dinner through the bars, but she didn't touch it. He grinned at her growing apprehension. "Well go on, eat it. You will need your strength."

"I already told you, I cannot sing for him."

"You can do anything you want."

"I cannot," she repeated.

"I know you do not want to do this, but you must think of the bigger picture. Once you have the count where you want him, he will get careless, and you can escape. You can have the last laugh, but you have to play along for a little while."

"I could never sing in front of people. My voice just freezes in my throat."

"You can practice on me. Pretend I am your audience. Imagine me in a long evening gown."

Viola giggled, but it didn't last.

"Sing something."

She shook her head. "I do not think I could. Besides, you are only one person; it would not be realistic."

"I am only trying to help."

"I know you are, and I appreciate what you are trying to do, but it is hopeless. I will never give in to the count, and I do not care what he does to me. I have already lost."

The boy paused at the door. "I thought I knew you, but I guess I was wrong."

"What do you mean?"

"You told me you were on your way to attend a singing school when you were kidnapped."

"Yes?"

"Now, correct me if I am wrong, but the purpose of attending a singing school is to learn to sing, yes?"

Viola rolled her eyes. "Yes."

"This is just a wild guess, but the purpose of learning to sing is so that you might perform."

"I assume so, but since I never made it to the school, I obviously missed the class on performance."

"Well, you seem to get by just fine without it. You are the biggest performer I have ever met!"

"What do you mean by that?" she asked, her voice rising.

"This whole drama of yours about being afraid to sing is an act—it has to be. I have heard you sing. I sat outside this wall in the freezing cold every night just to hear your voice, and even though I do not know much about music, I know enough to realize that no one could sing like that if they did not love it. And if you really loved it that much, you would want to share it with everyone. You are using the count as an excuse to feel sorry for yourself and withdraw into your shell, but you have not lost unless you sit back and allow it to happen. You still have this amazing voice, and it is time for you to move on. So use it!"

The boy heard someone walking above them, near the steps. "I have to go," he hissed. "Remember, you can do this!"

Viola stared in disbelief as he left. She kicked the bars as hard as she could, hoping that it would make her feel better, but she only succeeded in injuring her foot. How dare he say those things about her, as if he knew what it was like to sing in front of a crowd of strangers? He knew nothing about what she'd suffered, so he had no place passing judgment on her. She didn't care what anyone said because there was no way that she would sing at the gala tomorrow night. It would accomplish nothing, and she would be giving away the last thing she owned that was truly hers.

As the sun rose through the trees on the morning of the count's gala, the echo of hooves sounded across the bridge. A horse-drawn wagon came to a stop in front of the castle doors, and two men jumped down, lifting something heavy and awkward from the wagon. The viceroy directed them to an upstairs room, where they happily left their burden, veiled in a sheet. Viola sat on the bed in the room, eyeing the viceroy disapprovingly.

"What are you doing in here? And what is that?"

He pulled the sheet from the object, revealing a large, ornate mirror. "I am delivering a gift. You should feel very privileged—the count had this mirror brought in especially for you."

"What do you mean brought in?"

"In case you have not noticed, there are no mirrors in the castle. The count is very superstitious, but he wanted you to have one so you could get ready."

"How very kind of him," she said sarcastically.

He surveyed her from the top down. "I suggest that you get started as soon as possible; it looks as though you have a great deal of work to do. There is a hot bath waiting for you, but do not dawdle. A servant will come in awhile to fix your hair." He pointed to a lone garment bag, hanging in the closet. "The count has requested that you wear that dress. When it is time for you to sing, the boy will come and fetch you."

Viola feigned disinterest until the viceroy left, locking her in from the outside. She slid down from the bed and slowly made her way to the mirror. She hadn't caught a glimpse of herself in more than two years, and the girl who stared back at her seemed a complete stranger, someone she would be frightened to approach in the street. Her hair was overgrown and matted, hopelessly full of knots. She was definitely thinner, her ribs, knees, and elbows painfully prominent under her skin. Covered with a thick layer of dirt, she was like a trinket that had been pushed carelessly onto a high shelf and forgotten.

Perhaps the girl she remembered was still there somewhere; there was only one way to find out. She opened the door that led into the bathroom, hardly able to contain her excitement over the giant tub filled with hot water. She picked up the new bar of soap and pressed it to her nose, drunk on the heady scent of lilacs. But before her bath, she wanted a quick peek at the dress. She tiptoed to the closet, easing down the zipper on the bag until just a glimmer of pearly silver showed.

A deafening crash of thunder cracked in the kitchen, the lightning splitting the sky and illuminating the room just as the lights went out. Kaitlin squealed.

"Oh, dear," Viola said nervously. "Where are the candles?

They have to be in one of these drawers, but I can't see a thing," she said, fumbling for a nearby drawer handle.

"Never mind the candles, we don't mind the dark. Get back to the story!" Megan said desperately.

"Wait a minute. I think I found something," Viola announced. She switched on a flashlight, shining it directly into Megan's eyes.

"Now what are we going to do?" Kaitlin asked glumly.

Viola put on her most sensible look. "We're going to do what I always do when the power goes out—finish the ice cream!"

"Yay!" Kaitlin cheered.

"You'll have to count me out after those s'mores," Megan said, groaning and patting her belly.

"Don't be a stick in the mud; it's tradition. Besides, we might as well eat it—it's only going to melt in this heat and go to waste."

"The power could come back any minute," Megan argued.

"You're right. Best to take advantage of the situation while we can." Viola took the carton of fudge ripple out of the freezer and retrieved three spoons from the drawer. Despite her protests, Megan dug her spoon into the carton, searching for a nice, gooey pocket of chocolate to ease the sting of her abruptly interrupted bedtime story.

* Twelve *

Kaitlin peeked around the corner into the kitchen, where Viola was busy measuring spices and powders from different containers into a metal bowl. She hummed faintly as she worked, a scratchy rendition of "Happy Birthday to You" that was so quiet, it took several minutes for Kaitlin to identify the tune. Viola meticulously sifted the flour onto a sheet of wax paper before adding it to the bowl and stirring all the ingredients together. As she clapped her hands, she watched the flour disperse in a cloud, hanging briefly in the air before dissipating. Viola brushed her hands on her apron. "Good morning, birthday girl," she said matter-of-factly without turning around.

Kaitlin was mesmerized by the flurry of baking, and the sudden voice startled her. "I can't see them, but I know they must be there."

"What can't you see, dear?"

"The eyes in the back of your head." She watched as Viola creamed the butter and sugar in another bowl. "What kind of cake is it?" she shouted over the hand mixer.

"It's a surprise."

While Viola was busy mixing, Katitlin snuck to the garbage can. She lifted the lid as inconspicuously as she could, rummaging through the top layer of trash.

"Have you lost something, Katie?"

She dropped the lid sheepishly. "I was trying to cheat by looking at the box."

"What box?"

"You know, the box the cake mix came in."

"This isn't that kind of cake," Viola said haughtily. She began adding the eggs one at a time, making sure each was incorporated before she moved onto the next.

"Why do you do it like that?" Kaitlin asked curiously.

"Because the recipe says so."

"Wouldn't it be easier to just throw them all in at once?"

"Probably, but it might not turn out the same. If I'm going to go to all this trouble, I want it to be perfect."

"What if the recipe said to stand on your head while it was baking? Would you do that too?"

"What a very strange idea. Why would I want to stand on my head?" Viola said in astonishment.

She shrugged. "I don't know. It makes about as much sense as the eggs. Who was the first person that was brave enough to eat an egg, anyway? When you think about it, it's kind of gross."

"Who wants a present?" Megan sang as she strolled casually into the kitchen.

"Me! Me!" Kaitlin said eagerly, dancing around her mother.

Megan laid the hastily wrapped package on the table. Kaitlin hovered over it, examining it from all angles. "Can I open it now?"

"I don't see why not."

She eased off the curly ribbon and tore into the paper, revealing a hardbound book she'd been pestering her mother for. It was the last in a series she'd been reading, and she was desperate to know the ending. She squealed. "But you said we had to wait for the paperback."

"I wanted it to be a surprise. Happy Birthday, sweetie."

"I've been *dying* to read this—I can't wait to see what happens! Thanks, Mom!"

"I thought that maybe while the cake is baking, you girls might want to hear about the gala."

"The gala—it sounds so glamorous," Kaitlin said appreciatively with stars in her eyes.

Megan lifted the lid on the garbage nonchalantly. "What kind of cake is it? I don't see a box."

Viola rolled her eyes. "It's a very special cake. I think my mother made one like it for me when I was a little girl."

"You mean you don't know?" Kaitlin asked.

Viola scrunched up her face in deep thought. "I have this picture of a cake in my head, but I'm a little fuzzy about when or where I actually saw it. Maybe I only dreamed about it. Anyway, it's going to be out of this world."

Megan scanned the counter, looking for anything strange. "Not literally out of this world, right? There isn't any . . . fairy dust in it, is there?"

Viola laughed heartily, the hissing noise reminiscent of a snake with the giggles. "Of course not! You can't eat fairy dust. Well, not twice anyway."

Megan blinked. "It will kill you?" her voice squeaked, an octave higher than usual.

"It will kill *you*," she corrected. "I have enough fairy blood that I would survive, and Katie might just pull through, even though her heritage is fairly diluted. But you, my dear, would be a goner for sure."

"I thought you said almost everyone had a fairy somewhere in their family."

"I was trying to cheer you up. Besides, do you really want to take that chance?"

"I can't believe we're really debating whether I want to risk my life by ingesting fairy dust. Do you even have any fairy dust?"

Viola looked crestfallen. "No."

"Then I guess I'm safe either way. Now, I want to hear about the party."

"The gala," Kaitlin corrected.

"Right—the gala."

Viola took a deep breath, closed her eyes, and smiled as she exhaled. "It was the most thrilling night of my life. It was like a dream, really. You should have seen the table in the dining room. I swear it was as long as a football field, and it was covered with every sort of dish and delicacy that you could imagine. There were even some things that no one wanted to eat."

"Like what?" Kaitlin wondered.

"Oh, like broiled dragon with prickly pears."

"Broiled dragon." Megan repeated the words skeptically.

Viola waved her hand impatiently. "It was scaly. Maybe it was just some sort of big lizard, I don't know. Anyway, it was very sad. And there was a poached swan in pomegranate sauce, surrounded by a flock of tiny roast quail."

"That's terrible."

"It could have been worse. At least we didn't know the swan."

Kaitlin laughed. "Who knows a swan?"

"The last swan at the castle—he was supposed to be the one on the plate. But he managed to escape his fate. The count never liked the swans in the moat; I think he was a little bit afraid of them, so he didn't mind when they slowly disappeared as dinner for the toothy fish. All but one and I think he only managed to survive on sheer meanness. He was a sleek black swan with icey blue eyes that cut right through you, and he was missing one webbed foot, courtesy of one of the fish that tried to eat him. Apparently he won, because the other fish never bothered him again. Anyway, the count tried to convince the viceroy to catch the swan so they could serve it at the gala. He'd heard that serving swan was considered very elegant. But the viceroy refused. He said he had no intention of getting bruised and battered by a swan that was probably too old and tough to be eaten anyway.

"So the count decided he was going to do it himself. He walked down to the moat early one morning, before the sun rose and the sky was still purplish and quiet. He surveyed the bird as it swam confidently through the lily pads and weeds that crowded the water, holding a large net at the ready. Before the count knew what was happening, the swan came out of the water onto the grass. It hobbled toward him, hissing loudly, its marble blue stare never leaving his. When the swan was close enough for him to throw the net, it unfurled its impressive wings, beating them threateningly. The count was awed. He truly had never seen a more majestic creature, in spite of its flaws. The swan held his ground, refusing to back down from the challenge, and he respected that. He went back into the castle, telling the viceroy to add a more docile swan to the caterer's list."

"It's just like a fairy tale," Megan sighed.

"I wonder what swan tastes like? Chicken?" Kaitlin said.

"I can't wait to find out if you sang that night," Megan said, her hands clasped so tightly that her knuckles were white.

"We're almost there, so you only have to be patient a little longer. Now, where were we?"

THE GALA

"Have you found your voice yet, little songbird?" the count inquired.

Viola stood before him in the dress. It must have been the way the firelight shone against the fabric, but he was having a difficult time keeping his eyes on her. He remembered reading someplace that you shouldn't stare directly into the sun, and this dress seemed to have much the same effect. He couldn't help feeling that it was somehow doing irreparable damage to his vision. It was the color of starlight, but the intensity was blinding, as though she had fallen from the heavens; a solar flare in human form.

The skirt consisted of flouncy, filmy layers that looked like spun sugar, falling delicately to the floor. When she stood, she appeared to be floating, and when she walked, the dress rippled as though it had a life and consciousness of its own. It was definitely the otherworldly gown the count desired, but instead of being pleased, he found himself disturbed. Arrayed in this dress, Viola was a goddess who had suddenly come into her full powers. He had the strangest impression that the dress somehow knew who she was, and he felt inferior in her presence. But he made every effort to brush it off, hoping that his guests would share his awe.

She did not reply.

"I wanted to give you a bit of . . . encouragement before your debut. By the way, that dress really does suit you. It is quite a remarkable transformation. Do you know where it came from?"

"I was there, watching you bully that poor woman. Judging by the end result, I suppose you were right; fear is a powerful motivator."

"Sadly, no. Miss Hastings proved to be, how shall we say, not up to the task. You should have seen the pathetic rag she presented me with. No, I had to go to a more seasoned seamstress to achieve the desired results."

For a fraction of a second, Viola wavered. The brilliance of the dress was not enough to gloss over her uneasiness, and the count felt the balance of power shift in his favor. "You know, I believe I have discovered something, my dear. As steadfast as you have been in refusing me, in my life I have learned that everyone has their weak spot, and I think I may have discovered yours. You seem to be fearless as far as your own comfort and well-being are concerned, but I wonder, how long would you hold out when someone you cared about was suffering?"

Viola's lower lip trembled, but she blinked back the tears that welled up, unwilling to give him the satisfaction of seeing her wilt. She did not trust her voice to be as solid as her resolve, so she said nothing.

He clicked his tongue disapprovingly. "You disappoint me, Viola. I thought you were more intelligent. Do I really have to spell it out for you?"

She swallowed her apprehension, throwing back her shoulders and standing at her full height, summoning the last of the courage she possessed.

"Very well, then. Let us see if this persuades you. The dress you are wearing tonight was sewn by your mother—your *blind* mother. Do you see that swordfish, hanging over the mantle? I was with your father in his boat when he caught it." He pointed, using his finger in a stabbing motion to punctuate his words.

Each admission made her flinch and her cheeks burned as though he had physically struck her.

"I want to be very clear, so that no one can ever say there was any misunderstanding between us. I know who your parents are, and I know where they are. I have been within inches of them. And if you refuse to sing at the gala, I will not hesitate to make things very difficult for your family. Your parents will pay for your disobedience." He pulled his dinner jacket down, straightening it in one swift motion. "Now, if you will excuse me, I would not want to neglect my guests. I am looking forward to finally discovering if your voice measures up to my expectations."

. . . ✶ . . .

"Viola?" the boy whispered, standing in the doorway.

She looked in his direction but did not reply. She stood still, frozen where the count had left her. He was right, and she knew it. It was one thing to put herself into harm's way, but quite another to throw her unsuspecting parents to the wolves. This was it—she'd come abruptly to the end of her options. No matter what choice she made, she would lose something dear to her.

He glanced in either direction, making certain there was no one in earshot. "Has something happened? Are you unwell?"

"Yes," she said shakily. Her voice was so small, and suddenly everything was moving so quickly. She was a tiny speck, hurtling toward her imminent destruction at an alarming rate.

"Yes, you are unwell, or yes, something happened?"

"Both."

He looked perplexed. "You are not making any sense."

"No matter," she said resolutely. "It looks as if I will be singing after all."

A wide smile split the boy's face. "That is wonderful! From the expression on your face, I thought you had lost your best friend."

"I am doing my best to prevent that from happening."

"We do not have much time, so you will have to explain that to me later. You're really going to do it," he said in amazement.

"I do not seem to have any choice." She felt the resignation stealing over her like an anesthetic, numbing her to any residual pain.

"Listen, I know you think this is the most terrible thing in the world, but if singing to a crowd of stuffy rich people is the price of your liberty, then it is well worth paying. In the end, you will see that I am right."

Viola looked lost, gazing around the room blankly. It was

as if she'd woken there after a long sleep and couldn't remember where she was or how she'd arrived. She could feel herself shutting down.

The boy snapped his fingers in front of her face, startling her from her trance. "Hey! If you are going to do this, you might as well give it your best effort. Who knows if you will ever get a chance like this again, right?"

"That is what my mother said when I left for school." When she thought about her mother, she had to fight back the painful lump that rose in her throat without warning. She looked into the boy's eyes and tried to smile. "She made this dress; did you know? Even if she did not know it was for me, she still made it. Her hands touched it, maybe only hours ago. The count said that to upset me, but he made a mistake. I feel stronger wearing it now that I know. It is like my own suit of armor."

He stared at her, really studying her for the first time since he'd entered the room. From the tiny red tea roses woven through her hair to the elegant slippers on her feet that sparkled like diamonds, she'd been completely altered. Viola had gone from grubby to glamorous almost instantaneously. There was a kind of warm white light that emanated from her, softening her features yet bringing her beauty into sharp focus at the same time.

She eyed him strangely. "Why are you looking at me like that?"

He wasn't sure how long he'd been staring, and he looked away, embarrassed. "It is nothing," he mumbled hastily, cursing his voice for cracking.

"I look silly. It is too much; I feel as if I am on display."

"Well, you are."

"What if they all laugh at me?" she wailed.

"Trust me when I say that no one is going to laugh," he said sincerely.

"Then why do you keep staring at me like that?"

"I just never realized you were so pretty."

She ducked her chin shyly, unable to think of anything to say. Her face was hot, but the roses in her cheeks only added to her loveliness. The boy looked at the clock on the wall. "We must go right now. I did not realize it was so late," he said nervously. Suddenly, he was all business. "You will stand on a platform under the stage, and when it is time, I will raise it. After the performance, the curtains will close and you will wait behind them for me to come and get you. Are you ready?"

She nodded hesitantly.

"Once we leave this room, I cannot speak to you. It is too dangerous; someone might see us. So I will say good luck now. You have nothing to worry about—you will be fantastic."

"Thank you . . . for everything. I am not certain that I could have done this without you."

They walked silently down the corridors of the castle. As they neared the stage, the volume of voices grew louder. Viola felt sick when she imagined how many people must be in the room, but she forced herself to think about something else. The boy pointed to a door that led to a staircase, and the stairs took them to a large room underneath the stage. The orchestra boomed somewhere beyond them; the harsh sounds of instruments being tuned was amplified by the wooden floor. Viola felt jittery. The low hum of muffled voices competed with the cacophony of the discordant strings and horns.

The boy pointed to the platform, and Viola obediently stepped onto it. He waited for the music to begin—the signal for him to raise Viola into the sea of staring eyes. Every second she spent waiting was torture. Now that she was here, she just wanted to get this over with. The sooner she began, the sooner it would be finished. Suddenly, the instruments stopped tuning up, the talking began to fade, and the world grew quiet. She was aware of the blood pulsing through every vein and pounding in her ears until it drowned out everything else, even her own terror. The strains of a familiar piece of music began, and the boy grinned at her. She managed to grin back.

. . . ✶ . . .

Viola ducked behind the curtain of crushed moss green velvet as it closed. It was impossible to tell which was louder—the deafening applause, or the beating of her own heart. She flattened herself against the wall, digging her fingers into the crevices between the stones. She felt so light that she was afraid if she didn't somehow tether herself to the earth, she might just float away. If this is what performing was like, she could understand why people craved it. She felt as if she'd discovered the answer to a troubling question, and when the light went on in her brain, she could see that the answer was the key not only to her question, but to all the questions. Her senses were heightened, and everything around her looked somehow . . . different. This new feeling of being invincible coursed through her body like a drug, and now that it was finished she wanted to relive her brief time on stage again and again in her mind.

She had begun by singing very softly. In fact, the audience had needed to strain to hear her. But as her confidence grew, she gradually began to get louder, each note leaving them breathless and eager for the next. Every person in the audience felt as though she were singing only for them. In fact, later, when they discussed their favorite parts over dinner, no one could agree on exactly what she sang. One man was convinced he heard an aria from a Mozart opera, while another swore it was Puccini. It was very peculiar, for it seemed that everyone heard the music they most wanted to hear.

At the end of the performance there was one last note that went on and on, so full of longing, so achingly beautiful that the audience was moved to tears. When she was certain that there could be no breath left in her body and she could hold the note no longer, her voice faded away into the rafters, mingling with bits of colorful confetti that fluttered down onto the stage and the crowd like bright paper birds raining from the sky.

It was the perfect end to a flawless performance. People remarked that the little soprano must have been unaware of the surprising spectacle that would accompany her finale, as she stared in wonder at the storm of spectacular colors. Even the count grudgingly admitted to himself that it was impressive. He had to give the viceroy credit for his dramatic flair.

The enthusiastic clapping finally subsided, changing to conversation. Viola could hear people abandoning their seats and preparing themselves for the next stage of the evening. She peeked through a crack in the curtains, watching as the crowd began to filter out. There would be dancing, then a lavish dinner. Already, she could hear the distant sound of violins as the orchestra began a waltz. She swayed unconsciously to the sweeping music, her numerous layers of skirts floating around her like clouds. She imagined the grand ladies of the ballroom in their gowns, choked by layers of corsets and strands of jewels, spinning around by candlelight on the glittering floor made of seashells. She envied their freedom and the ease with which they moved not only across the dance floor but in the world.

The boy appeared finally, and though he did not speak, his face was wreathed in smiles. Another waltz was beginning, and on impulse, he bowed to Viola and offered her his hand. She curtsied to him, imagining what a strange looking pair they must make; she in her dress made of starlight and he with his ragged clothing and brown bare feet. He gingerly clasped her hand, putting his other arm carefully around her waist. She put her hand on his shoulder, and they began to slowly twirl.

It was as if they had been waltzing together for years, gliding across the darkened floor in perfect time with countless other couples in the grand ballroom across the hall. But it was over almost before it began. Viola broke the spell by stepping heavily on the boy's foot. Her cheeks reddened with shame, but her mortification quickly turned to giggles when the boy began hopping around, holding his injured foot and laughing uncontrollably. When he finally caught his breath, he ran toward her, growling playfully. She shrieked and ran in the other direction, but there was no way she could outrun him in her finery. He grabbed her, tickling her ribs while she shook with silent laughter, each blissfully unaware of the eyes smoldering in the darkness like hot coals, watching them.

. . . * . . .

On their way back to Viola's cage, the boy took a detour. He put a finger to his lips, poking his head into a room with dimmed lighting. Since he could still hear the instruments, he wasn't worried about being caught. He signaled for Viola to follow him, and she went through the door cautiously.

She'd never been in the dining room before, and already she could see why the count saved this part of the evening for the finale. Everything about the room suggested unbridled opulence. Inside, candles flickered, casting looming shadows on the wall that urged wandering eyes upward to a mural of a large tree filled with vibrant butterflies. The entire ceiling sparkled with bits of something shiny embedded in the butterfly wings, reflecting like fractured stars. Along one wall, there were enormous windows that stretched from nearly ceiling to floor, draped with heavy midnight blue curtains. It was dark outside now, but she imagined that during the day the room afforded an amazing view of the grounds.

Although the décor of the room was spectacular, it was the table that captured her attention. At every seat there was a bowl, three crystal glasses, three spoons, two knives, and seven different forks. Who could possibly need seven forks for one meal? Bottles of champagne rested on ice in silver buckets, just waiting for someone to pop the corks and begin the celebration. Evenly spaced every few feet across the table were small topiary centerpieces that grew an assortment of miniature fruits for guests to harvest and sample.

Viola heard a noise, and the boy grabbed her hand and dragged her into the shadows. They crouched behind the curtains, trapped, half expecting to see the count himself walk through the door. Luckily, it was only a few servants pushing their rolling trolleys laden with tureens of steaming soup. They moved from seat to seat, quickly ladling hot, creamy soup into each waiting bowl, so it wouldn't have time to get cold. Viola's stomach growled at the smell of roasted butternut squash and rosemary. The boy frowned.

If the food was ready, the guests could be only minutes behind. Viola and the boy took the opportunity to sneak out when the servants retreated to the kitchen to refill their tureens.

The boy dragged Viola down the hall as she stomped her feet and complained, in case they happened to run into someone. She thought it best that, for the sake of appearances, she should be as unpleasant to him as she possibly could. The boy played his part as well, looking appropriately blank and disinterested. He stopped by the kitchen on the way back to pick up Viola's dinner, which consisted of a hard roll and a rather shriveled looking ear of corn. Viola caught a glimpse of the harried servants putting the final touches on a glazed swan, roasted potatoes that glistened with butter, trays of unidentified tarts with dollops of cream or drizzles of caramel, an enormous bowl of caviar, and some sort of baked fish, decorated with circles of lemon and something weedy. And that was just the beginning! Aside from the swan, which she thought was sad, the food made her mouth water, and she wished that she could have explored the entire kitchen, tasting and sampling at her leisure.

Once back in her room with the door safely shut, the boy launched into his praise, unable to keep silent any longer. "You were amazing! It was like you had no fear at all. I knew you could do it!"

"What are you talking about? I was terrified!"

"Maybe at the beginning, but admit it; you loved singing for those people."

She paused thoughtfully. "You know, it was strange. I was so worried about it until I started singing, and then everything just seemed to fall into place. For the first time in years, I felt like I was in control of my destiny; I could have sung for hours."

"It only took about a minute for the entire room to fall in love with you. You were brilliant."

"All right, enough of this flattery. It is time for you to pay up."

"I am afraid I do not understand," the boy said slowly.

"Now, do not pretend you cannot remember what our deal

was. On the night that I sang at the gala . . ."

"I promised to tell you my name," he finished.

"Exactly." She folded her arms expectantly. "Well?"

He hesitated.

"I am waiting."

"I cannot tell you my name," he blurted out finally.

"Unbelieveable! We had a deal. I fulfilled my end of the bargain, and now you will not tell me your name? Do you not trust me?"

"You have it all wrong. I truly cannot tell you my name . . . because I do not have one."

"That is silly. Everyone has a name," Viola argued.

"I cannot remember it."

She was astonished. "How does one forget their own name?"

He shrugged. "I must have suffered some sort of shock when I was brought here, and since I arrived, no one has ever called me anything but 'Boy.' 'Boy, do this,' and 'Boy, fetch that.' "

"You mean you have no name at all?"

"Well, I must have at some point."

She brightened. "Maybe I could name you! After all, when we escape, I am going to have to call you something."

"I will have to think about that," he said wryly.

"Come on, it would be fun!" she begged.

"That is what I am worried about. You might take advantage of the situation and give me an old lady name like Francis or something."

Her eyes narrowed. "Francis is my mother's name."

"I thought you said her name was Claire," he stammered.

"Her name is Francis, but she goes by her middle name, Claire."

"There, you see? She does not want to be an old lady either."

Viola giggled despite her efforts to keep a stern expression on her face. "I promise I would give you a really good name, something you would like."

"I am still not sure it is a good idea."

"But promise me you will at least think about it."

"I will."

"Will! That is the perfect name for you! In fact, you look just like a Will."

"Hmmm . . . Will. It is not horrible."

"See? I said you could trust me," she said smugly.

"I do not want to commit to anything right away. This is a big deal. You are saddled with your name for the rest of your life, and I want to be sure it is the right one."

"Well, I think Will is a great name, at least for now. When we get out, you can always just ask your parents what your real name is."

The boy looked away, not wanting her to see his face before he could regain his composure.

"What is it?"

"The count told me that my parents are dead." His voice was flat and withdrawn.

"It might not be true, you know. We cannot trust anything he says."

"I did not believe him at first. I thought it was just a way to keep me here. He knew that if I had nothing left, there would be no reason for me to try to leave. So I wrote their names and our address on a piece of paper and gave it to someone I trusted in the stables, to check on them. He said there were different people living there—no one had seen or heard from my parents in over a year." His eyes were shining with tears, and he wiped them away angrily.

"I am so sorry. I can only imagine how you must feel. The count told me something . . . about my mother. He said she was blind."

"We *are* going to get out of here," the boy interrupted suddenly. "I am going to get you home to your family, I swear it," he said firmly.

"But, how?"

"Never mind that. You must be tired—you should eat your dinner and get some sleep. I have a feeling that your performance tonight is just the thing to set our escape plan in motion."

"What plan?"

"I have an idea, but I need to think about it. I will see you tomorrow." He locked her in the cage and turned to go.

"Good night, Will."

He shook his head, smiling, with his hand on the door. "Good night, Viola."

. . . ✶ . . .

"By the way, I must compliment you on the way you handled the arrangements. The confetti at the end of Viola's performance was nothing short of magnificent. Whatever made you think of it?" The count was not one to give undue praise, but he felt that in this situation, the viceroy had gone above and beyond his expectations.

"It is true that I put a great deal of time and effort into the preparations. Unfortunately, the confetti was not a part of my careful planning; I only wish I could take the credit."

The count looked baffled. "Who, then? I would like to congratulate them personally."

"Is it not obvious, Excellency?" the viceroy said, flashing a mysterious smile. "The girl did it."

"What is this nonsense?"

"Did you notice a peculiar . . . feeling of some sort when she was singing?"

"I felt a little short of breath, I suppose. But I assumed that was just the anticipation."

"I think not. You see, people respond differently when she sings in their presence; actual physical manifestations that present themselves in ways that can be wonderful or decidedly unpleasant. I myself do not enjoy listening to her because I feel as if my heart might explode at any moment. But judging from the general response tonight, I would say that most people have a more positive experience than mine." He paused for effect before continuing. "There were no plans to release that confetti tonight," he said emphatically. "The girl did that all on her own."

"Do you think I am so foolish as to believe that Viola has some sort of magic powers? That she can make things happen, simply by wishing them into existence? If that were true, she would hardly allow herself to be kept prisoner in a cage."

"Ah, but that is the interesting part. It is just possible that she has not yet discovered her abilities. I think, Excellency, that now might be a prudent time to consider what might happen if she ever learns to channel these powers and use them at will. Perhaps you might be wise to think about getting rid of her, before she can become a more serious threat."

"Are you mad? Did you hear how the crowd roared tonight? She is going to be famous—a prodigy known throughout the world, and she will belong to me."

"And her mother?"

"What of her mother?" the count huffed.

"She is blind, Excellency, not deaf. If the girl is to be that well known, surely the day will come when her mother will hear her and recognize the voice of the child she thought was dead."

"I will deal with her mother later. Besides, who would ever take the word of a raving blind woman over mine? She would be as easy to crush as a dried-up moth. Now, I really must return to my guests, if you will excuse me."

"Did no one think it was strange that Viola did not receive an invitation to dinner?" the viceroy asked archly.

"Of course I asked her to dine with us, but I could hardly force her to attend when she was so worn out from her debut. Once I explained that she preferred an early dinner and rest in her quarters, everyone was very understanding."

"You do think of everything, Excellency."

"And now, without further ado . . . birthday time!" Viola exclaimed in her dry whispery tone.

"What?!" Kaitlin yelped. "You can't stop there. As the birthday girl, I order you to keep telling the story."

"But it's time for cake."

"I suppose a short intermission for cake would be okay," she said grudgingly.

"You can look now!" Viola said.

Kaitlin opened her eyes to see a gigantic three-layer cake, complete with pale pink frosting, fresh flowers that sprouted near the edge of each layer, and ten flickering candles.

"Grandma, it's beautiful!" she said in admiration.

"Hurry and make a wish so you can blow out the candles!"

Kaitlin closed her eyes briefly, her lips making a sort of unintelligible mumble. She took a deep breath and blew until every candle was extinguished, so her wish would be sure to come true. Viola and Megan clapped politely.

Viola rose from her chair. "I'll get the plates."

The phone rang, and Megan grabbed it. "Hello?" She listened patiently for a minute before smiling in understanding. "Yes, I see. I'll get her." She held the phone out toward her daughter. "I have an urgent call for Miss Kaitlin Patterson."

Kaitlin took the phone. "Hello?" she said hopefully.

"Is this my daughter, Kaitlin, who's getting so grown-up that I probably won't even recognize her the next time I see her?"

"Dad!" Kaitlin said, her face lit up in perfect joy. "I was afraid you forgot."

"How could I forget your big day? Have you had a good birthday?"

"You should see the cool cake Grandma made. We're just about to cut into it."

"You're a lucky girl. I used to wait all year for my birthday to roll around, just to have a bite of your Grandma's cake. Listen, I don't have much time, but I just wanted you to know that I love you, and I wish I was there."

"I wish you were here too, Dad. Do you want to talk to Mom for a minute?"

"It's okay—I have to go, but she'll understand. I'll talk to you soon, okay?"

"Okay. Bye, Dad."

"Happy birthday, sweetie."

When Kaitlin hung up the phone her eyes looked a little teary, so Viola cut a large wedge of cake and quickly set it in front of her granddaughter. "Now, it's impossible to be sad when you're eating cake, so let's get started!"

Kaitlin reluctantly forked a bite, feeling marginally better when the buttery frosting hit her tongue. She quickly swallowed it, following it with a larger piece. The cake tasted of tiny wild strawberries and golden sunlight. "Grandma, are you sure you didn't use any fairy dust?"

Megan froze mid-bite, the fork barely touching her lips.

"Of course I didn't, dear. Why do you ask?"

"Because this is the best cake I've ever had," she mumbled. "It tastes like summer."

Megan gingerly put the bite in her mouth, tasting hundreds of wild violets growing in the tall grass by a cool stream. "Incredible," she marveled. "How did you do that?"

Viola beamed. "I'm glad you like it. And I saved the best for last." She disappeared around the corner, and returned with a garment bag that she gingerly handed to her granddaughter. "I just knew I was holding onto this for a reason."

Kaitlin carefully lowered the zipper on the bag and gasped, followed by Megan's own sharp intake of breath. It was exactly as Viola had described it, yet infinitely more spectacular than either of them had imagined. Looking as fresh as if it had been sewn yesterday, the translucent layers were unveiled as Viola removed the dress from the bag. It seemed to ripple in pleasure, as though it reveled in the thought of being worn again after so many years. When Kaitlin touched it reverently with one hand, she could swear that her fingertips tingled.

"Wow," was all Kaitlin could manage.

"That's really it, isn't it?" Megan said in disbelief.

"Yes. That's the very dress my mother sewed, all those years ago. And now it belongs to you."

Kaitlin's eyes widened. "Do I really get to keep it?"

"As long as you promise to take excellent care of it."

"Cross my heart and hope to die," she said solemnly. "Can I try it on?"

"I'm not entirely sure it will fit," Megan said doubtfully. "You might be too tall."

"I don't think we need to worry about that, dear. You're forgetting the fairy dust."

Kaitlin nodded, taking the dress to the bedroom and closing the door behind her. Although the feathery layers of starlight gave the illusion of weightlessness, she couldn't believe how heavy it was. The material felt smooth, except where trails of pearly beads interrupted the flow of the fabric. She took her clothes off, easing down the zipper and shimmying into the gown. It took her a while to get the zipper back up, and for a minute, she was worried that it would be too small. She mentally scolded herself for repeatedly accepting the extra pancakes her grandmother offered her at breakfast. But as she worked at it, she had the oddest feeling that the dress was molding itself to fit her body.

She made her way slowly to the full-length mirror on the closet door, lifting her skirts so she wouldn't trip on them. As she gazed into the mirror, she was so lost in the vision of the dress that it took her awhile to notice that the face of the girl in the dress was not her own. Although she should have been frightened, she was more curious than anything else. The girl in the mirror was smaller, and her face was thinner. But they shared the same mischievous grin; the resemblance was unmistakable. Kaitlin didn't know how it was possible, but she was certain she was staring at an incarnation of her grandmother as a child.

"Grandma!" she shouted, looking away from the mirror momentarily.

"What do you think she's doing in there?" Megan wondered

aloud. She sat at the kitchen table with Viola, methodically tearing a napkin into shreds while she waited for her daughter to reappear.

"She's probably just admiring herself in the mirror. You know how girls that age are."

"I've been thinking about something."

"What is that, dear?"

"If that's the dress that you wore, the night of the gala . . ."

"Yes?"

" . . . and you lost everything when your house was destroyed in the sinkhole . . ."

"How is it that I still have the dress?" she finished.

"Don't get me wrong—I'm not questioning your story," Megan said quickly. "I just wondered."

"A week before the house was sucked into the ground, I noticed that the dress had a small tear in the skirt, and as I didn't inherit my mother's talent for sewing, I thought it best to take it to a seamstress and have it mended. It was in her possession at the time, so it was saved."

"That was lucky."

"Do you believe in heaven?"

Megan was taken aback by the question. "I believe that there is something after this life," she said carefully.

"I like to think my mother is in heaven, looking after me. I don't think it was an accident that I decided to take the dress in to be fixed that week. It's all I have of hers."

"Grandma!" Kaitlin yelled, her call muffled by the closed door. They both jumped.

"I'll be right back," Viola said, her bones creaking as she stood. "She probably just needs help with the zipper. It sticks sometimes."

"What is taking you so long?" Viola hissed, peeking through the door.

"Come and look!"

Viola stood next to her, surveying her granddaughter in the dress. "You look beautiful. I knew you would."

"No, the mirror, Grandma. Look in the mirror!" Kaitlin pointed frantically.

She squinted closely at the glass. "Don't worry, that chip was always there. I'm not going to accuse you of breaking it."

"Not that," Kaitlin sighed in frustration, turning back to face the mirror and show her grandma her amazing discovery. But to her dismay, the only two people in the reflection were herself and Viola; the elderly Viola.

"Just what am I supposed to be looking at?"

"I thought I saw something," she said timidly. Now that she thought about it, she felt silly. Of course the younger version of her grandmother wasn't in the mirror. Obviously, she'd told her story in such detail that Kaitlin was able to imagine her in the dress.

"It's getting late. It's probably just your eyes playing tricks on you."

"I guess so. Can you show me where the fairy dust is?"

She pointed to a seam. "Anywhere there is thread, there is fairy dust."

"I expected it to . . . sparkle." Her voice was hollow with disappointment.

"It does. You look like the brightest star in the sky."

"It just looks like ordinary thread to me."

Viola paused in the doorway. "Don't you see, Katie? It isn't the fairy dust that makes the dress sparkle; it is the person who wears it."

After the euphoria from the dress and the sugar high from the cake wore off, Kaitlin suddenly found herself quite sleepy. She struggled to hold back an enormous yawn but couldn't quite avoid it entirely.

"Off to bed with you, daughter," Megan said, kissing the top of her head.

"But I'm not tired!" she protested.

"Don't think I didn't see that yawn, however much you tried to hide it."

"But if I go to bed, I'll have to take off the dress."

"All good things must come to an end," Viola said. "Besides, it's yours now. You can try it on whenever you like."

Kaitlin stood on her tiptoes, giving her grandmother a quick peck on the cheek. "Thank you for the awesome dress, Grandma."

"You're very welcome. I'm glad you like it."

"You get to bed. I'll be in soon. And make sure you hang up that dress; don't just leave it in a heap on the floor," Megan said.

"Like I would do that."

"If memory serves, that's where I usually find the rest of your clothes."

Kaitlin rolled her eyes. "Good night, Mom. Good night, Grandma."

* THIRTEEN *

Kaitlin lay in the darkened room, wondering what was taking her mother so long. Despite how drowsy she'd been in the kitchen, she was having a hard time falling asleep. Her eyes refused to close as she imagined her grandmother as a little girl, bravely going on stage and singing in front of all those strangers. She rolled over onto her other side, punching her pillow and trying to get comfortable, but it was no good. She sighed. Something had to be done.

She crept down the hall and poked her head into the kitchen. "I can't sleep," she announced.

"Maybe a glass of warm milk would help," Viola said helpfully.

"No, but I think I know what would."

Megan grinned.

"All right," Viola sighed. "But only because you're the birthday girl.

THE ESCAPE

"I must say, your repeated refusals to sing for me made me question your skill, but as it turns out, I had no cause for concern. Your voice is the most impressive and unusual thing in my collection." The count faced the window, nibbling on a flaky croissant while the sun warmed his face. He finally turned to face Viola, giving her an uncharacteristic smile. "Why did you not just sing for me when I asked you to? You could have had a more comfortable place to stay, delicious food, and you could have saved us both all this trouble. I cannot understand why anyone with a talent like yours would not flaunt it every chance they got. No one should have to beg you to sing."

"Oh, I enjoy singing very much. It was just the audience I objected to," Viola said. She returned his smile, but hers was cold and distant.

He clicked his tongue disapprovingly. "See, there it is again. Why do you have such disdain for me? We could have such a rewarding friendship if you would only give me a chance."

Her eyes darkened. "You kidnapped me and took me away from the people I love. What could possibly convince me to give you a chance?"

"I see you are determined to think the worst of me, but I can be patient. Perhaps as the years go by, you will see it is in your best interest to look on me a little more . . . favorably. And as a show of good faith, I brought you here today to give you something."

"There *is* something I would like very much."

"And what would that be?"

"Let me go home," she pleaded.

"How many times do I have to tell you—you *are* home. But after your remarkable performance, I wanted you to have something. After all, I got something I wanted, so you should have something you want as well."

"There is nothing you could give me that would please me," Viola repeated, turning away stubbornly.

"What about an unscheduled walk in the forest?"

"Alone?"

"Well, I would not feel right about sending you on your own. There are all sorts of animals wandering around the woods, and I could not bear it if anything were to happen to you."

"You have no need to worry; I can take care of myself."

"Still, I would feel better if someone went with you. Unfortunately, the viceroy has some other business to attend to, and as much as I would love to accompany you on a ramble in the woods, I am far too busy. I thought that perhaps you might consent to the boy as your companion."

Viola's heart immediately began pounding in her chest, but

she tried to keep her outward composure calm. This was the chance they had been waiting for. She cleared her throat nonchalantly. "I suppose that if I must go with someone, the boy will have to do, even if he does refuse to speak to me."

The count laughed suddenly, the amusement evident on his face. "My dear, the boy speaks to no one. From the time I took him from his parents, he has never uttered a word."

"I know why you wanted me, but why did you take the boy? Does he have some special talent?"

"I took the boy to set an example. I made his parents a loan, and despite numerous promises, they would not repay what they owed."

"You mean they *could* not repay it," Viola challenged.

"They should never have accepted the loan if they were unwilling to commit to the terms."

"I hardly think that the terms they agreed to included surrendering their child."

"I admit I came up with that consequence after the fact, but it was definitely effective. Once that story started to circulate, people found a way to pay me. It is amazing what you can accomplish, when properly motivated. But then, I hardly need tell *you* that, do I?"

The boy appeared at the door to the study, holding the manacles in one hand apprehensively.

"Ah, perfect timing! Your escort awaits."

The boy fastened one of the manacles around Viola's hand, linking the other to his own. He winked boldly at her when his back was to the count.

"I do not see why these are necessary. There is no way I could overpower him—he is obviously much stronger than I am."

"It is for your own good. Sometimes when we are not thinking clearly, we make split second decisions that are not in our best interest. I am just making it harder for you act on those impulses."

They were almost out the door when the count called out with a word for each of them.

"I hope you have a lovely outing, my dear. And, boy, you can be certain that I will hold you personally responsible for any harm that might come to my songbird. You may go."

. . . ✶ . . .

They were many steps into the woods before either of them dared speak. The boy was the first to break the uneasy silence.

"See? I told you that the count would get careless, once you did what he wanted. He has given us the perfect opportunity to escape, and we never had to plan a thing!" He took the key from around his neck, ready to unlock the restraints.

"Stop!" Viola hissed.

"What do you mean, 'stop'? This is our chance."

"I know, but this is too easy. Something is wrong."

"You are paranoid. The count does not trust you, but he must be convinced he can trust me; otherwise, he would never have allowed me to take you out. That is where he made his big mistake."

"Or maybe he is just setting us up. He might have had us followed, just to see what we would do. Keep walking; it looks strange if we are just standing here. Maybe he suspects that you can speak. You heard what he said—he has eyes everywhere!"

"He is only trying to scare you with talk like that," the boy scoffed.

"I think we should wait until next time."

"That is the trouble; there might not be a next time. We have to take advantage of this chance now. Who knows when he will decide to let me take you for a walk again?" The boy had to lengthen his stride to keep up with Viola, who had taken the lead and was dragging him along behind her.

"It is too big of a risk. If someone is following us and we try to run away, I will never see the light of day again. We need to wait, give the count some time to let his guard down."

The boy stopped suddenly, and with the short leash of the restraints, Viola was jerked to an undignified stop herself. "Do you trust me?" he said quietly.

She thought for a minute before answering. "Of course I do. You are the only friend I have."

"Then believe me when I say this is our best chance. We will be able to move faster without the restraints, and as long as we keep moving, everything will be fine. Are you with me?" His eyes challenged hers, and she finally nodded her acceptance. He unlocked the manacles, and Viola rubbed her wrist where it was sore. After taking a quick glance around, the boy motioned ahead.

"We have to keep moving," he said decisively, but before they could go, there was the unmistakable sound of a twig snapping. The boy grabbed Viola's arm and yanked her down behind a massive tree trunk. They both held their breath and waited to see what would happen. After what seemed like an eternity, when there was no further movement, the boy whispered, "It must have been a deer or something."

"It sounded bigger than a deer."

"Since when are you the expert in forest noises?" The sudden crackling of leaves underfoot was deafening in the woodland quiet.

"There it is again," Viola hissed.

"Be quiet! Do you want them to find us?"

"Oh, so now it is a 'them'? We cannot just sit here and wait for them to search us out! We need to move."

"If you move, they will get you for sure. Our only hope is to be as quiet as we can and pray they pass us by."

"I cannot just sit and hope for the best—I have to do something!"

"Sssh, I think I hear voices." The boy cocked his head, straining to translate the muted sounds into words. There were two voices, and they appeared to be arguing. The closer the men got to where Viola and the boy were hiding, the more words they were able to decipher.

"If they went this way, we would 'ave seen them by now. I ain't seen nothing the last ten minutes but trees, and they all look the same," one man said glumly. "I think we should circle back the way we came, since we obviously lost 'em."

"You better hope we ain't lost 'em. The count ain't very forgiving when people make mistakes, and he was very clear about bringing the girl back alive." He grinned. "He wanted the boy back too, but he weren't so particular about the condition he was in."

The boy gulped loudly, trying to swallow the tickle that suddenly materialized in his throat.

"We're wasting too much time. We 'ave to circle back before they get too far away. Come on."

Viola sighed. The men were going in another direction, and they just might get out of this alive. The boy looked down to see several red ants crawling on his leg, and he quickly brushed them off. The men froze at the sound.

"Did you 'ear that? I think it come from over there," he said, pointing toward the tree.

"It is over, they have us. We are going to have to run for it!" Viola said desperately.

"Viola, wait!" the boy hissed frantically, but it was too late. Viola shot out from behind the tree, taking off into a dead run. The boy had no choice but to follow her.

"There they are! You grab the girl, and I'll go after the boy. We can't afford to lose 'em again!" The men dashed after them, cursing as their feet pounded against the hard ground.

Viola sprinted as quickly as she could, but the forest was an obstacle course of downed trees and awkward rocks, slowing her escape significantly. She glanced over her shoulder whenever she dared, feeling comforted to see the boy close behind her. It wasn't long before she was out of breath, and she found it hard to keep moving, but she knew there was no other alternative. She ran even when the searing pain in her side made her want to double over in pain, even when her vision started to get blurry from lack of oxygen and she was afraid she might pass out. She ran until she had no strength left, and she knew that if she kept going, her lungs would explode.

When Viola hurled herself down into a small embankment, she finally collapsed. She lay on her back like a fish flopping around on the sand, feeling that every breath would surely be her last. She knew that her desperate gasping for air would make her easy to track, but she couldn't control it. She fully expected the boy to jump down beside her at any moment, and when he tried to drag her to her feet, she was prepared to tell him to leave her behind.

But he didn't come.

After awhile, she rolled onto her stomach and peeked through the weeds, but she couldn't see anyone. The idea that she'd somehow managed to lose her pursuers was an excellent prospect, but where was the boy? The last time she had looked back, he was only a few feet behind her. She heard it from their own lips—she was the one they really wanted. So why would they take him and leave her behind?

Viola lay on the ground until it began to get dark, her muscles sore from her flight. She had come to two startling conclusions. First, that the boy must have been captured, and second, that she had no intention of trying to rescue him.

. . . ✶ . . .

It was getting dark, and Viola could feel the damp starting to seep into her dress. If she wanted to find a dry place to spend the night, she would have to move fast. She brushed herself off and started to scout out her surroundings. There was a tree that looked like it would be easy to climb, and being in the air would keep her safe from whatever was lurking on the ground, looking for an easy meal. But she was exhausted and didn't think sleeping in a tree sounded comfortable or safe. It wouldn't do her any good to escape the prowling animals if she fell out of the tree and broke her neck.

The next spot she stumbled onto was a small cave. It looked dry, and it would keep her out of the wind. But she reasoned that if it looked warm and cozy to her, she probably wasn't the first person—or beast—to think so. The idea of being awakened by the growling of an angry animal made her move on. After all, you can't reason with a wild animal, and they don't appreciate intruders.

At the rate that the trees were being swallowed up by the

darkness around her, Viola knew that she was running out of time. She found a large tree with a generous dusting of fallen leaves under it, and she pushed them into a makeshift bed. Lying on top of the leaf bed, she snuggled down until she was partially covered by the leaves, hoping they would provide some warmth and protection from the elements. Every time she shifted to find a more comfortable position, the leaves made a crunching noise that was deafening in the darkness. Viola prayed that there was nothing hungry in the vicinity, because the sound of the leaves would lead it right to her.

As tired as she was, the utter blackness of the forest and the occasional howling of animals made it impossible to sleep. She might as well have climbed the tree; at least she would have been safe there. She focused on keeping as still as she could, her eyes wide open in the dark night. Viola found herself wishing that the boy were there with her. No matter how frightening the forest was, she knew that he would make her feel better about it. But instead, she was there alone, and she couldn't help worrying that he might have landed in an even worse situation than she had.

Viola tried to blot out the image of the boy being brought before the count. What punishment would he inflict on the person who lost his prized songbird? She shook her head, refusing to feel guilty for what happened. After all, didn't she tell the boy that running was a mistake? Didn't she try to convince him to wait for another opportunity? Whatever trouble he was in now, it was not her fault.

She squeezed her eyes shut, hoping for the oblivion of sleep to come quickly and allow her a few hours of peace. But it was a long time before her wish was granted.

. . . ✶ . . .

Viola walked through the forest. The sky above her was overcast and gloomy. The trees were bare, their naked branches heavy with ripe black birds. She didn't know exactly where she was going, but there was a low humming noise that she found familiar and comforting, and she was following it. She strolled at an easy pace, the humming getting stronger and easier to detect. She had no idea how long she'd been tracking it, or how much time had passed before she found a door in her path. It did not seem strange to her to see a free-standing door in the woods. She only knew that she was drawn to whatever was behind it. She stepped closer until she was directly in front of it, putting her hand tentatively on the knob. The vibration was now something she could feel more than hear, coming from the ground into the soles of her feet and filling her whole body. She only hesitated a moment before turning the knob and pushing the door open.

On the other side of the door, it was winter. The world was covered in glorious fluffy snow lying undisturbed on the ground. Every branch of every tree was delicately iced with powder. She stepped through the door, her feet leaving prints as she entered her new wintry environment. She could see her breath in the air, but there was no chill to accompany it. The sun was huge in the sky, and she could feel the warmth on her shoulders. The humming sound seemed to have a life of its own here, and she continued to follow it into a clearing, where she discovered a slender woman with wings.

The woman was completely covered in butterflies below the neck, so many perched on her that Viola could not tell what color her dress was, or if she was wearing one at all. Her face had a familiarity that she could not trace, but Viola was certain they had met before and felt at ease enough to approach her. The woman had a serene smile, and she extended her butterfly-covered arm, beckoning Viola to approach.

"Am I dead?" Viola finally squeaked timidly.

"No, you are only dreaming," the woman said evenly. The tone of her voice was soft, like falling snow.

"Are you dead?"

"I am a messenger. I have a message for you, Viola."

"How do you know my name?"

"I know a great deal about you, but there is little time to explain."

Viola could finally see that the humming noise was coming from the butterflies. Their wings opened and closed rapidly, and now that she was in closer proximity, she could separate the vibrations into individual high-pitched chirping that sounded like communication.

"Yes, they are talking to each other," the woman said, reading her thoughts.

"I do not speak butterfly. What are they saying?"

"They say that they have been anxious to meet the girl with the beautiful voice, and that they would very much have liked to sing with you, if there were time."

"You said you have a message for me?"

"Yes."

"Is it about my parents? Are they all right?"

"It is not about your parents. That is another story. I am here to tell you about the boy."

Viola's cheeks colored. "What about the boy?"

"He is in great danger, and you are the only one who can help him."

"Me? What can I do? I am only little."

"You are small in size, but you have great power."

"I cannot compete with the count."

"You have two very powerful weapons that the count could not hope to match."

"I have no weapons. The count has an entire wall of swords—did you know that?"

"Your weapon is more powerful still. Do you know what it is?"

Viola shook her head silently.

"Your goodness."

"My goodness will not help me free the boy. Goodness is not a weapon," she argued.

"But your goodness takes an unusual form. You have more strength than you imagine, and it is manifested in your greatest treasure—your voice."

Viola unconsciously touched her throat. "The count wanted me for my singing. My voice has been my curse."

"Your voice is capable of defeating the count and rescuing the boy."

"How can that be?"

"By using your power against him. It will not be easy, but it is possible. You must have complete faith in yourself—there can be no shred of doubt in your heart. You must put all of your energy and strength and goodness into one piercing note, and you will be victorious. The count will be unable to stand in your presence."

"Are you saying I can defeat the count . . . by singing?" she asked incredulously.

The woman smiled, but there was sadness in her eyes. "Yes. But such a victory does not come without a price."

"I have nothing to give you."

"The cost, I am afraid, will be the thing you value most. With your efforts, your voice will be shattered. You will never be able to speak above a whisper, and you will certainly never sing again."

The woods draped in white were completely silent, except for the chattering of the butterflies, which was more animated than ever. Their wings fluttered more rapidly now, blues, pinks, greens, and yellows all bleeding together. Viola stared at the woman, agonizing over the impossible choice she had delivered. All she ever wanted was to sing, and this twist of fate struck her as unbelievably cruel. She raised her eyes to meet the woman's, and although hers were filled with encouragement, Viola felt nothing except cold. The place inside where she felt pleasantly warm before had now been replaced by a chilly emptiness.

"I cannot do what you ask. It is too much," she said finally, her voice flat.

"Could you expect to accomplish something so great without sacrifice?" the woman asked gently.

"I cannot," she repeated.

"You can. But the choice is yours. I want you to remember what I said—there is no room for doubt or fear, or you will surely fail, and you will only have one chance. If you do not succeed on your first attempt, your voice will already be too damaged to try again."

Tears rolled down Viola's cheeks, falling unnoticed into the snow.

"Each of us has one story worth telling, one moment of glory and triumph or grief and despair; something that defines us. Your moment has come, Viola, and the outcome is entirely in your hands. Good luck on your journey, wherever it takes you."

Viola woke with a start. Her face was warm from the sun, an impossibly wonderful sensation after her long confinement in the cage. She squinted through the bright rays, trying to decide what time it was. Judging from the heat of the sunshine, it must be at least midday. But maybe the sunlight just felt warmer to her because she'd been deprived of it for so long. She'd forgotten how delicious it was to sit in the sun and get toasty.

Her stomach growled, reminding her that it was way past breakfast time. She rolled over and was rewarded with a shooting pain in her back and a mouthful of leaves. She spat out the leaves and rubbed the sore spot, wincing. She was famished, but definitely not desperate enough to eat dried leaves. For the first time, she wondered what she could find to eat until she reached her home. Maybe she could find some berries or mushrooms, but she had no idea which ones were safe to eat.

She noticed two pale pink butterflies hovering in the air above her, chasing each other upward in a spiral, climbing ever higher. Suddenly her dream came back all at once, like lightning: the door, the snow, the butterfly woman and her strange ultimatum. Despite the comforting rays of the sun, Viola shivered. As crazy as it all seemed in the light of day, she thought back uneasily to the day she'd screamed at the boy to leave, and the sudden appearance of the ice on the bars of her cage. The idea that her voice was the key to destroying the count seemed ridiculous, but she knew now what she had to do. She only hoped she wasn't too late.

Megan could only stare, her mouth open in shock. For the first time since her mother-in-law began spinning her perilous tale, she thought that she might grasp the ending, and it was not at all what she expected.

"Close your mouth, dear. You'll catch flies," Viola advised.

"You did it, didn't you?" Megan said finally, her voice filled with amazement.

"You saved the boy. That's why your voice is so weird!" Kaitlin said triumphantly.

"You're both getting ahead of the story. I'll tell you the rest tomorrow because it's way past your bedtime, Katie."

"But . . ." she protested.

"No buts. It is past midnight, and therefore you are no longer the birthday girl. The sooner you go to sleep, the sooner it will be tomorrow."

Despite her protests, Kaitlin was asleep almost the minute her head hit the pillow.

Megan quietly unzipped her laptop from its case and took a seat on the floor against the wall. She knew that the odds were against her, but she hoped that Kevin would be online because she really needed to talk to him. She waited while the computer booted up, glancing in Kaitlin's direction occasionally. When it was ready, she opened the Instant Messenger and typed a short message to her husband.

`M: Honey, it's me. Are you there?`

She clicked "Send," and sat back to wait. She leaned against the wall, closing her eyes briefly. Behind her closed lids, she could see Viola as a little girl, walking on the beach as she sang. What an awful burden she'd lived with, and what a terrible choice to have to make. And she had made her choice—Megan was sure about that. If she had any doubt about Viola's story before, she was positive now. Her voice, or lack of it, was the last piece of the puzzle. It made her unbelievable story . . . believable.

Megan opened her eyes, but found no reply. "Come on, Kev, where are you?" she muttered under her breath. She typed an additional message, sending it across the thousands of miles between them.

M: Please be there.

Her thoughts raced through her mind like fireflies, trapped in a glass jar on a muggy summer evening. A message popped up on her screen.

K: Megan, is everything all right?

She let out a huge sigh of relief.

M: I can't believe I caught you! Everything is fine—I just have something really important I needed to tell you. What are you doing?

K: Eating lunch and checking my email. What are you doing up so late?

M: Your mother has been telling us more of the story. I know you're going to think I'm crazy, but she has to be telling the truth.

K: What did she tell you this time?

Megan hesitated a minute. She'd been in such a hurry to find her husband that she hadn't considered what she would say when she found him.

M: You know how I told you your mother said she was kidnapped by an evil count and kept in a cage?

K: How could I forget?

M: Well, there was a servant boy who lived in the castle. He brought her meals, and he was nice to her. She decided to call him Will, because he couldn't remember his real name. She and Will managed to escape, but they were followed and had to make a run for it. She got away, but they caught him. She was so glad to finally be free that she decided not to try to rescue him. She didn't want to risk getting recaptured.

K: My mother had a brother named Will. He died in an accident a long time ago.

M: That's odd. They weren't related. It must be a coincidence.

Megan frowned.

K: Maybe she's just confused, and she's incorporated people she knew into one big adventure. Is that the end of the story?

M: No. She fell asleep in the woods that night and had a dream. She went through a door and found a woman who told her how to use her voice . . . as a weapon.

K: A weapon???

M: She said Viola had the power to defeat the count by singing, but there was a price. Her voice would be ruined, and she would never sing again. I wish you could have heard her. I think the decision broke her heart.

K: Honey, you don't really think this all happened, do you?

M: It must have! Don't you see? That's why her voice is so soft; she used it all up trying to save the boy! I always thought it was scratchy because she used to be a smoker or something, but this makes sense.

K: Listen to yourself. This does NOT make sense. There is a perfectly reasonable explanation for her voice, and it has nothing to do with this fairy tale she's invented.

Megan was starting to get a little bit irritated with Kevin for dismissing her explanation so quickly. She typed her answer one letter at a time a bit more roughly than was necessary, the keys loud in the darkness.

M: Well? What's your explanation then?

K: When my mother was a young woman, they found a tumor in her throat. She had it removed and it was benign, but her vocal cords were nicked during the surgery. Although she made a full recovery, I'm told her voice was never the same.

Megan considered this new information, delaying her response.

K: You're disappointed, aren't you? You *wanted* it to be true!

M: How do you know that mine isn't the true version and yours is the made-up one?

K: Think about it—which story is more logical?

M: But you weren't here. You didn't hear her. She's so sure about it.

K: I believe you. She might even think she's telling you the truth, but you know what the doctor said. She's in the first stages of Alzheimer's, and everything is jumbled up in her mind.

M: He said it *might* be Alzheimer's.

K: I know this isn't what you want to hear, but this story she's been telling you just isn't possible.

Megan knew she wasn't going to convince him, and he hadn't even heard the more questionable parts of the story yet. She understood now what Viola said at the beginning, and why she'd never told Kevin the truth in the first place. When it came to fairies, sons didn't really come into it. She decided to just change the subject.

M: How are you doing? We haven't had a chance to talk about anything but your mother in ages.

K: I'm doing okay. I miss my girls a lot, but I'm all right. Now that it's almost over, are you glad you went on the trip, even though I couldn't go with you?

M: Yes. I'm really happy that Kaitlin and I had a chance to get to know your mother better.

K: Good. I'm afraid lunch is over, and I'd better go. You'll have to let me know how the story ends.

M: I thought you already knew the end. ☺

K: You know what I mean. This is ten times better than any bedtime story she ever told me. Give her and Kaitlin my love.

M: I will. I love you, sweetie.

K: Love you too.

Megan shut down the computer and quickly changed into her pajamas. She slid into bed and curled up next to Kaitlin, still thinking about Viola's tale, and Kevin's very different version of events. Megan loved her husband more than she could say, but she knew that in this case he was wrong. Even though she was pretty sure she knew the ending, she was still considering different scenarios when she finally drifted off to sleep.

⋆ FOURTEEN ⋆

"Are you going to tell us the rest of the story?" Kaitlin asked. She was alternating between taking bites of a warm brownie and a slice of buttered cinnamon toast. "You're running out of time, you know. Our plane leaves first thing in the morning."

"I think that's a good idea," Megan said quickly.

"I can't believe it's been two weeks already. I'm going to miss you both so much when you go home tomorrow. The house will be so quiet," Viola whispered, stirring a spoonful of brown sugar into her oatmeal.

Megan grinned. "You'll probably be glad to have some peace for a change; a little time to yourself."

"No, I'm afraid after all this company, I might feel a little lonely once you've gone."

Kaitlin brightened. "I have an awesome idea! Why don't you come and live with us?"

"That's very sweet, Katie, but I'm sure I'll be fine. Living alone just takes some practice. I used to talk to myself a lot, but eventually I stopped. I guess I just ran out of things to say."

"What did you talk about?" Kaitlin asked.

"Oh, all sorts of things: the weather, books I'd read, things I had to do that day. It was something to pass the time."

"That sounds awful."

"It wasn't bad. I always found myself to be fairly good company."

"Couldn't you find another friend to play cards with, like Fern?"

"I'll never find another person who makes peanut brittle like she did. No, I'll be just fine on my own. Don't you worry about me."

Kaitlin shrugged. "Well, the offer is open, if you ever decide you'd like to live with us." She glanced at her mother, who had a thoroughly amused expression on her face.

"You said that as nonchalantly as if you were inviting Grandma to dinner instead of asking her to stay forever."

Kaitlin blushed. "I guess I should have asked you first."

"She's right, you know. You're always welcome to come and live with us, if you ever wanted to," Megan said seriously.

Viola placed her age-spotted hand over Megan's younger one. "I appreciate that, dear, but I've still got some life in me yet. I'm perfectly capable of taking care of myself."

"It's not about that. It's about having your family around you."

"You mean, in my twilight years?" Viola asked, her eyes sparkling and lively.

"I mean there's nothing wrong with letting someone help you. Kaitlin and I would be happy to have you, and we'd let you cook any time you wanted."

Kaitlin nodded her approval.

"I really am flattered by your kind offer, but I don't want to leave my little house. Besides, it will give you an excuse to take another vacation soon to visit."

"But you will keep it in mind?" Megan pressed.

"I will. So . . . I guess it's time for the end of the story," Viola said abruptly.

Megan perked up perceptibly. "Are we getting close?"

"I should hope so, since you're going home tomorrow. I would drag it out a little longer, if I thought it would persuade you to stay."

"I wish we could. But if I don't get back to work, they might decide they could do without me, and Kaitlin will be starting school again before long."

Kaitlin groaned.

"I know; you have your own lives. Well, you have a plane to catch, and we don't have any time to waste."

THE END

"I did warn you about trusting her." The words stood out against the stark silence in the count's study, the only other sounds coming from the cheerfully crackling fire. The flames created a friendly glow in the darkness as they made flickering patterns on the walls, but they did nothing to warm the spirits of the boy. He stood in the middle of the room, and the count hovered near the fire, the shadows making his features look more threatening than usual. "You should have taken me more seriously when I told you how dangerous she was. You put yourself on the line for her, and where is she now? She left you behind to take the fall at the first opportunity, just as I said she would. Still, I suppose there are some lessons in life that we insist on learning the hard way."

The boy said nothing, staring stubbornly ahead at eye-level.

"There is no use pretending any longer. My men in the forest heard you speaking to my little songbird. I always suspected that you were hiding something from me, and I must commend you for your deception. Hiding the fact that you could speak for years on end was a remarkable feat. In fact, I think that I might be able to use you. You have proven that you have definite potential, and I am convinced that if you put yourself into my hands, there is a great deal I could teach you. If you play your cards right, you might even be the next Count Diavolo when I am gone," he said innocuously.

The boy finally turned his eyes in the count's direction. "There is nothing you could teach me that I would be interested in learning," he said, deliberately enunciating each word.

He shook his head in disappointment. "Insolent boy. I offer you the world, and you spit on it and throw it back at me! You would do well to think carefully before you choose sides. The girl to whom you show such loyalty did not afford you the same courtesy. When she is back in her cage, you might regret your hasty alliance."

"You have her?" he said anxiously.

The count smiled, enjoying watching the boy squirm. "Not

yet. But it is only a matter of time."

The boy relaxed a little, returning his smile. "If you do not have her by now, then she is long gone. She is free and probably halfway home, where she will tell everyone what a monster you are. By this time tomorrow, *you* could be the one behind bars."

"I think not. Viola is like you, young and impetuous. She is not smart enough to go home and fetch the police to deal with me. She will come back here . . ."

"She would never come back here," the boy said, his voice steely and adamant.

The count ignored the interruption. "She will come back here . . . for you."

"She has been alone in a cage for over two years, and you really think she would risk her newfound liberty just to come back here and fetch me? I am nothing to her."

"Do not lie to me. I know you are friends. I saw the two of you dancing, the night of the gala." The count began pacing thoughtfully around the room. "Human nature is so fascinating, don't you think? For reasons that are unclear to me, she sees something in you worth risking everything for, and since you helped her to escape, I can only imagine that you feel the same. You, who have no special gifts that would endear you to her, and yet she favors you and insists on treating me with nothing but disdain. She is still a child, but one day, she will be the most famous voice on stage. She will have the finest wardrobe and the best of everything—I will see to that. And one day, she will thank me for it. What can you give her?"

"I already gave it to her. When she grows up, she will become whatever she wants, and she will make her own decisions. There will be no bars to confine her, and she will fly to the highest clouds in the sky for the sheer joy of feeling the wind on her face. I gave her that," he said, grinning defiantly.

The count slapped the boy hard across the face, but even that couldn't wipe away his triumphant smirk. "If only we could go back and change the ridiculous things we did and said when we were young; all our black and white notions of right and wrong. Tolstoy once said that if we could be vaccinated against love in our youth, we would be much better off. But we all have the opportunity to make our mistakes, and you are no exception. Viola would never just leave you here—she would be too tormented by the idea of you suffering the consequences of her escape. When she returns, you will both be back where you started, and you will see that all your loyalty and bravery were for nothing."

Despite his previous efforts at bravado, the boy could not hide the worry that now stole across his face like a dense fog.

"Now, I am certain that you have a lot to think about. Viceroy, would you escort the boy back to the dungeon, where he can wait for his friend to return?"

"With pleasure, Excellency."

The count poured himself a glass of Scotch and lit some candles. He pulled his armchair around until he could see the door. He knew that very soon now, Viola would come through it with some half-baked scheme to rescue the boy and save the day. He thought how amusing it would be to see her back in her cage where she belonged. He swirled the drink in the glass, smiling as he settled into his chair to wait.

Viola had no idea which direction the castle was in, but she decided to trust her instincts and go in the direction that the two pale pink butterflies were headed. They never got too far ahead of her, but occasionally she would lose them as they flittered off on their butterfly adventures. She would stop and sit to rest until her guides rejoined her, and they set off again together. She followed them through one day and night. When the sun began to rise, the sky was the same pinkish hue as the butterflies and they vanished, evaporating into the larger canvas.

In the woods just ahead of her, Viola recognized the embankment where she had hidden when she was too exhausted to run anymore. She knew she was getting very close now to the edge of the forest and that just beyond that was the Castle Diavolo, and her destiny. She couldn't deny she was terrified of meeting the count again. The woman in her dream had cautioned her that she could not be successful if she had any doubts, and no matter how many times she practiced summoning her courage, she was disappointed to find that her heart was still filled with fear.

She walked until she came to the clearing where the castle became visible. Viola closed her eyes, pushing away the feelings of dread that crowded her chest and focused on picturing the forthcoming battle with the count in her head. Her heartbeat quickened, and she imagined gathering all her strength into one mighty howl. The woman hadn't been very clear on what would happen then, and Viola's feelings of inadequacy began to prey on her, picking at her defenses like hungry birds. What if nothing happened? What if she opened her mouth and only a tiny squeak came out? What if she was too late and the count had already dealt with Will?

Viola forced the horrible questions from her mind. She stepped out of the woods and began the last leg of her journey toward the castle. She knew one thing for sure, and that was that if she spent too much time thinking about everything that could go wrong, she would lose her nerve and run away. Maybe this was just one of those things in life for which there was no preparing, and since she only had one chance before her voice was too weakened, practicing was not an option. No, the only way to discover if it was really going to work was to try it, and aside from her sadness at the thought of her voice being permanently damaged, there was no reason to put it off any longer.

There was no one in sight as she neared the castle. She decided that the best way to enter was through the servants' entrance in the back, where there was less chance of being caught. She slipped through the door unnoticed and crept noiselessly through the halls, looking for something that seemed familiar. She was going to go directly to the count's study; Will said he spent most of his time there. She would deal with him first before trying to locate Will. Still, she'd only been in the study a few times, and the castle was massive.

Viola heard voices and ducked into a darkened room, waiting for them to pass by. The narrow crack of light coming through the partially opened door didn't provide much clarity, but from what she could see, the room appeared to be full of painted masks: splashes of color with haunting scowls and gaping sockets where the eyes should be. Each was more frightening than the last, and she didn't waste any time getting out of there as soon as the conversation and footsteps disappeared into the distance.

After wandering down what seemed like several miles of corridors, she turned a corner and saw a room where the door was open, an eerie, flickering glow spilling out into the hall. She swallowed hard. She recognized it as the heavy wooden door that led to the study. She tiptoed toward it, peeking around the edge of the door. She jumped back quickly, for the count himself sat in his armchair, facing the door. She knew that he'd seen her because she had glimpsed the white of his eyes, shining in the blackness like a clever cat. She forced herself to breathe quietly, waiting to see what his next move would be.

"Look who has flown back to her nest," his voice boomed, lingering in the hall like an invitation.

This was it—the moment of truth. She could run or she could face him, but whatever path she chose, there was no turning back. She took a deep breath, and forced her feet to carry her into the room. "You mean my cage," she retorted.

He opened his palms toward her in a conciliatory gesture. "I guess it is all in your point of view. Were you out of your element in the outside world with all its dangers? Maybe you need my protection after all."

"I told you before; I can take care of myself."

"Your actions speak louder than your words, my dear. I have heard stories before of animals that escape from zoos, only to return to their cages. They say it is because after their captivity, the animal cannot survive in the wild. They know no other life. But I suspect that it has more to do with the fact that secretly, deep down, they enjoy being kept."

Viola felt the anger flare inside her. This was good: the more he goaded her, the more she wanted to strike out, and she knew that she would need every bit of daring she could summon to do what needed to be done. "I did not come back because I was afraid of the forest, and I am certainly not here because I missed the accommodations."

"Then why did you return? Could it be you found your sainted parents and discovered that they were happier without you?" His eyes glittered with barely concealed enjoyment, and she hated him for the twist of pain the words caused in her gut. She felt herself hovering on the edge of losing control, but there were still some things she wanted to say, and she needed a little more time to collect her rage before directing it at the count.

"I came back because of Will."

"I assume you mean the boy. And you have given him a name? How very quaint."

Viola said nothing, her eyes narrowing into angry slits.

The count laughed heartily. "You cannot be serious. After you managed to elude my men in the woods, you were willing to throw it all away for a servant? A nobody? I am curious—what is it about him that makes you take leave of your common sense?"

"He is everything you could never be. He is good and courageous and selfless."

"He is worthless. I dropped him in the moat as punishment for setting you free. The fish are very hungry, especially since there are no swans left to devour. I have been considering the same fate for you, but it is not too late for you to change my mind."

Viola's frame shook, her grief and guilt and fury building until she could no longer separate them. When she closed her eyes, she saw fireworks exploding; feeling the hot spray of sparks desperately seeking an outlet. She forced herself to stay in the moment, but her own voice was unfamiliar in her ears. "What makes you think I would allow you to dispose of me so easily? Did you think I came here to face you without a plan?"

"Well, it seems I may have underestimated you," he said sarcastically. "Go on, little songbird; do your worst." He folded his arms across his chest and waited.

For just a minute, Viola wavered. She was assaulted by images from the night of the gala, singing on the count's stage and the pure, boundless joy she'd known and would never know again. But Will's life was worth more than her voice, and she was determined that even if she was too late to save him, his death would have meaning. She knew now that she could never live with herself if she didn't at least try.

She drew in a large breath, filling her chest with as much air as it would hold. She threw her head back and sang one clear note, forcing away her anxiety and doubt, and she felt the vibration from the shrill power pass through her. She put every spark of love she had into her song, feeding it with thoughts of her happiest moments, and she felt it grow stronger and more focused.

The count clutched uselessly at his throat, his face turning from bright red to an unnatural shade of blue as he struggled for air. It seemed that Viola was somehow siphoning all the oxygen from the room, using it to support her unwavering note, and he knew exactly when she ran out of useable air because he felt the burning pain as she took it directly from his own lungs. He gasped, staggering toward her as he flailed his arms.

If the situation weren't so dire, Viola might have laughed; the mighty Count Diavolo was trying to swat her like one of his butterflies. The count dropped to the floor, writhing and scratching the ground. He pointed wildly at Viola, and she could barely glimpse something wholly unexpected in her reflection in the windows—a set of glorious, shimmering wings. The look of terror on his face was unimaginable and he went limp and still, just seconds before Viola felt her voice being torn from her throat. Her breath came in short gasps, and she tentatively touched her throat with her fingertips. She half expected it to be raw and bloody, as if a sharp claw had physically torn her vocal chords from the skin. She watched as her iridescent wings slowly dissolved into the air, becoming less and less visible until they disappeared completely.

The count was still lying motionless on the carpet, and Viola was having a difficult time convincing herself to go near enough to check if he was breathing. She could see the glint of metal around his neck, the key to the dungeon, and she knew she would have to take it from him. She eased toward him until she was near enough to grab it, and she yanked it free with one quick tug. Edging against the wall toward the door, she fled into the hall, where she nearly tripped over a woman lying on the cold stone floor.

Viola was horrified. She hadn't considered the possibility that other people besides the count might be affected. She crouched down close to the woman, placing her fingers carefully against her neck, searching for a pulse. She was incredibly relieved to discover that it was strong; the woman was only unconscious. She forced herself to her feet. The count had lied to her before, and she could only hope that he'd fabricated the story about Will as well. She had to believe that he was still alive, to stick with the plan and focus on finding him and escaping.

As she ran through the halls, people littered the floor where they fell, as if a sleeping spell had been cast on all the occupants of the castle. Viola ran down the steps that led to the dungeon, thinking that was the most likely place for the count to keep Will. She turned the key in the lock, praying that he would be on the other side of the door. Her heart sank when she saw that the cage was empty.

Then she saw Will lying on the ground facing a wall. Viola crossed the room to where he was, dropping to her knees and tentatively rolling him over so that she could see his face. It was bruised, but he appeared otherwise unharmed. She shook him violently until he finally opened his eyes. She was overjoyed and tried to say his name, but when she spoke, nothing happened. Not only was there no sound, but she could not even imagine now how she ever formed words, much less sang.

Will focused his eyes on Viola, and for a moment they were blank. She wished that she'd asked the woman more about the damage her voice was capable of. Could it be she'd wiped his memory clean?

"Viola?" he said finally.

She smiled, pulling him into a tight hug before sinking back against the wall. Whatever the consequences of her actions might be, she had two things to be thankful for: her friend was alive, and he knew who she was.

"How did you get in here? Why did you come back?"

She shook her head, taking his hand and tugging it in the direction of the door.

He sat up straight. "What is the matter? Why will you not answer me?"

She stood abruptly, still pulling his arm toward the exit. When Will attempted to stand, his legs were too wobbly to support his weight. Viola put his arm around her shoulder and helped him to the door. They moved slowly down the hall as she half-dragged him next to her. He was quiet now, and he seemed to have given up asking why she wasn't speaking. As they staggered toward the front door, they stepped gingerly over the sleeping heaps on the floor.

At the door, Viola had an idea. She leaned Will against the wall for support, racing back down the hall to the study. She carefully eased her father's swordfish from over the mantle, lugging it back to where Will was waiting, half asleep against the wall. She maneuvered him and the fish through the door and into the cool, brisk early spring air, steering them away from the castle. She stopped when they reached the moat where she deposited the stuffed fish, watching as it wriggled in the tall weeds until it disappeared in the murky water. It wasn't long before a wide spray of mist burst from the water as her father's fish wrestled with one of the count's. She occasionally caught a hint of silver arcing out of the depths.

As much as she wanted to see the outcome, she didn't dare wait around to watch the battle. Will seemed a little more alert now, and she grabbed his hand, pulling him toward the forest. As they hurried along, she noticed shoots of grass sprouting under their feet at an alarming rate. She stopped briefly, turning around for one last look at the castle. The trees were bursting into bloom, their collage of wild colors erupting across the sky, announcing their liberation from the count's tyranny. Viola and Will turned away from the display. With their backs to the castle, they disappeared into the woods without looking back.

. . . ✶ . . .

Viola and Will hid in the tall grass surrounding her parents' home. She chewed nervously on her fingernails, watching the house for any signs of inhabitants.

Will leaned closer. "What are we waiting for?" he whispered loudly.

"I am not ready yet," Viola rasped, her voice almost inaudible against the hissing of the weeds, brushing together in the breeze.

"Oh, come on. After all this time, I am surprised you did not run all the way. We have been sitting out here for hours now; what are you waiting for?"

She glanced at Will uneasily before her eyes resumed their careful study of the ground. She hesitated. "What if they do not remember me?"

"You are their *child*. Of course they will remember you."

"But I do not look the same. And my voice . . ." she trailed off.

"Listen to me. Your parents are in for a shock, and it might seem a little strange for a while. But believe me when I say that they could be nothing but overjoyed to see you again."

"Are you sure?"

"Positive."

"All right. I guess I am ready."

"Good, because I was beginning to worry that we might have to spend the night in the weeds."

She giggled, but it sounded more like the soft rushing of the grass. Taking his hand, she led him toward the house and knocked on the door.

"Come in," a voice called, floating through an open window.

Viola took a deep breath before she turned the doorknob and stepped inside.

Claire sat on the couch in the small living room, deftly working at a patch of delicate lace, but her eyes were blank. At the sound of the door she stood, placing the dress carefully on the cushion next to her. Her eyes looked past them, but her smile was friendly.

"Who is it, please?"

Viola tried to speak, but a sob caught in her throat. She finally managed to croak out one word.

"Mum?"

The color drained from Claire's face. In the darkness that constantly surrounded her, she could see the glow of the fairy thread. Her darling child, alive, and wearing the dress she created for the count. She held one outstretched hand to the daughter she couldn't see. Viola ran into her arms, hugging her mother tightly as they soaked each other with showers of tears. Will turned to go, feeling that he was intruding on a private scene, but Viola beckoned for him to join them. She took his hand and placed it in her mother's before introducing them.

"Mum, this is Will," she whispered. "He is going to live with us now."

"Did Will ever find his mom and dad?" Kaitlin asked.

Viola leaned back against the chair, exhausted but pleased that they'd finally reached the end of their journey together. "The count told a lot of lies in his time, but there were two things he told the truth about: my mother was indeed blind, and if Will's parents were still alive somewhere, we never found them."

"So Will came to live with you?"

"My mother was so grateful for all he had done that she took him in and raised him as my brother."

"I would love to meet him someday," Megan said.

"Will died a long time ago, dear."

Kaitlin was confused. "I thought you said he was here the other night?"

"Well, he still stops by to visit on occasion," she said, as if this were completely normal behavior.

"How did he die?" Kaitlin asked.

"When he got older, he learned to fly an airplane. He loved it so much. He felt about flying the way I did about singing. But one day he didn't come back. They searched the mountains until they found the wreckage, but they never found Will. Usually he visits on our birthday."

"You had the same birthday?"

"It was a little joke we had. Will's birthday was another of the things that was lost, along with his real name. So I told him that he could share mine. We always celebrated together—I think that's why he picks that day to visit."

"I wish I could have known him." Megan's eyes burned, shining with unshed tears.

"You do, just like you know me and my mother and grandmother. And as long as you remember them, when I am gone, they will live on in you."

"Thank you, Viola, for sharing your life with us."

"Yeah, Grandma, it was a really good story," Kaitlin added.

"It was my pleasure. Maybe we should go sit by the pool and let Katie swim for a while."

Megan rose from her chair, unable to stop a small chuckle from escaping.

"Why are you laughing, dear?"

"You really did have wings after all. Kaitlin was so convinced that you did, and I didn't believe her."

Viola squeezed Kaitlin's shoulder with her bony fingers. "My wings are on the inside, just like hers."

* Fifteen *

"Are you sure you have everything?" Viola asked for the fourteenth time.

"Yes, I think it's all here," Megan said, absently patting the suitcase on the ground next to her. They were having breakfast in the airport while they waited for their plane. She picked at a small plastic bowl of sliced melon and berries, pushing them around but not really eating much.

"This bagel is dry," Kaitlin commented.

"Have some more cream cheese, dear," Viola said, pushing it across the table.

"That's not it. It's just that, after brownies for breakfast, everything else seems boring."

"I was thinking exactly the same thing!" Megan said, laughing.

Viola beamed. "Actually, I brought you a little bag with some treats for the plane, and there just happens to be some brownies in there."

"Well, let's break them out. No harm in one last brownie breakfast."

Viola distributed the brownies, and they munched them in relative silence.

"I think that when Kevin gets home, we should plan another trip," Megan said, wiping the chocolate from the corner of Kaitlin's mouth.

"Well, you girls just let me know when you're coming, and I'll be sure to have the pool ready."

Kaitlin smiled mischievously. "We'll have to make sure to remind Dad to bring his suit. I can't wait to go swimming with him!"

A voice announced on the overhead speaker the final boarding call for their flight. They gathered up their bags and walked the short distance to the gate. Viola hugged her granddaughter tightly.

"Good bye, Katie. You work hard in school and do what your mother tells you, okay?"

"I will. And I'll take really good care of the dress, I promise."

Viola smiled. "Good girl." As she pulled away, Kaitlin caught a glimpse of something hanging on a golden chain as thin as thread, just beneath the neckline of her shirt. Her eyes widened.

"Is that . . ."

Viola nodded.

Megan looked confused. "What?" She carefully lifted the necklace, uprooting the spiral shell from its hiding place. "That's pretty," she said nonchalantly.

"That's right, you don't know! It must have been when you were emailing Dad!" Kaitlin said excitedly.

"Don't know what? What is it? You have to tell me!"

Kaitlin locked eyes with Viola. "Sorry, Mom, but there are only two people on earth that know that story; right, Grandma?"

Viola's eyes beamed with approval.

"Maybe when we come back to visit, you'll tell me then?"

"We'll think about it," Kaitlin said, grinning so wide that it threatened to split her face.

Megan hugged her mother-in-law, wondering how someone could be so strong and so fragile at the same time. "I want you to know that, no matter what happens, I believe you," she said fiercely.

Viola pulled away. "I know you do. Maybe the next time you come, you can tell me your story."

"It would pale in comparison to yours."

"I'll be the judge of that."

Viola waved until they disappeared down the long corridor that led to the plane. She began the long walk back to her car, but on impulse, stopped and hurried back to the gate. She approached the attendant at the desk. "I need to see someone who is on the plane," she said earnestly.

"Who do you need to see?"

"My granddaughter. There is something I need to tell her; something I forgot."

"I'm so sorry, ma'am," the woman said, "but I can't allow you to board the plane without a ticket."

"Perhaps you could just send her back out, then; just for a minute? I'd be very quick."

"I am sure you would, but the plane is already pulling away from the gate," she said, pointing.

"I see," she whispered, her voice resigned.

"Is there anything I can help you with?" the woman asked kindly.

"No, thank you. You've been most kind." She sighed deeply. "I suppose I will have to tell her about the Last Fairy next time."

Book Club Questions

1. Would you have wanted to live in the time of Viola's childhood? Do you think you would have been tolerant of fairies or not? Do you think you would have liked to be a fairy?
2. How would you react to Viola's story in Kaitlin's situation? In Megan's?
3. Viola and Kevin both have different versions of the events of the story. Which do you believe? Do you think Viola is sane or senile?
4. Which character do you relate to most, and why?
5. Who is your favorite character?
6. Discuss the metaphor of butterflies as a recurring theme.
7. There is a quote at the beginning of the book by G. K. Chesterton: "Fairy tales are more than true—not because they tell us dragons exist, but because they tell us dragons can be beaten." Do you agree with this quote in relation to the book? Who do you think represents the dragon in this case?
8. Would you like to have a grandmother like Viola? Why or why not? What stories have your grandparents passed down to you?
9. Viola has to give up her voice, something very important to her, to save Will. Do you think she made the right choice? What would your decision have been?
10. Why didn't Kaitlin want to share the story about the shell necklace with Megan at the end of the book?

About the Author

Aubrey Mace lives in Sandy, Utah. She attended LDS Business College and Utah State University. When she is not writing, she enjoys cooking, traveling, gardening, playing the cello (badly), and spending time with her family.

You can visit Aubrey at her website: www.aubreymace.com. And be sure to check out Aubrey's first book, *Spare Change*, and her newest novel, *Santa Maybe*, coming fall 2009.